HÔTEL TALLEYRAND

BOOKS BY PAUL HYDE BONNER

HÔTEL TALLEYRAND
SPQR

HÔTEL TALLEYRAND

A Novel

by PAUL HYDE BONNER

CHARLES SCRIBNER'S SONS

New York 1953

Copyright, 1953, by Lilly M. Bonner

PRINTED IN THE UNITED STATES OF AMERICA

All rights reserved. No part of this book may be reproduced in any form without the permission of Charles Scribner's Sons

[A]

To the Memory of
A. E. T.

La raison du plus fort est toujours la meilleure:
Nous l'allons montrer tout à l'heure.

—La Fontaine

There are many things in this book that are real, such as Paris and the Hôtel Talleyrand and the Forêt de St. Germain, and even the Economic Cooperation Administration, the United States Senate, and the Communist Party; but the people who move about in these familiar settings are all as purely imaginary as the creatures of La Fontaine. The *clef* to this *roman* unlocks a door to a make-believe world wherein the reader can find the moral to suit his taste.

HÔTEL TALLEYRAND

CHAPTER ONE

S. LIVINGSTON LOCKE examined his face in the mirror with considerable satisfaction. He found it strong, handsome, dignified, and with just the right look about the eyes to give the impression of wisdom and authority. It was eight o'clock of an April morning, and Locke, who was known to his family as Sam and to his associates in banking and government as Livy, was shaving in the ultramodern bathroom of his rented house in Neuilly. Ever since his beard had begun to require daily attention with a razor, he had enjoyed these matutinal Narcissus dialogues with his own image. They were the staff conferences at which the plans for the day were exposed and agreed upon. This morning, however, the planning had been interrupted by a dream—a fantasy of his sleeping mind which had been both flattering and disturbing. Flattering in that it had suggested a promise of bigger and better things in the world of diplomacy; disturbing in that it had found him floundering and helpless in the face of blatant infidelity on the part of Eleanor, his wife. Although he tried his best to concentrate on a detailed recall of the flattering episode, nevertheless his efforts were continually blocked by repeated emergence of the unlikely and shocking sequel.

He had dreamt that he and Eleanor had arrived in full evening dress at a state reception. The details of the long black

Cadillac, the chauffeur in livery, the entering of a great arched doorway guarded by cuirassiers in shining patent-leather boots, pipe-clay breeches, red-and-gold tunics, and silver helmets trailing long plumes of horsehair were very clear in his mind. He remembered Eleanor saying to him as they walked up the broad staircase covered with Turkey-red carpet, "Well, Sam, here it is. This is what you always wanted." In the dream he had glanced at her quickly to see if she were being caustic and bitter, but there had been no sign of such a thought on her face. On the contrary, her expression had been one of breathless anticipation. Then, at the top of the stair, he had seen the major-domo, who had apparently recognized them, for, before they had reached the landing, he had turned his head and announced in clarion tones which carried above the hum of conversation, *"Son Excellence l'Ambassadeur des Etats Unis et Madame Locke."*

From that point on the dream had developed phantasmally, even though it had been as clear, and seemingly as consequent, as the arrival at the reception. The courtiers, or diplomats, or whatever they were, who stood in solemn line waiting to be greeted were so heavily bedecked with medals, orders, sunbursts, and broad bands of ribbon as to be grotesque—like the chorus of a musical comedy; and their wives, too, had an opulent, Alice-in-Wonderland air of burlesque, each one plump as a partridge, with masses of pink, naked flesh bulging from her strapless gown as if pushed up by the squeezing of stays, and each one wearing a bland, inane grin, while the diamonds, emeralds, and rubies resting on each cushiony bosom shot forth continual flickers of variegated rays. Yet, during the dream, he had found nothing abnormal about either the deportment or appearance of these people. He had kept moving along the line, extending as it did from one tapestry-hung salon to another, solemnly shaking alternately a thin and bony or a fat and pudgy hand, mumbling words of greeting, sometimes in English and sometimes in French.

It was somewhere along the seemingly endless line that he had become conscious of the fact that Eleanor was no longer with him. His immediate reaction had been one of acute annoyance. He remembered thinking to himself, how like her to ignore protocol and go wandering off with one of those fat dowagers to look at some silly picture or to talk about her children. The mere thought of it made the face in the mirror flush. The anger of the dream rose up in him and came to a boil. His razor had reached the deep declivity in the center of his chin. He stopped its progress and regarded his image, which was now half ruddy skin and half billows of white shaving soap. The anger that lit his eyes and set the line of his mouth into an even, unwavering aperture gave him, he fancied, an added air of rock-bound determination.

He realized quickly that it was unfair, even preposterous, to be annoyed by something which Eleanor had done in a dream, and yet he could not escape the thought that she might well have behaved that way, and this was enough to justify the sudden recurrence of the rage. The trouble with Eleanor was that her interests were so shockingly circumscribed and unimportant. Power, position, world affairs were matters of which she was entirely oblivious. He might still be in Wall Street for all she cared. After three months in Paris she had shown no more interest in the European Payments Union than she had in the Ulysses Power & Light reorganization in their New York days. The trouble was deep-seated—she had absolutely no ambition. She was quite content to lead a life of reading novels, going to concerts and picture exhibitions, talking highfalutin nonsense with her few intimate friends, and looking after her children. Many would say that he was blessed with a good wife, but those were the fools who mistook the wifely role for that of a housekeeper or companion. What he missed in her was that modicum of guile which would be forever forcing the social issue into the paths that would help his career. It was always he who had to propose the dinner party and suggest the list of guests. Left to herself, she would have sat at home and read, or dragged him to some insufferable musicale where Bach would be played by three scarecrow women on three tinkling harpsichords.

As far as he could remember now, it was anger rather than concern that had subtly changed his dream action from greeting into search. He had had a fixed desire to find her and tell her off. With this change in his own deportment, there had coincided a change in the character of the reception. Instead of being lined up to receive the guests, the heavily decorated men and their consorts had begun to mill around in little groups, talking animatedly as they wolfed sandwiches and drank champagne. He had had to push his way through or around these knots of people, who either ignored him or scowled at him, which had served only to increase his annoyance. It had been Eleanor who had caused him to behave boorishly.

In the dream it had seemed hours that he had wandered thus, peering at every cluster of people, standing on tiptoe to look over their heads into every corner of every room. His anger had steadily mounted. There had been no place where she could have hidden. Each salon had only two doors—not doors really, but great doorways framed in marble. Had she escaped? Had she gone home without him in order to demonstrate her revulsion at all this pomposity? If she had, it was the last straw. She had no right to destroy his career at the very apex of its development. He would have to deal with her. How, he did not know. Divorce was, momentarily at least, out of the question. The Senate and the public would not approve of that, and the State Department was only too sensitive to the views of the Senate and the public. He had been seized with a stifling frustration. Would he have to continue to put up with this sort of behavior on her part? Would this be but the first of a series of horrifying acts of the American Ambassadress which would make him the laughing stock of diplomatic Europe?

His search had become more frantic, more hurried. For the third time he had made the circuit of the salons. And then, suddenly, he had seen the little door half hidden by a large tapestry. A knot of people were standing in front of it, drinking and laughing. As he had approached them they had stopped laughing and looked at him, their faces solemn and worried. He had tried to push through the group, but they had not budged.

"I beg your pardon," he had said, politely but with a certain air of command, "but may I trouble you to let me through that door?"

"There is no door," one of them had replied in broken English.

"Oh yes there is," he had insisted, "right there behind the arras." He remembered now how pleased he had been with himself for using the word "arras" instead of the more American "tapestry."

They had all looked where he had pointed and shaken their heads, as if they did not believe their own eyes. Another of the group had spoken, an old man with a white beard which almost hid the large decoration suspended beneath his white tie on a scarlet ribbon. "It used to be a door," he had said, "but it is no longer used."

"I must open it," Sam had said. "I am looking for my wife. She has disappeared."

"*Tiens, tiens,*" a fat woman had said, "the American Ambassadress has disappeared. This may be serious, gentlemen. This may be a *cause célèbre*. This may be the subject of questions in the Chamber."

"Has she not, by chance, returned to the Embassy?" another one asked.

"She would not have dared to leave without me," he had protested, though he had not been nearly so sure as he tried to appear. He had made an attempt to push through them to reach the door. There had been a chorus of "No, no, you must not! It is forbidden. One does not enter the private apartment of the—"

"I insist," he had said grandly, "in the name of the Government of the United States of America."

At this they had all looked very frightened and had stepped slowly aside. "Ah, *ces Américains, ils n'ont pas de honte*," the old man with the beard had said, shaking his head sadly.

Sam had stepped forward, pushed aside the tapestry, and turned the handle of the door. It had not been locked and had opened inward. He had stood there transfixed. He was dimly aware that the group were peering over his shoulders. He could hear the gasps of their astonishment as they observed the sight which had struck him dumb—his wife, Eleanor, reclining quite naked on a great canopied bed, while a rather stout, middle-aged man in resplendent uniform was trying to embrace her but was being thwarted in the attempt by his sword, which prevented him from raising his left leg. Someone behind Sam had remarked, "*Le Maréchal! Pensez, à son age!*"

Then he had waked up, crimson with rage, his heart beating wildly.

It was, of course, preposterous. The sort of thing that comes from reading Nancy Mitford. Eleanor was the last woman in the world to go jumping into bed with some strange officer like a lady in a play by Arthur Schnitzler. She was the soul of wifely, motherly rectitude whose interest in sex had become sublimated. To be sure, she was attractive, more attractive now at thirty-four than she had been as a girl of twenty. She had grown in depth, in perception. She understood, these days, that she had an obligation, a responsibility to perform correctly the role of Mrs. S. Livingston Locke. It was plain silly to start worrying about Eleanor. Her trouble was not men. If she had a fault, it was that inherent lack of ambition. She would be quite content if tomorrow he should announce that he was chucking it all to retire to a farm on the Tidewater of Virginia, or on the Eastern Shore of Maryland. Maybe the dream—that part about Eleanor, at least—was but an echo of his own conscience. He had been neglecting her recently. It must have been a month since they had had what she used to refer to in the early days of their marriage as a "party." Not that she seemed to care one iota, except for the flattery involved.

(Sam liked to think that she was cold and accepted sex merely as a necessary, though boring, means of providing another generation of Lockes. This suited him, for he lived with the fear that overindulgence might weaken his power to advance. It had been one of the earliest problems he had discussed with his face in the mirror. But it had resolved itself, as usual, to his satisfaction.)

He forced his mind back to the first part of the dream, the reception, the part which really interested him. What was it Eleanor had said to him as they mounted the carpeted stairs? "This is what you always wanted." It wasn't quite true, but it was good enough. He had never wanted to be an ambassador when he was in Wall Street, for the very good reason that such a thought had never crossed his mind. He had wanted to be a partner in the firm; then he had wanted to be a senior partner and a figure of solid respect in the Street; and, of course, all along, ever since he had left Groton, he had wanted to be rich enough to adorn himself with all the trappings of aristocracy—to be, in other words, as close as an American can come to the equivalent of a British peer. It was only after he had steadily, carefully, and painstakingly accomplished all these steps (planned each morning at the shaving mirror) that he had consented to come to Paris as the Chief of the Fiscal and Payments Branch of the Office of the Special Representative of E.C.A.

As far as he was concerned, the dream had accomplished one good thing—it had served to point a goal. From now on his morning dialogues with the mirror would be devoted to plotting the course. With sound planning, he would achieve this, just as he had achieved every other goal. Now that he thought of it, he would, as a matter of fact, make an excellent ambassador. Diplomacy, he had already observed during his three months in Paris, was a matter of selling the other fellow a bill of goods, convincing him that what you wished him to do was to his best interest and profit. It was the banking business all over again, but easier, because the bill you were selling in this game had already been wrapped up for you by E.C.A. or the State Department. You were not required to stick your neck out with ideas and policies. In fact, any diplomat with his own ideas of foreign policy was a menace who should be summarily dismissed from his post. His success had hinged on the refusal to deal with anything but facts, tempered, of course, by a cold and critical analysis of the history and character of the men with whom he was dealing. Yes, by temperament and training he was singularly well equipped.

"Good morning, Your Excellency," he announced to the face in the mirror.

CHAPTER TWO

WHILE Sam had been shaving, Eleanor, with a flowing blue chiffon peignoir over her nightdress, was taking her croissant and café au lait in the bow window of the small second-floor library, which overlooked the garden in the rear of their house. Her blue eyes were focused on the European edition of the New York *Herald Tribune*, but her mind was concerned with a young man named Walter P. Haines whom Sam had brought home with him from the office the evening before, so that they could "talk shop" during dinner and later over coffee and cigars. She had taken a fancy to Walter Haines from the moment he had walked into the drawing room and shaken her hand with a firm grip and said, "It's a pleasure, Mrs. Locke," in a way which sounded as if he meant it.

She had scarcely addressed a word to him all evening. At dinner, Haines and Sam had taken up where they had left off at the rue St. Florentin. It had been, to her, a very involved and abstruse discussion, having to do with Belgium's predicament under the European Payments Union. It did not interest her, but Haines did. He had talked well and with complete assurance. The thing that had fascinated her was that he had been *telling* Sam, and not, as usual, Sam telling him. What was more, Sam had listened intently, interrupting only when something got by him which he had not understood. It had been like teacher and pupil, only this time Sam had been the pupil. But there was more than this quiet air of authority about Haines that interested her. She had a feeling that his body was as lithe and solid and controlled as his mind. He was like an overtrained athlete who was as tight-strung as a piano wire. He had been stating his views in a quiet, precise monologue, but his voice had had an undercurrent of frustration which had aroused her curiosity. Although his words had been directed to Sam, he would turn to her from time to time as if she, too, were an important segment of his audience. Each time he had done this he had put down his knife and fork and looked at her, straight in the eyes. There had been nothing fresh or flirtatious about it. He had simply looked at her—into her—as if it were necessary and important that she should understand, not what he was saying, but that he needed her sympathy.

Now, the unusual thing about this breakfast reverie of Eleanor's was that she had not thought about a man in this particular and delicious way for at least ten years. She had married when she was twenty. Sam had been thirty-one and was considered by her mother and her mother's friends to be the most eligible of the bachelors who had spent their weekends at Southampton that summer. He was Groton, Harvard, class of '27, and at that time a promising junior partner in the banking house of Gwenn, Thackeray & Co. Furthermore, he had been tall, handsome, a sound golfer, and an ardent, if somewhat erratic, tennis player. No question, he had been a model for mothers. Even in those days he had taken himself and his job so seriously that he limited his drinking to two cocktails before dinner and one whiskey and soda after. The young men of his generation had thought him likely to succeed, but a stuffed shirt. The young girls had considered him eminently suitable for marriage, but rather a drag on a party. Eleanor had won him without even trying. She had been pretty in a distrait, languorous sort of way, and she had had the added attraction of an income of ten thousand a year from a family trust fund. Marriage had not interested her particularly, but when he proposed she had not been able to think of any good reason for not accepting. Everybody said that she had made a brilliant match, so she had assumed it must be so. There had never been any burning, devastating passion. She would have welcomed it, but her mother had given her to believe that it was a strictly unsound emotion, indulged in only by movie actresses and women who had illicit affairs, and that it always ended in disaster or divorce. Either of these conditions, she had always tacitly assumed, was her mother's definition of "a fate worse than death."

Well, looking back on it, she had played the game. She suddenly checked her thoughts and blushed. There had been one brief—yes, brief and beautiful—exception. She had not recalled that episode for years, and it seemed now so remote, so foreign to her present life, as to be almost the story of another person. She smiled to herself for having felt the hot flush of color come to her face and neck. It had been a mere reflex, she argued, devoid of any sense of personal guilt. She was safe these days, so safe from that disassociated past that she could allow herself the amusement of thinking through the whole story without any more identification than she would give to a character in a novel. Then she let her mind reweave a pattern of the past.

During the first year of her married life with Sam her ardor had made her proudly possessive. She had existed only for him. Nothing else mattered, no person, no incident could shake the solid intensity of her devotion. He had responded politely, thoughtfully, attentively, but without passion. Gradually she had become aware of the fact that his attitude toward her was that of a man who had acquired a suitable, even attractive, possession which was a necessary adjunct to the mode of life he had planned for himself. He respected her with the same diligence with which he respected all the other classic habiliments required of his station and objective. It was proper that he should have a wife and that she be a lady of impeccable connections who would grace his dinner table and add luster and one or two children to his name.

When, after a year, it had dawned on her fully that the satisfying response to her own love would never come from Sam, that he was so thoroughly controlled by the reasoned calculations of his mind that he could never—not with her, at least—let his passion spend itself recklessly, she had descended into a pit of deep depression. The outlook of a lifetime of duty and sweet obedience without the leaven of those moments of thoughtless, joyous, satiating love was grim and awful. She remembered now, with a shiver, the hours she had spent endlessly revolving the problem, looking at it from every side, but never from the angle of divorce. That, at no moment of frustration, or even anger, had ever entered her head. It must have been her mother's conditioning which had automatically ruled out that solution. But her unhappiness had been acute. Her desire to be loved had become an obsession.

Then she had been rescued.

She let the croissant in her hand fall back on the plate and, closing her eyes, she brought back the sequence of events. It was another April, and Sam was out of town on business. Clara Hitchcock had asked her to dinner—not a party, just a few old friends and a transient Englishman. It was the latter, the stranger, whom she sat next to at dinner. He turned out to be a Captain Derek Dunglass of the Scots Guards who was on his way home from a fishing trip in the Bahamas. He flirted with her outrageously, much to the amusement of Clara, who considered her as safe from tomcats as a churchmouse, being convinced, as everyone was, that she was hopelessly in love with her husband.

The method of his approach was new to her. Unlike the men she knew and had grown up with, he was not only gay but disarmingly frank. He admitted that he was bursting with ardor after a fortnight of trolling a bonefish off the Bahama Banks and could think of nothing more agreeable than popping into bed with her and staying there until his boat sailed. She tried to appear shocked at the forthrightness of this proposal, but she could not bring it off. He had a way of making his china-blue eyes laugh while his mouth, under a bushy red mustache, whispered indecencies as if they were the most natural thoughts in the world. He was like a big untamed spaniel that one would rather stroke than scold.

At the end of the evening he insisted on escorting her home. Clara said laughingly, "I'm afraid you're wasting your time, Captain." To which he gallantly replied, "No time spent with Mrs. Locke is wasted." As they stepped into a cab, he ordered the driver to take them to the Hotel Norwich. "But I don't live there," she said. "No, but I do," he answered with a laugh. She realized at the time that she should have protested, but the sum of the past year had stilled all reason. She sat back on the seat happily and let him kiss her. The tickle of his mustache was exciting.

When they reached his suite, she walked into the bedroom, ostensibly to take off her cloak. She remembered now, with a kind of ironic pride, how she had closed the door and calmly proceeded to undress. Quite naked, except for her stockings and her pearls—some innate sense of wickedness told her to leave them on—she turned on the lamp by the bed table, turned off the main switch, and lay down on the old-rose silk cover on the bed. Then she called in a casual voice for the captain to bring her a drink. "Righto!" he answered, and she heard him pouring the whiskey and dropping the ice cubes into the glass. As his footsteps crossed the living room, her heart started to pound. He opened the door and stopped, glass in hand, to look at her. "I say, you are lovely!" he exclaimed. It was the last word he uttered for a long time.

She had never forgotten that speech.

For some time after his departure she had worried about the wantonness of her behavior. There had been a fear, a deep, insistent fear, that she had discovered something in her character which, if not kept under strict control, might well send her spinning down a road that led to decadence. But with pregnancy and children this fear had gradually subsided, and she had been able, as Sam had assumed, to sublimate sex. The next eleven years had been devoted to her children, her home, her friends, and to the suitable framing of Sam's ever increasing position in the world of finance.

Now, sipping her café au lait in Neuilly, it seemed to her that she had done her bit with admirable loyalty—more, really, than Sam deserved. Not that she felt herself a martyr, for she had done it even more to suit herself than to please him. The fear, as much as anything, had forced her into a pattern of behavior. But thirteen years was a long time. The shadow of forty was on the horizon, giving the days, it seemed to her, a quickening tempo in their passing. She was still handsome, her skin was still soft and her body smooth and well formed; she could still display it with pride. But for how long? Her mind's eye formed again the picture of Derek

Dunglass. She wondered if he had become a stodgy Colonel Blimp, with a scrawny, self-righteous wife. Then the outline of him blurred, transforming itself gradually into the semblance of Walter Haines.

She threw the newspaper on the floor. "This is too silly," she said to herself, and got up to take her bath.

CHAPTER THREE

WHILE Sam Locke was shaving and his wife, Eleanor, was sipping her café au lait in the bow window, Walter Haines was drinking an *exprès* and eating two sugared buns at a bar in the rue Cambon, just off the rue de Rivoli. He liked this spot for his second cup of coffee—his first had been a Nescafé made in his bedroom on an electric ring—because it was close to his office in the rue St. Florentin, and because it had not yet been discovered by his fellow workers at the Office of the Special Representative of E.C.A. He had no desire to talk. At this hour he preferred the company of his own thoughts, which at the moment were engaged in reviewing the dinner of the night before. It had been gracious of Livy to ask him to his home. He knew his boss well enough to realize that it was out of the ordinary for him to invite anyone not of his rank or social position to sit at his table. Although he was inclined to ridicule this sort of snobbery, nevertheless he was flattered, and besides, he enjoyed talking to Livy, who had a quick, accurate grasp of economic matters, although he was astonishingly ignorant of the broader theories of money and credit. He wondered if most successful bankers relied on trained assistants for the solution of their more esoteric problems. He was aware that Livy used him, parroting Walter's phrases at meetings with the high brass of

O.E.E.C. But this did not bother him. His day would come in due course. He could afford, at his age, to wait patiently. There were plenty of regular officers in key posts in Paris and Washington who were aware of his ability. In the meantime the temporary fellows like Livy Locke, drafted from Wall Street or industry to hold ephemeral titles of rank, could spout the wisdom fed them by career wet nurses like himself.

It was not so much Livy and his chameleon quality of assimilation that interested Walter this morning as it was Mrs. Locke. She had struck him right between the eyes. He had never imagined that Livy's wife would be like that. He had supposed that she would be a coldly artificial society woman, with no interests beyond clothes, parties, and canasta. The woman he had met last night was not that at all. He had known it instinctively, the moment they had shaken hands. Whether or not she was an intellectual, or cultured in the aesthetic sense, he had no idea. She had said very little, as he and Livy had monopolized the talk. But that she was sentient and impressionable, he knew. He could guess it from her eyes and the way she watched him while he talked. He wondered how she had ever come to marry Livy Locke. One could never figure out what made people mate. She seemed so direct and straightforward and free from guile, which were the last things one could say of Livy, who operated on what the French called *"arrière-pensées."* Well, he had better put Mrs. Locke out of his mind. It was enough to keep her filed away as a sample of the type of girl he would pick, when and if.

Walter's knowledge of the world, that is, the world of social intercourse and mores among cultivated people, was as limited as his knowledge of women. He had never had the time, let alone any strong desire, to interest himself in either. Oh, he had had his crushes and his dates at Ohio State, and, on occasion, he had dated a couple of Waves in Washington, but these had been transitory diversions which had left him untouched. Besides, girls seemed to tire of him quickly. He had no light touch. He had never learned to kid and josh. He preferred a good bull session on some topic of the moment, such as the effect of reconversion to civilian production on prices and credit, or (he liked music) the relative merits of Bartók and Stravinsky, or (he read what he called "good fiction") which of the three, Faulkner, Hemingway, or Marquand, was the most likely to survive in the history of American letters. The girls were willing to go along with this sort of thing for only a limited time, then—at Columbus—they wanted to turn on the juke box, and—in Washington—to go to the Shoreham or the Carlton. Sex, of course, had a habit of raising its ugly head from time to time. One of the reasons he liked this Paris post was that he could get rid of it here quickly, economically, and without the need for argument or conversation.

He remembered suddenly that this was the day for his methodical semimonthly visit to a discreet and high-class establishment in the Cité Pigalle, near the Place Blanche. Somehow the idea did not appeal to him this morning. The very thought of going through that sordid pantomime with the ignorant, submissive, and colorless Jeannette, his "regular" at the Maison Nicole, was repugnant to him. The drive and devotion to work often left him like this—drained of physical desire. He was just not in the mood, that was all there was to it. Not today, he decided emphatically, and got up to pay the cashier at the end of the bar.

Walter lived in a small flat in that portion of the Quai d'Orléans which faces the Quai de la Tournelle on the Left Bank. His passion for the Ile St. Louis was such that he had been willing to wait a year in order to get these attractively furnished, though sparingly heated quarters, with an antique geyser in the bathroom that was forever threatening to blow him out into the Seine. On his salary as a Class 3 officer, plus allowances, he could easily have afforded a larger, more modern apartment in one of the fancier *arrondissements*, like the eighth, or in Passy. But he was at heart an aesthete with antiquarian leanings who derived satisfaction from the sense of history which covers the Ile St. Louis with a mantle of dignity.

In fact, Walter was a lonely and dedicated scholar who had risen the hard way. Born in a small town near Portsmouth on the southern border of Ohio, he had had to work for his education. His father had been a country doctor, whose patients— farmers and mill hands—could not afford large fees. Walter had jerked sodas while going through Portsmouth High, and had found himself a part-time job as a bookkeeper with a brokerage house in Columbus which had paid him enough to get through Ohio State with a B.A., *cum laude*, in economics. He had graduated in 1942, just in time to go to the Great Lakes Naval Training Station and become, nine months later, a snappy lieutenant, j.g., with a brand-new and proudly employed nautical vocabulary. The Navy, however, had been smart enough not to waste his special knowledge on a destroyer or an LST. They had shipped him off to the Bureau of Aeronautics in Washington, where he had spent the first three years of the war helping a Philadelphia lawyer with four strips argue the Navy's case for more aluminum and alloy steel before the Priorities Committee of the War Production Board. By the spring of 1945 he had attained the rank of lieutenant commander and had been marked down in Washington as a serious, hard-working, and capable young man. A week after V-J Day a friend of his in the State Department had asked him casually if he had considered taking the short-cut exam for the Foreign Service, then open to service personnel. He hadn't thought of it, but after a careful scrutiny of the field and its prospects, he decided that it would suit his temperament better than a civilian job—two of them, with good pay, had been offered to him. He had never regretted the decision.

Now, as an economic analyst loaned by the Department of State to E.C.A., he was Livy's assistant. It was a good job, even an important job, giving him, as it did, the power to weld the economic forces of Europe together, through the mouth and over the signature of S. Livingston Locke. The Department was smarter than most people realized. They had foreseen from the beginning that E.C.A., brimming with noble zeal, its ranks filled with the big names of business, all fired to pluck Europe out of the poorhouse and teach her the tricks of mass production and fat profits, was likely not only to stub its toe on the hard rock of ancient tradition, but to convince the recipients of our aid that we were those very imperialists which the Soviets accused us of being. So the Department had, with good grace and the air of a helpful partner, contrived to fill many secondary posts in the new organization with experts who had been carefully briefed in the basic tenets of our policy and who, by being the draftsmen of reports and pronouncements, would smooth the rough edges of eager novice attitudes. Not that Walter had much to fear from Livy, who, as a banker, was schooled in caution. On the contrary, Livy was one of the few who left the molding of policy in the hands of Washington and counted on his assistant to embellish the stark instructions with the embroidery of technical vernacular.

Walter walked down to the rue de Rivoli and turned right under the arcades of Mansart on his way to the Hôtel Talleyrand. He walked rhythmically, neither slow nor fast. It was his natural gait, never altered even under stress, and expressing his thoughtful, contemplative nature. The sun filtered only faintly through the early morning mist, painting the budding lime trees of the Tuileries and the gray walls of the Jeu de Paume with a delicate, chastened wash. It was a luminous color which intensified the subtle and variegated tones of gray —the Paris that Walter loved, not as a Frenchman loves it, but as only a boy from southern Ohio can love the object of a youthful dream.

CHAPTER FOUR

THE same sun which had tinted the corner of the Tuileries Garden for Walter Haines's pleasure had found a hole in the mist directly above the point where the rue Spontini crosses the rue de Longchamps, allowing one of its more powerful beams to penetrate the bedroom window and splash itself in golden revelry on the yellow Chinese carpet of Monsieur le Comte Christian de St. Avit. The count was annoyed at this presence of light. He felt, with that grumble of resistance and discontent which conveys the deep sleeper into consciousness, that no one, not even Le Roi Soleil himself, was privileged to pull him from the peace of oblivion into the rude and noisome world of fact. He distrusted the wakened world, and for good reason. In a violent gesture of insubordination he heaved his body away from the sunbeam, tried vainly to cover his tousled blond hair with the hem of the sheet, and sank his face so deeply into the pillow that all evidences of the new day were blotted out. But it was no use. The sun had won. He was awake.

With a roar of rage he threw the covers from him, swung his feet to the floor, and sat up. Another day. Another bloody (*"sacré"* was the word he used) day. What day? Not that it mattered a damn. Tuesday, perhaps. Yes, it must be Tuesday, because he had dined last night with Philippe and Michèle de

Gramont and the invitation had been for Monday, the tenth of April. Ergo, it was Tuesday, the eleventh of April, which was staring him in the face. The knowledge conveyed nothing to him. A blank day. Well, at least that was something to look forward to—a day of uninterrupted thought, of contemplation, with a little reading and a little planning. He picked up his wrist watch from the night table and looked at it. Eight-thirty. A reasonable hour, neither too early nor too late. He yawned, ran his thin, aristocratic fingers through the unkempt ringlets of his taffy-colored hair, opened the coat of his reseda-green silk pyjamas, and scratched his chest. This was no special gesture for April eleventh. It was his accustomed method of rubbing out the last dregs of sleep before he rose to his feet, put on his yellow shantung robe, closed the tall window through which the sunbeam had sought him, and rang for old Etiennette, his maid.

Christian de St. Avit's bedroom was a fairly accurate indication of the nature of the man. It was in impeccable taste without being feminine. The furniture, all but the bed, consisted of original pieces of the period of Louis XVI, some from a family château near Mont de Marsan, which had been sold after the death of his father, and others—the Jacob chairs and the gilt-mounted Sèvres vases—from the *hôtel* of his aunt, the late Marquise de la Tour d'Albi in the Boulevard St. Germain. The color scheme throughout, carried even to his pyjamas and dressing gown, was green and gold; not that they were his racing colors or had any other significance, but in order to reflect and complement the tonal effect of the three pictures that hung on the walls. He was very attached to these paintings, which he had unearthed in the provinces during the war and had acquired at prices which were a fraction of those demanded by the galleries in the rue La Boëtie. The one above his bed was a small portrait by Corneille de Lyon of a lady in an olive-green velvet dress, with dark, searing eyes, and a pearl-trimmed fillet on her smooth raven hair. Over the marble chimney was a landscape by Fragonard, a towering mass of billowy trees, with an antique statue half hidden on a patch of sunlit lawn. The third, hanging above the marquetry commode which served as his dressing table, was by Cézanne and showed a hill town of southern France as seen through an opening of heavy green leaves.

His other rooms in the flat were in equally good taste—a bathroom, and a large living room, which had a table at one end, where his meals were served when he ate at home, which was infrequent. He had no interest in the kitchen and Etiennette's bedroom, which were her province and which he never entered.

"*Bon jour, Etiennette*," he said, as the old woman pushed the door open without knocking. She carried a tray and copies of *Le Figaro* and *Combat* under her arm. Christian sat down on a striped satin fauteuil and waited for her to place the tray on a small table and bring them both to the exact position at the left side of his chair which he demanded. Having adjusted them correctly, she surveyed the objects on the tray—teapot, hot-water pitcher, cream pitcher, toast, marmalade, butter, knife, spoon, and napkin—to satisfy herself that all was in order before handing him the newspapers. All the while, in fact even before entering the room, she kept up a running fire of talk, like an old hen scolding an errant chick. He had come home very late. It must have been very late because she had not fallen asleep before midnight and she had not heard him come in. Furthermore, he had left the light on in the foyer, which was very extravagant. Oh, how his dear father would have raged to find a light burning in the morning since the night before. And how had he found Monsieur le Marquis de Gramont? She hoped that marriage had settled him down.

What a scamp he had been as a child when he used to visit at Mont de Marsan, always sneaking into the kitchen to steal a bite to eat just when cook was busy preparing dinner. And those horrible white mice of his. Ah, she would never forget the day when he had brought one of those creatures into the room of Juliette, the underhousemaid, while the poor girl was having a quiet nap. He had put the mouse on Juliette's bed, then watched from the door. When it had crawled up on Juliette's neck she had merely sighed in her sleep. It was only when the filthy creature had tried to crawl down that nice opening between her breasts and under her corset that the poor girl had awakened. When she saw what was going on, she leapt out of bed and tore off every stitch of clothes she had on. Then she saw young Monsieur de Gramont staring at her. My God, was she furious! And he only ten years old at the time.

Christian paid no attention to her chatter. He poured himself a cup of tea and opened the copy of *Combat*, his favorite newspaper because it delighted in puncturing the pomposity of politicians. Etiennette was like the furniture; she had been with him ever since he could remember. She had been his nurse as an infant, his refuge in school days, and his maid-of-all-work ever since he had taken up his bachelor existence in Paris. During the war she had, at his command, dressed like a gentlewoman and played the role of owner of the flat in order to divert the attention of inquisitive, rapacious German officials who wished to know the whereabouts of a certain Captain de St. Avit, a former occupant, who was suspected of being a dangerous member of the Résistance. Their suspicions were, of course, correct, but they never found out anything from Etiennette, who had snubbed them haughtily, saying she knew nothing concerning former tenants. The sentiment between the old woman and her young master was stronger than either of them would have admitted. Whatever complaining they did, and there was much on both sides, was a shield to cover a deep affection.

There was much to be said in defense of Etiennette. Christian was no easy person to care for. He did not conform to the traditional pattern of young French noblemen. True, he did not have a job, but neither did he lead the glamorous life of wine, women, and song which, according to Etiennette, was expected of a bachelor of twenty-eight with money and position. It was that awful war, and those frightful, boorish Germans who had done it, she was convinced. They had robbed her Christian of his youth. All he did these days was to read and talk of politics with that young Dominican, the Abbé d'Albret. She had an inherent, Jacobin distrust of the cloth. They were up to no good, particularly this one, this d'Albret. He was too smooth, too articulate, too serious. It would be better if the count had a mistress instead of a confessor, one of those ripe, jolly girls from Normandy, like the kind his father and his grandfather had had before him. A man needed that—above all, a man of his position. It tended to keep him relaxed and normal, with his feet on the ground. Yet here he was, sleeping alone every night and knitting his pretty brow over politics. No wonder he was distrait and forgetful, not putting out the lights, and not coming home for dinner last Friday after she had prepared him some beautiful *rognons de veau* with spinach and little onions. Poor dear boy, the war had taken his joy of life, and now that Abbé was plotting to ensnare him for the Church.

In a sense Etiennette was right, but Christian was a good deal more than a mere product of the war and the Free French underground. He was perhaps a typical example of the effect of the modern world on a civilization which had fostered the analytical mind from Rabelais to Voltaire, and from

Diderot to Henri de Montherlant. It amused him to dissect the people of his era solely to uncover their weaknesses. The good in man he took for granted as something part animal and part divine. He was much more concerned with the evidences of greed, ambition, self-esteem, and deceit which were stultifying the growth of Europe's hard-won freedom. He believed in the force of reason, but his dissection disclosed few leaders within whom this force was not either bent or blunted by prejudice or pride. He was a cynic whose only faiths were history and his own powers of induction.

Christian de St. Avit saw no point in writing down his own thoughts, which he fancied as being brilliant and iconoclastic, any more than he would entertain the idea of becoming a politician or a civil servant. With unerring perspicacity he considered it a thorough waste of time for him, an unknown young man of twenty-eight, to attempt to reform the governments of the Western world. He much preferred talking, either to women of wit and perception, or to those few of his men friends of whose integrity he felt assured. Contrary to Etiennette's belief, he enjoyed the society of women, that is, of certain amusing and emancipated women. He eschewed the sentimental ones, even though they might be as beautiful as Helen. He wanted no aftermaths of tacit beliefs in eternal faithfulness. They must assume, as he did, that any words spoken on a bed or in a boudoir were poetic expressions of immediate desire and ceased to be binding the moment the front door was closed and either he or the lady was in the street. That, according to Christian's code, was civilized behavior between ladies and gentlemen who were not unfortunate enough to be married to each other. He realized that the obligations of family would eventually require that he take a wife, and that she produce little St. Avits. He was, after all, an only son on whom rested the responsibility for the survival of an ancient name, if for no other reason than to prove that the pre-Napoleonic aristocracy was less perishable than two empires and a string of republics. But there was plenty of time yet for that step. He counted on seven more years of contemplative research and subtle spreading of "La Doctrine de l'Empire."

If you had asked Christian to define the doctrine of empire, he would have explained (if he had had confidence in your sincerity) that it had to do with a return to a medieval concept of the unity of European Christendom and was not to be confused with the aims of the few frustrated monarchists still crying in the political wildernesses of France, Italy, and Spain. He would have told you that his only fixed belief was that the fate of Western Europe would be disintegration and Bolshevism unless its component nations would unite under a single governing body. But the Federalists and the earnest men at Strasbourg had gone about it the wrong way. He doubted Europe's ability to achieve the federal form without a moral emblem, stronger than a mere banner, which, placed above the melee of politics, would become the symbol of unity for the masses. His knowledge of the intuitive historic sense within the European mass mind had brought him to the conclusion that this symbol must be a king-emperor. He did not care what family or individual was selected for the office, although he had a sentimental predilection for the Bourbons because of their universal identification with European ruling. He also had a fancy that the capital of the Empire of Europe (the name he had chosen for it) should be at Aix-la-Chapelle, where the Emperor and his parliament could derive moral sustenance from the pervading spirit of Charles the Great. Christian was aware that his most powerful ally in spreading the doctrine was Catholic Action. Whether he had sold them the idea, or they him, or whether both had arrived coincidentally at the same conclusion, no one knew. It was interesting, however, to note that Etiennette had put her finger on the agent of liaison, the young Abbé d'Albret, who of late had become the constant companion of Christian.

On this April morning, as he drank his tea and smiled over the barbed comments of *Combat*, he was unaware of the existence of Mr. and Mrs. S. Livingston Locke or Mr. Walter P. Haines. It is safe to say that Sam Locke would have considered him a playboy and a symbol of French aristocratic decadence (he eventually did). Such an appraisal would not have bothered Christian in the slightest (nor did it ever). He looked upon the working colony of Americans in Paris in much the same way as Professor Fabre had regarded a colony of ants. He found them interesting as a species, but he was convinced that their tireless, unalterably focused energy made them completely unable to comprehend the workings of the European mind. They were fascinating to observe, but as companions he would as soon have Fabre's insects. In fact he had stated only the evening before, at the de Gramonts' dinner, that as long as civilization had to be saved it was a pity that the saviors were so lacking in wit.

CHAPTER FIVE

THE fifth member of this oddly assorted Parisian pentarchy to awake on that eleventh day of April was a young lady of rather deceptive appearance. On the street, or at a table of a café terrace, one might not have accorded her a second look. Not because she was not handsome to the nebulous point of beauty, but rather for the reason that she went out of her way to disguise her natural good looks, which she considered a detriment to her career. She accomplished this by affecting an unkempt, pedagogical dowdiness which was by no means inherent in her character. She never used any make-up, never wore a hat; she let her hair, which had no one color but ranged from dull gold to shining copper, fall as it wished, and dressed in nondescript tweeds. To the casual passer-by she looked like the typical Sorbonne exchange scholar one finds in the bars and rabbit-warren night clubs of Montparnasse. Those few who did give her a second look—they were the knowing males who could penetrate a disguise—dismissed her as a disciple of Jean-Paul Sartre and therefore too engrossed in intellectual mannerisms to be much fun, in or out of bed.

Had they been privileged to see her as she opened her eyes, stretched her lovely white arms, and shook her varicolored mane, they might have thought differently. For she was one of those rare women who are beautiful on waking. Even on that cot, which served as bed by night and couch by day, in that shabby room, furnished only with a cheap dresser, a deal table, and one chair with a broken, dangling cane seat, the simple fact remained that her beauty was enhanced by a dilapidated frame.

She had not opened her eyes because she had finished sleeping; it had been the noise as of someone knocking that had awakened her. She waited for the sound to recur. If it had been caused by the broom of the concierge sweeping the stair, she would turn over and finish her sleep. She looked at the man's watch on her wrist. It showed nine-thirty, which was too early in the day for her comrades to be up and about. Unless, of course, there was some special, urgent message. Then the knock was repeated on her door.

"Who is it?" she called.

"Georges," a male voice whispered hoarsely through the keyhole. "Let me in."

"Wait," she said, jumping out of bed and pulling on a belted raincoat over her cotton nightdress. In her bare feet she went to the door, slid the heavy bolt, then called, "Come in," as she went back to the bed and sat down.

A tall, swarthy young man opened the door quickly, slid into the room, and, turning, took a swift look at the hallway before closing the door and shooting the bolt back into place. He was the leader of her cell in a very special and highly classified apparatus of the French Communist Party and was known to her by the name of Georges Persan. He was dark and beak-nosed enough to have Persian blood, which may well have been the reason for the alias, but his speech was that of a French scholar who had been born, but not educated, in the Midi. She was quite aware that the name he used was not the one which had been given him at birth, just as he was aware that she had not been christened Germaine Brisson.

"What gives?" she asked. She did not use the exact equivalent of these words, but it will serve as a rough translation of the argot she purposely employed when talking to her cell comrades.

"You've got the job," he said brusquely, sitting down on the cane chair and tossing his battered felt hat on the table.

"What job?" she asked.

"The one you wanted," he answered, twisting his thin lips into a lewd smile.

"Don't be a jerk," she said angrily. "One doesn't *want* a job in this game. One does what one is told."

"And sometimes what one is ordered to do turns out to be nice work."

"All right, come clean. What is it?" she demanded coldly.

"The Marshall Plan job," he said, with the leer still on his lips and his black, beady eyes watching her intently.

"You call that nice work, shacking up with some lousy American?" she snapped at him.

"Smart clothes, a beautiful apartment, a big bathtub of an American automobile to ride around in. Don't kid yourself, Germaine, it's a soft assignment."

She looked at him appraisingly. "Sometimes I wonder about you, Georges," she said, "the way your mouth waters for all those bourgeois trappings."

"Just what are you trying to imply?" he asked, his eyes narrowing.

"Just what I said," she replied coldly. "You've got secret longings which don't fit the Party principles. You can talk the dialectics, but deep down you're full of envy—envy for the cheap eyewash of capitalism." She didn't really mean this, knowing perfectly well that Georges Persan was one of the most trustworthy and dedicated of the whole lot in her apparatus. What made her say it was the knowledge that the envy which was consuming him was for the man who was to become her lover. Georges had had those black Oriental eyes on her for months. That was why he came with his bit of news at nine-thirty in the morning, hoping to find her in bed. Well, he was mistaken. There were only two motives in the world which could make her go to bed with any man—the Party and love. She didn't love Georges. In fact, she found him physically repulsive—more repulsive even than his sidekick, Le Boiteux.

For a minute or two Persan was speechless with rage. He stood up and faced her threateningly. "You have made a very serious accusation," he said, sucking his breath in between his teeth after pronouncing each word. "If I see fit to report this to Comrade Crépuscule you will find yourself in very profound trouble, my dear friend."

She laughed. "Don't talk nonsense, Georges. Sit down and cool off." She pulled a pack of cigarettes out of the pocket of her raincoat and handed it to him. "Here, smoke one of these, it will quiet your nerves." She laughed again. "Imagine you going to Comrade Crépuscule and saying to him, 'Comrade Brisson accuses me of a secret yearning for the cheap claptrap of bourgeois capitalists, and I think she should be severely punished for uttering such disloyal lies.' Can you picture Crépuscule's reaction? Can you see him raise that big head of his from the pile of papers on his desk and look through you over the top of his spectacles? Can you hear him say, 'Very interesting, my dear Comrade Persan, very interesting indeed, and what was it, by chance, that you might have done or said which caused Comrade Brisson to have these suspicions?' And right away you would be on the defensive, and you would become nervous and splutter and stutter, as you always do when you talk with Crépuscule, and before you'd realize it you would be confessing the very deviations of which I have accused you in fun."

"So now you say it was only in fun," Georges said stiffly.

"Well, maybe not so much fun as malice. Frankly, I did not like the way you spoke about this assignment of mine. All you have to do is to tell what the job is and how the cover works. Whether I enjoy the work or not is outside the question, and, what is more, it doesn't concern you. Now, let's cut out the nonsense and get down to business. I can't wait all morning. I want to get dressed and have some coffee."

Persan knew he was beaten and he was not very happy about it. The door was locked and he could rape her, of course. But there were too many hazards to that approach, the biggest of which was that she was probably stronger than he was. He decided to let the matter rest for the moment and get on with the instructions with as much dignity as possible. "The objective," he said pompously, "is the securing of documents of the Marshall Plan group of nations on their economic and rearmament plans. Not the stuff that is given out in the press releases, but the high-level secret agreements. The point is that we wish to obtain documentary proof that the United States is using its dollars and military production as a means of achieving complete domination of the countries of Western Europe. You understand what I mean?"

"Perfectly. Go on."

"To do this you must gain the confidence of one of the more highly placed bureaucrats of the E.C.A. office in the Hôtel Talleyrand. Your command of the English language should aid you in this. Now, we have made careful inquiries and have discovered that French employees of the E.C.A. are not allowed to work in any office where secret material is handled. Therefore it would do no good for you to apply for work there as a typist. Instead you will contrive to meet one of these higher officers and cause him to take you as his mistress. This should not be difficult for the reason that these Americans, I understand, consider it a weakness not to have a girl friend, even if their wives are living here. Being a primitive people, the male ego is very strong, which means that any man who cannot boast of his sexual prowess is shunned as an outcast."

Germaine shuddered. "And this is what you call nice work. Very good—you don't have to go into any more noxious sociological details—what's the cover?"

"Did you ever hear of Madame Nicole?" Persan asked.

Germaine shook her head.

"She is a reliable comrade who runs a brothel of the highest class in the Cité Pigalle. She has reported that one of her regular clients is an American who works in the Hôtel Talleyrand. Now listen carefully. It is his habit to visit her place once a fortnight. The next time he arrives, he will be told by Comrade Nicole that his usual girl—one Jeannette—has left Paris to go to Algiers, but that there is a new girl of exceptional charm who has never done that sort of work before—"

"True enough."

"Don't interrupt me. The new girl will be Comrade Brisson, who will take a taxi the moment she gets the call and go directly to number 48 Cité Pigalle."

"What's his name?"

"Comrade Nicole will introduce you. From then on it is your affair, but, mind you, Comrade Crépuscule will expect results. In order to receive the call, you will wait each evening at the White Dove bar from eight until eleven-thirty. He usually arrives at Comrade Nicole's about ten o'clock."

"Let me repeat the data," Germaine said in a businesslike voice. "Madame Nicole, 48 Cité Pigalle. Where is that?"

"Near the Place Blanche, I believe."

"The regular girl of this man is named Jeannette and she has gone to Algiers. Anything else?"

"Yes, the White Dove, where you wait each evening for the call."

"Good. Where, and how often, do I report?"

"Every Thursday at eleven in the morning you will walk across the Pont Neuf from the Quai du Louvre toward the Quai de Conti. Whatever documents or information you have obtained will be placed in the inner fold of a copy of *Le Figaro* which you will be carrying. You will stop at the parapet, near the statue of Henri IV, and look into the river. As you do this, you will place the copy of *Le Figaro* on the parapet, holding it firmly down with both hands so that the wind will not open it. A woman will stop and ask you to direct her to the Hôpital de la Charité. You will tell her that it is in the rue des Saints Pères. She will ask you how one finds the rue des Saints Pères. You will take a pencil from your bag and on the margin of *Le Figaro* you will write, 'At the Left Bank turn to the right and follow the quays to the end of the Quai Malaquais, where you turn left into the rue des Sts. Pères.' Then hand her the newspaper and return to the Quai du Louvre."

"Will it be the same woman each week?" Germaine asked.

"Not necessarily, but it will always be a woman," Georges replied.

Germaine repeated the sentence to be written on the margin of the newspaper in the flat voice of one committing something to memory. "Good," she then said, rising to her feet, "I shall be at the White Dove this evening, and every evening following until the call comes." She held out her hand. "Goodbye, Georges, you may tell Comrade Crépuscule that I will do my best."

Persan shook her hand listlessly and rose to his feet. It was plain that he was disappointed by the miscarriage of his plans for the morning. He blamed himself for having needlessly aroused her ire and, being essentially a weak man with a deep sense of inferiority, he twisted his own failure into resentment against Germaine. He put his hat on the back of his head and fastened the belt of his raincoat. "Do you still believe me to be a doubting deviationist?" he asked bitterly.

She laughed again as she walked over to the door and loosened the bolt. "Don't be stupid, dear friend. You know very well why I said that. It was to protect myself from you."

"Why should you do that?" he asked.

She hugged the raincoat about her and her eyes flashed. "Because I'm not that kind of a girl and you know it, and Le Crépuscule knows it. You two have given me this assignment as some sort of a test—of loyalty, of God knows what—but I shall do it. I shall prove to you that no sacrifice, no matter how degrading, is too great for the Party." She opened the door. "Now go, Georges, I want to dress."

He went out without a word.

She closed the door, locked it, and went back to the bed and lit another cigarette. It was a strange life she led, among strange people. Not that she had any regrets, or the slightest doubts. Characters like Georges Persan were offensive to her, to be sure, but they were unimportant molecules in a vast and powerful force which would finally, by the power of its own unquestionable rightness, drag all the peoples of the world into the haven of Marxian socialism. That the means were at times sordid in no way affected or mitigated the beauty of the ends to be achieved. On the contrary, the very mire through which one fought was, in itself, a purifying agent. Every last link with her bourgeois past had been irremediably severed. As far as she knew her family believed her to have been captured and killed by the Germans. She had cut the umbilical cord when she had flown from England to join the F.T.P., the Francs Tireurs Partisans, which was the Communist-controlled branch of the Maquis, having nothing to do with the De Gaulle-inspired F.F.I. Fighting with them, she had risen to the rank of captain, and then, after the war, she had become a confidential party worker under the name of Solange Ramé, until the day had come when she had been recommended for the most trusted work of all—the apparatus of Comrade Le Crépuscule, which was engaged in espionage for the Cominform. That was her second rebirth, under the name of Germaine Brisson.

She was peculiarly well equipped for her new work. Her father, a professor of English literature at the University of Toulouse, had insisted on her leaving France when the threat of the German armies darkened the skies in 1940. He had forced her to go to the home of an Oxford professor with whom he was on friendly terms of pedagogy. She had been only thirteen at the time, but she had rebelled against leaving him, leaving her brother, leaving France to go to England and comparative safety. The bitterness invoked by her exile had made her a difficult, uncooperative guest in her new English home. It had turned her mind toward a search for revolt against a world that could create such situations of moral cruelty. She had soon found young undergraduates who suffered as she did, and from them learned of the Communist Manifesto and *Das Kapital*. Through them she found her way into the British organization aiding the Free French underground.

She put out the cigarette and started to dress hurriedly. There was a lot of planning to be done and she wanted to get to the bar on the corner of the rue d'Angoulême, where she could drink her coffee, read *L'Humanité*, and think.

CHAPTER SIX

LIVY LOCKE bounded out of the official Citroën the moment it stopped in the courtyard of the Hôtel Talleyrand. As he hurried toward the door at the left corner of the *rez de chaussée* the chauffeur came running after him, poking a sheet of paper, secured to a clip board, in front of him.

"Vous avez oublié de signer, Monsieur Locke," the chauffeur said.

Livy halted and whipped out a pencil. He had been so intent on his immediate plans that he had forgotten to sign the chauffeur's trip coupon which would eventually tell the administrative section that he had been fetched on the morning of April eighth at his house in Neuilly. He signed and rushed on, hardly acknowledging the cheery greeting of two stenographers in the elevator. When the car stopped at the second floor he walked quickly out, and down the corridor to his suite of offices, which looked out on the rue St. Florentin, facing the Ministry of Marine. On the side of the door was a neat cardboard sign which read, "201. Fiscal and Payments Branch. Chief, S. Livingston Locke. Ass't Chief, Walter P. Haines." The door opened on a reception room, where sat the secretary and the typist who served them both. Unlike the offices of the Special Representative and his deputy, which were on the Rivoli side, these held no vestige of the elegance so beloved by Baron Edouard de Rothschild. They had probably once been servants' rooms, but now, completely reconstructed, they were like any modern business offices, severely plain, with cream walls and green trim, puce carpet on the floor, maps of France and French Equatorial Africa hanging on the walls, and durable, efficient metal office furniture.

Livy was quite happy with this décor. He considered it highly suitable to the work in hand, more suitable, in fact, than the fancy frescoes of naked caryatids and the gaudy Empire furnishings in the offices of the ambassadors. He believed it important that his callers from among the fiscal experts of O.E.E.C. should be given a sample of stark simplicity under cold neon light. He would, of course, have abhorred it in Wall Street, where his office was the replica of a paneled Georgian library; but here, as a missionary teaching thrift, productivity, and honest taxation, it was better that he appear in surroundings of monastic integrity. He had seen his visitors eyeing the effect with an amazement which he concluded was salutary.

As he strode across the reception room toward the door on the left that led to his private office, Miss Callery, the secretary, and Miss Kleinholz, the typist, greeted him in unison. Without glancing in their direction or altering his stride, he said, "Good morning," and disappeared into his own room. Neither of the girls was in the least offended by the brevity of his greeting. They knew him well enough to realize that it was the result of preoccupation. As bosses went in government, he was a good one, and their unit of measure was the degree of impersonality a man could adopt while at work without being rude or abusive.

Janice Callery swung around in her chair and faced Shirley Kleinholz. "Tell Mr. Haines that Mr. Locke is in his office.

He asked me to let him know when Mr. Locke came in," she said.

Miss Kleinholz got up and walked over to the door on the right which led to Walter Haines's office. As she did so a buzzer sounded and Miss Callery picked up the telephone. "Bring your book in, Callery"—it was Locke's voice—"I have some letters to write. And tell Kleinholz that I will take no calls for the next half-hour. Naturally that does not include either of the ambassadors."

"Mr. Haines said he wanted to see you first thing," Miss Callery said.

"Tell him to make it nine-thirty." He hung up.

When Miss Callery went into his room he was leaning back in his chair, playing with an ivory paper knife. His eyes were fixed on a multicolored graph of the progress of Europe's gold and dollar reserves which hung on the wall opposite his desk. He was deep in thought and oblivious of her presence. She pulled a chair up beside his desk, opened her book to an unused page, and waited, pencil in hand, for him to speak. It was a minute or two before he realized that she was there; then he sat forward in his chair and put his elbows on the desk.

"Is the door shut tight?" he asked.

Miss Callery got up and walked over to the door, trying the handle. "Yes, it is," she said, and came back to her seat.

"Now, listen, Callery," he said in a lower key than his normal voice, "the letters I'm going to give you are not only personal but strictly confidential. One copy for my personal file and that's all. You understand, don't you? No copy for the O.S.R. files."

"I understand," she said flatly, without a flicker of interest appearing on her deadpan face. It was nothing more than the mask of a good secretary. Inside, she was consumed with curiosity. The whole build-up, from his hasty entrance with its curt greeting, to the orders that he was not to be disturbed and the closed door and the lowered tone of voice, had created an atmosphere of suspense worthy of a murder mystery. She waited expectantly for the fateful words, hardly daring to breathe, yet outwardly placid and businesslike.

"The first letter," Livy said, poking the point of the paper knife into the blotter, "is to Lewis Pomeroy, of Pomeroy, Greenough and Sedwitz. You'll find some letters from him in my file. I think the address is 14 Broadway." He reclined once more, still fiddling with the paper knife. "Dear Lew—spell it L-e-w. After three months of dealing with the diplomatic representatives of the Marshall Plan nations I find that my experience in the banking game, together with my education and background, parenthesis, I have always spoken French, parenthesis, have turned out to be good diplomatic assets. I was surprised to discover that I was more adept at trading and suasion and making these foreigners think they were gaining their point when it was really the U.S.A. that was gaining, than most of the men who have come over here with E.C.A. from industry or the law. They are good men, some of them, but there is a rigidity about their thinking which takes the form of outspoken frankness in their dealings with their foreign counterparts. Now, you know as well as I do that this approach does not get one very far in Europe. They react badly to it here. It is considered dictatorial and mannerless. It puts their backs up, and you are licked before you start. Paragraph. The point I wish to make is that I feel I owe it to my country, parenthesis, not to the present administration, parenthesis, to put this ability of mine to its best possible use during the present world crisis. You will naturally ask if I am not already doing this. The answer to that is twofold, colon, I am doing it to the utmost in a position of distinctly secondary importance, but I could be of far greater service in a key post, or, as they would say in the Foreign Service, in a chief-of-mission post, which to you and me means an ambassador or minister. Paragraph. You are aware that jobs of that caliber are not handed out for ability alone. Ability may count, but political considerations are the paramount factor. You know your Washington and you will understand what I am driving at. A flea will have to be tactfully placed in the right ear, together with the thought that I am willing to contribute up to twenty thousand to the party coffers. I want to make it clear, however, that there will be no contribution until my nomination by the President has been approved by the Senate. Paragraph. I am not interested in just any post so that I can wear a title. I want to do a job in the spot where my talents and training are best suited to obtain results. This means in any of the civilized countries of Western Europe. Paragraph. I have every confidence that you can handle this discreetly and well. Best regards. Sincerely."

Locke sat up straight in his chair and looked intently at Miss Callery. "Now you can understand why this is so highly classified," he said.

Miss Callery allowed the slightest suggestion of a smile to curl the corners of her lips. "Don't worry, I get it," she said.

"No one must know," he said sternly.

"They won't," she said. "Not from me."

"Very good," Livy said, seemingly reassured. "Now, let's get on with the second letter. This is to Richard Feinstedt of Hilling, Breed & Co. They're on Pine Street somewhere."

"In New York?"

"Of course New York," he answered impatiently. "They're the bankers. Look 'em up in the directory for the right street number. Dear Dick: Just a line to tell you that I am not altogether happy about the way things are going over here. Not the E.C.A. part of the job, dash, that is going better than anyone could hope for. Quite frankly, it is the political angle that has me worried. From where I sit, which is pretty close to the hub of the European wheel, I get a picture of hesitancy and lack of force in the presentation of our policy. It seems to me that too many of the men who represent the State Department in key European posts are inhibited by—"

"Are what?"

"Are i-n-h-i-b-i-t-e-d."

"Thanks."

"—by seeing both sides of the problem. They listen to the weeping of the local ministers of state, then read instructions from Washington, and are unable to decide who is right. This comment does not apply to Dick Beale, who has not only had E.C.A. experience but is a solid banker of the type we both admire. Paragraph. I am writing you this because I am aware that you are called upon by the White House from time to time for advice on matters of policy and people. You know me well enough to appreciate that my motives are disinterested, except for the fact that, being a good American, I want to see us represented over here only by the most able men, dash, the kind of men who can hew to the line without doubts or misgivings. You and I know that it is the quality in management which makes a business successful. Diplomacy is no different. Paragraph. I know that you will treat the contents of this letter with the utmost confidence. Kindest regards. Sincerely."

Miss Callery looked up from her notes. "Is that all?" she asked.

"No, there's one more," Locke said. "It is to Congressman George Alexander. You can address it to the House Office

Building, Washington. Dear George . . . Oh, by the way, do you know how to address a congressman?"

"Yes, of course," Janice Callery said emphatically, as if to imply that it was a stupid question. "That's the first thing you learn when you work in government."

Livy smiled for the first time that morning. "You used to work for the Reconstruction Finance Corporation, didn't you?"

Janice repressed the laugh that almost exploded from her lips. "During the war, yes. I was the secretary of one of the directors."

"Good," Locke said, "then these letters won't surprise you." He glanced at her, expecting some sort of conspiratorial comment, but she was silent, her eyes averted, giving the impression that she was patiently waiting for him to continue his dictation. She was not bad-looking, Livy thought, in her pert Irish way. There was a faint suggestion of freckles under the surface of her smooth skin. This meant that it was soft to the touch. The jacket of her tailored suit was open, displaying a handkerchief-linen blouse, lined with little tucks and ruffles, which fitted her figure like a glove. He wondered if she had bought it at Beresford's. These girls with their pay and allowances could often afford things which even Eleanor found too expensive. When she lifted her eyes and caught him looking at her breasts, which the blouse maintained in high relief, he quickly picked up the paper knife and examined it.

"Where were we?" he asked.

" 'Dear George' was all you gave me," Janice answered. She was actually blushing with delight. It was the first time he had ever noticed her as a woman. He rose in her estimation. She even hoped now that he would be made an ambassador.

"Dear George," he repeated. "Knowing your great interest

in foreign affairs, I feel it my duty as a constituent to let you know how things are faring with this noble experiment of economic aid to war-devastated Europe. As you are well aware, the purposes of the Economic Co-operation Act were twofold, colon, first, to assist the friendly countries of Western Europe in regaining their economic stability through building adequate reserves of dollars and gold, and second, by thus raising the general standard of living, to lessen the appeal of communism among the European masses. Paragraph. As a legislator who voted for this act, and as my good friend and representative who advised me to make the personal sacrifice of coming over here with E.C.A., I feel that you have a right to know whether or not the public funds appropriated are achieving these purposes. They are. Happily, I can state that without fear of contradiction. The facts speak for themselves. If you will read the brief report recently published by this office, a copy of which I enclose, you will see what really remarkable progress has been made toward these objectives since E.C.A. was established in Europe in 1948. The kernel of the answer can be seen by the two charts on pages seven and eight. The first shows the changes in the balance-of-payments positions of each of the fourteen Marshall Plan countries, and the second shows the trend of the voting strength of the Communist parties in these same countries over the past two years. Paragraph. Who can read these figures without taking pride in being an American, question mark. My pride is even greater than the average, my dear George, by having had the priceless opportunity of helping to bring this situation about. This work, as arduous as it has been, as much of a sacrifice as it has meant, has given me a sense of dedication to my country which is worth more than money. It has given my life a new orientation. Believe it or not, if the powers-that-be ever tap me for a diplomatic post commensurate with my standing in the home community, I doubt very much if I could bring myself to turn it down. Faithfully . . ."

The telephone rang and Livy picked up the receiver eagerly, knowing that it could only be one of the two ambassadors. "Mr. Locke," a female voice announced, "Ambassador Carroway would like to speak to you. Just a minute please."

Janice Callery got to her feet, but Sam motioned to her to remain. She sat down again.

"Oh, Livy, this is Jim Carroway," the voice on the telephone said. "You may have heard that Senator Donegan has just arrived in Paris. I only learned about it last night from Dick Beale. Sherrill being away, it's up to me to do something about him, so Peggy and I are giving a little dinner tomorrow night, with a small reception after, so he can meet some of the O.E.E.C. people. We want you and Eleanor to help us out. Dinner will be at eight—informal dress. The Senator didn't bring a dinner jacket. Can you make it?"

Livy knew that it was a command, but even if it had not been, he would have broken almost any engagement to be there. Senator Donegan might be a useful string to his new bow. He was, after all, a member of the Appropriations Committee. "We did have a date with some old friends from New York who are stopping at the Ritz, but we'll put them off."

"You really don't . . ."

"I insist, Jim. This is duty, and duty at your house is a pleasure."

"Thanks, Livy. I'm sorry I couldn't let you know sooner. Give my apologies to Eleanor."

"No apologies necessary," Livy said. "We'll be there."

"Tomorrow at eight, then," Carroway said. "And try to make it on time, as Donegan is always punctual."

"On the dot, Jim. You can count on us."

"Thanks," Carroway said, and hung up.

Livy turned to Janice Callery. "Write those three letters in rough draft first. I want to go over them carefully before I send them out in final form."

Janice got up. "Very good, Mr. Locke. Is that all?"

Livy thought for a moment. "Don't let anyone see them—not even Kleinholz—and don't leave them around your desk. Put them in a sealed envelope and mark it 'Top Secret.' Keep the envelope in the safe until I call for it."

Janice nodded assent and started for the door.

"Get me Mrs. Locke on the telephone," he ordered, "and when I'm through talking to her, tell Mr. Haines he can see me."

When the door had closed he sat back in his chair with his thoughts. Yes, it was better to let those letters simmer for a while before sending them out. They were, after all, nothing more than the promptings of a dream, and he had no wish to live with the oppressive thought that he had taken a course, no matter how right, which had no stronger foundation than the inspiration of the subconscious. Dreams and nightmares were indistinguishable. Both were hallucinations arising from inner desires or fears and were usually induced by indigestion. This latest dream was no different. It had been a silly, whimsical fairy tale, having nothing whatever to do with reality. And yet it had impressed itself powerfully. Why? Had it, in truth, expressed an unformed, subconscious desire? The mere fact that he had dictated these letters in urgent haste, before reading his mail, before talking to Walter, before getting after the work in hand, must be a sign that it had touched a responsive chord.

The buzzer sounded and he picked up the telephone. He could hear Eleanor's voice saying, "Hello, is this you, Sam?"

"See here, Eleanor," he said in his most masterful, man-of-authority manner, "you'll have to call Sally Warren and tell her that we can't dine with her tomorrow night."

"My goodness, Sam," Eleanor said in a shocked voice, "we can't do that now. Why, Percy made that date from London by telephone over three weeks ago."

"Look, dear," Sam Locke said impatiently, "Jim Carroway has asked us to dine with him and help entertain Senator Donegan, who has just arrived. The Senator is on the Appropriations Committee. It's vitally important."

"But Percy and Sally are old friends, Sam," Eleanor pleaded. "And you always told me that he was Gwenn, Thackeray's best client."

"Look, Eleanor," Sam said, as if to a child with a low I.Q., "I just haven't the time now to explain the facts of life to you. You'll have to take my word for it that I know what I'm doing. You're in government now, darling. You're in the Foreign Service whether you like it or not, and Jim's dinner for the Senator is duty with a capital D. It's a command."

"What shall I tell Sally?" Eleanor asked in a plaintive, long-suffering voice.

"Tell her the truth. Explain that we are no longer our own bosses in these matters."

"They'll never understand."

"Percy will. Wait a minute." He flipped over the pages of the desk calendar in front of him. "Tell her we can make it on Thursday, if they are not booked. We have nothing for Thursday."

"I'll ask them to dine with *us* on Thursday," she said despairingly.

"That's fine. Jim's dinner is at eight o'clock and we are not dressing."

"I know—because senators don't travel with what they call 'tuxedos,'" she said sarcastically. "God, what a boring prospect!"

"Now, come . . ."

"Goodbye, dear," she said, and hung up.

He was annoyed because she had managed to touch him on the one weak spot. It was quite true. Normally—even yesterday—nothing could have made him cut a long-standing date with Percival Warren, Chairman of the Board of Ulysses Power & Light, a utilities holding company which had been financed and nurtured by Gwenn, Thackeray & Co. until it had become a rich and powerful property. Until this morning he would have considered anything which smacked of rudeness in his treatment of Percy Warren as sheer madness—cutting his own throat. Why had he done it, then? Was Jim's invitation in reality a command? He knew in his heart that there was no such thing as a command as far as Jim Carroway was concerned. With Sherrill, yes. Sherrill had been so long in the stratosphere of government rank that he expected his lieutenants to drop everything at his nod. But not Jim. Jim was a corporation lawyer on whom the laurels of rank rested lightly, like a paper hat on New Year's Eve. He would be the first to understand that dates with men like Percy Warren were not to be broken without risk. And yet he, Livy Locke, had done this very thing, just as he had dictated the letters, compelled by some unthinking inner force which was making a monkey of his accustomed careful, prearranged behavior.

In justification, one thing was clear in his mind. If it were really an ambassadorship that he wanted, then Senator Donegan was momentarily more important to him than Percy. He seemed to have cast the die at the shaving mirror. That was the moment when the dream had taken over command. But he was wise enough to know that things don't happen for wanting them. The achievement of any goal required tactical action. That's where he shone—and he knew it.

The door opened and Walter Haines stuck his head in. "How about it, Livy," he asked, "can you see me now?"

Livy smiled. The annoyance caused by Eleanor's probing had vanished. "Sure thing. Come in, Walter. Come in and sit down."

CHAPTER SEVEN

IT was obvious to Eleanor, who sat on his right, that Senator Donegan did not include small talk among his accomplishments. She had noted, during the soup, Peggy Carroway's desperate efforts to find a noncontroversial topic which would raise a glimmer of response, and she dreaded the moment when her turn would come to beard the lion. Since having had to break the date with the Percival Warrens she disliked the Senator on principle. He had become a symbol in her mind of all the stuffy, self-righteous powers of government to whom Sam had suddenly and inexplicably taken a fancy. There was something—well, dishonest was perhaps too harsh a word, but it was close to it—about Sam's *volte-face* that worried her. Ever since she had known him he had expressed a scorn of all politicians. He had implied—even if he had not stated it unequivocally—that improbity was a requisite characteristic of the profession. One had had the feeling when talking to Sam that he classified them all with gunmen and professional gamblers. The only man he had ever voted for with confidence was Wendell Willkie, because he had been associated in Sam's mind with Commonwealth & Southern and not with politics. In fact he had told her flatly that the only reason he had consented to work for E.C.A. was because it was run by Paul Hoffman, who was a businessman who could be trusted to stand up to the politicians. And yet here he was, breaking a date with the president of Ulysses Power & Light, the man whom he had always professed to admire extravagantly, in order to kowtow to this boor of a legislator. It was strange.

"The thing which most impressed me about Washington," M. Delvaux, the Quai d'Orsay man on her right was saying in French, "was the European quality of its appearance—the avenues converging on circles, the beautiful trees, and the classical architecture of the buildings. Not at all American, like New York, or Baltimore, or Philadelphia."

"It was thanks to General Washington," Eleanor said, also in French, with one eye on the Senator, who had finished his soup and appeared to be waiting for her attention. "He had the shrewdness to pick Major l'Enfant, a Frenchman, to plan the city."

"Ah, very interesting, very interesting. That explains it," Delvaux said, patently pleased to learn that the United States capital was a French creation.

"That's true, isn't it, Senator, that L'Enfant designed the city of Washington?" Eleanor said to Donegan in English.

"Who?" the Senator asked gruffly.

"L'Enfant," she repeated, realizing that it was her French pronunciation of the name which baffled him, but enjoying her moment of superiority.

"Who told you that?" the Senator asked, using the inquisitorial gambit to hide his ignorance.

Eleanor laughed lightly. "Mercy," she said, "how can one remember that far back. Was it my nurse? Was it my father? Or was it my first teacher? Can you remember who it was who taught you all you know about American history, Senator?"

"Yes, I can," he answered abruptly. "It was myself. Started

when I was a kid. Read every book I could get my hands on." He reached across her plate and picked up her place card. "Mrs. Locke," he read. "You're the wife of the tall, dark fellow I was talking to before dinner?"

"Yes," she said, and indicated Sam, who was seated on the opposite side of the table. "There he is."

"Talks like a diplomat," Donegan said. "Is he with the State Department?"

Eleanor smiled, still looking at Sam. "No, he's with E.C.A. Just an amateur volunteer from Wall Street."

"Banker, eh?"

"Yes, a partner of Gwenn, Thackeray."

"Hm. Handpicked by Sherrill. Well, maybe that's what we need over here, some hardheaded bankers who'll see to it that some of this money we're throwing around will get results." He suddenly lifted his head and looked at her, his beady blue eyes taking her in from under their awnings of bushy white eyebrows. He was a big, paunchy man, handsome in a rough-diamond way, with his florid skin and his crown of long white hair. "How does a good-looking girl like you like living over here?" he asked.

She leaned toward him. "If you promise not to tell the Committee on Un-American Activities," she whispered, "I'll confess that I love it."

"Woman's town, I guess," he said, smiling. "Clothes and perfumes and all that."

"Oh, there's a lot more," Eleanor said with mock earnestness. "There's the theater, and music, and art . . ."

"If you like it."

"Don't you, Mr. Senator?"

"I can take it or leave it alone. A good show's all right once in a while, but I can't understand them over here—not even at the Folies-Bergère."

"Well, you see, I speak French," Eleanor said consolingly, "and that helps."

"I thought that's what you were talking to the fellow on your other side," the Senator said. "Does your husband speak it, too?"

"Oh yes, just as well as I do."

"How does that happen?"

"We both learned it as small children in New York."

"Hm. Never had any need for it where I came from."

"My husband finds it useful when dealing with his opposite numbers in O.E.E.C. It's the one language they all understand." She was rather surprised at herself for giving Sam a leg up with this man whom she had made up her mind to dislike.

The Senator did not answer. He applied himself to eating a filet mignon, from the top of which he had carefully scraped all the sauce Béarnaise. Whether he wanted to or not, he left the impression that he had no wish to go on record as approving of an American civil servant speaking a foreign language.

Eleanor caught Peggy Carroway's eye, and the latter smiled as if in thanks for her having succeeded so well in extracting words from Senator Donegan. Poor Peggy, Eleanor thought, this is not one of her more successful parties. Yet it was not her fault. She had done all she could, but the situation was socially hopeless. Not even Lady Diana Duff Cooper could have kindled a spark among the fourteen people gathered around that table. It was the awful presence of the Senator that laid the cold, dead hand of mediocrity on everything. The mere fact that the men were in business suits and the women in short cocktail dresses destroyed whatever charm the dinner table might have had. The white tulips and jonquils seemed to droop in their Dresden bowls, and the service was slow and perfunctory, as if the butler and footman lacked interest in the proceedings. The company talked in low voices, only sipping Jim Carroway's second-string wines. They seemed afraid that Donegan might overhear some remark which he could store up against them and use in a speech on the floor of the Senate. They were all aware—French and Americans alike—of the extent of his power. They wanted him to return with a good report, yet they sensed his suspicion and distrust—his insular hatred of anything that was "foreign" and, not being related to bourbon whiskey or a ten-gallon hat, was therefore effete and decadent. Eleanor realized all this and it made her smile.

The Senator wiped his mouth, sucked the last bits of steak out of his teeth, and turned to her. "What are you doing tomorrow afternoon around two-thirty?" he asked peremptorily.

"Why, Senator, this is so sudden," Eleanor said, her eyes squinting with laughter.

The Senator grinned in response and put his big red right hand, with its enormous gold ring, on her arm. "You're just the girl I'm looking for to help me buy some gifts for the little woman."

"I'd better warn you then. My tastes are expensive."

"I'm not thinking of going to Cartier's," he said. "Just a bottle of perfume, and maybe a handkerchief or a scarf."

"Where shall I pick you up?" Eleanor asked.

"You've got a car?" he asked suspiciously.

"Yes, I have a car," she answered, looking at him with her eyes still twinkling. "And don't you worry. It belongs to my husband and doesn't cost the taxpayers a cent."

The Senator grunted. "You'd better drop by the Crillon. That's where they've put me up."

"Splendid!" she said lightly. "We won't need a car. Everything you're looking for is just around the corner. I'll be there at two-thirty."

"How about letting me buy you a lunch?" he asked in a gruff whisper out of the corner of his mouth.

"Sorry," she whispered back, "but I've got a date for lunch—with my children."

As the ladies left the dining room Peggy Carroway took Eleanor's arm and whispered, "Oh, Eleanor, I can't thank you enough. You were wonderful. Why, you actually made him smile!"

Eleanor chuckled. "His bark is worse than his bite. He's the kind who likes to frighten people into saying stupid things. I didn't frighten, so he gave up trying."

Peggy sighed. "Awful, isn't it, having to be nice to people like that? Jim says he's the senator who gives us the most trouble."

"I daresay he does," Eleanor said. "I think it amuses him to make a nuisance of himself. His constituents probably howl with glee whenever they read that he has insulted some groveling civil servant."

The men had stayed behind for their coffee and liqueurs. Jim Carroway moved down to his wife's chair, and the other men followed him, settling eagerly in the vacant chairs around the Senator.

"I've arranged a briefing for you tomorrow morning at ten, Senator," Carroway said pleasantly. "I hope that fits in with your plans."

"Make it ten-thirty," Donegan snapped. "And tell your people not to make long-winded speeches. I hear enough of those back home. Keep it brief. You can send all your reports and statistics around to the hotel. I'll read 'em when I get back."

"Very good, Senator," Carroway said, smiling. "Whatever suits you. It's your party. I've asked only the division chiefs to be there. However—"

"You're one of those, aren't you?" the Senator interrupted, pointing a finger at Livy Locke.

"That's right," Livy said, looking pleased at the unexpected recognition. "How did you know, Senator?"

"Your wife told me. She said you were a French-speaking banker from Wall Street. Sounds high-power to me. Just what are you going to sell me tomorrow morning?"

Livy was annoyed by the insolence of the question, but he checked any temptation to show it. Instead he took the attitude that it was friendly banter and replied, "The issue is oversubscribed, Senator. There is nothing left to sell. Tomorrow I'll tell you about it, just to whet your appetite for the next offering."

"I've made a date with your wife for tomorrow afternoon," Donegan said in a feint to throw Locke off his guard. "So you had better be good, because I'll be telling her what I think of you."

Everyone laughed, the two Frenchmen—Delvaux and another man, named Jouvois, from the Ministry of Finance, most heartily of all. The Senator had made a sally—a French sally, involving another man's wife—and the gloom had been dispersed. He was, then, human after all and could be reached, as all senators since Catullus could be reached, through a beautiful woman. Delvaux wondered if the pretty Mrs. Locke, who spoke his language with such a charming accent, might turn out to be a modern Lesbia.

Carroway did not let them linger over their brandy. The other guests had been invited for ten o'clock, and he wanted to get the Senator into the drawing room in plenty of time to receive with Peggy and himself. Gently but firmly he herded them out of the dining room and into the spacious salon where the ladies were seated in little groups on the régence chairs and *bergères* upholstered in dull pink brocade. As the Senator entered the room, his cigar jutting from his jaw, he stopped to take it all in—the putty-colored boiserie touched here and there with gold; the great Savonnerie rug, into which was woven an enormous wreath of pink flowers on a cream ground; the chandelier with its myriad crystal pendants sending off flashes of the spectrum like the facets of a diamond; the marquetry commodes, on whose pink marble tops stood Chinese vases mounted in ormolu; and the delicate, candy-box portraits of eighteenth-century ladies in elaborately carved frames. He turned to Carroway, who was standing expectantly beside him.

"You do yourself pretty well, Mr. Ambassador," he said.

"It's really magnificent, isn't it?" Jim Carroway said enthusiastically. "Thanks to the French Government, we have been able to lease it."

"Who's 'we'?" Donegan asked.

"Why, E.C.A., of course. You didn't think I could afford to live like this?"

The Senator grunted. "How do I know? It looks to me like you have a lot of wealth in your outfit, with fellows like Sherrill and that man Locke."

Carroway laughed uneasily. "They're bankers. We poor lawyers are not in their class."

"So Uncle Sam takes care of you, eh? Nice work. Wouldn't mind it myself. How much is this setup costing the taxpayers?"

"Make a guess?" Carroway said, forcing a smile.

"I'm not here on a guessing mission," the Senator said gruffly. "I'm looking for facts."

"We're getting this for twenty-four hundred a year, furnished," Carroway said. "And that's less than my rent allowance would be if I had to find my own place." He was nettled. He didn't like this kind of inquisition at a party given in the Senator's honor. "Where do you live in Washington, Senator?" he asked pointedly.

"At the Shoreham," Donegan answered, then looked sharply at his host. "What's that got to do with it?"

"I'll bet you pay more for your apartment there than the Government does for this," Jim Carroway stated. He was angry. If he had invited the Senator to some little flat in Passy, without decent wines or service or room for him to meet the bigwigs, he would have been criticized for not treating the Senate with the respect which was its due. You simply could not win with these bastards. He saw Peggy rise and motion to him. "Come with me, Senator," he said with a voice of command. "You are to receive with my wife and me."

Senator Donegan went along willingly. He was not in the least annoyed with Carroway, nor was he even concerned about the elegance of this great house in the rue Vaneau. Secretly he was proud of the fact that an American ambassador could receive him in circumstances of appropriate dignity. His questioning had merely accomplished his purpose—it had angered Carroway and thrown him off balance. That, to his way of thinking, was the correct approach with these brass hats of the executive branch. They should be taught at the outset who was boss, who held the purse strings. He was quite aware that men like Carroway and Locke considered him boorish. That was exactly the impression he wished to convey. It was in the good Jacksonian tradition, and his constituents loved it. To them he was the he-man who speaks his mind, and no folderols.

The thirty-odd guests who had been invited to come in after dinner to meet the Senator were all pretty much on time. For the most part they were high-level representatives of the fourteen Marshall Plan countries at O.E.E.C. and their wives. They were all seasoned enough as diplomats not to make the error of gushing over the Senator. They greeted him politely as they arrived, figuring that they would contrive to buttonhole him privately during the course of the evening. Walter Haines was among the five or six additional men who came from O.S.R. After shaking hands awkwardly with Mrs. Carroway and the Ambassador, he pumped the Senator's hand and said a dutiful "Glad to meet you, Senator Donegan." He tried to move on quickly, but the Senator held his hand.

"Where are you from, Haines?" he asked in a gruff but not unkindly voice.

"Southern Ohio," Walter answered, stating the fact simply and without a smile.

"Hmph!" Donegan grunted. "Bob Taft's bailiwick. You a Republican?"

"I'm a Lausche Democrat," Walter stated.

Another guest was waiting to greet the Senator, but before taking the outstretched hand he said to Walter, "I see they're passing wine over there. Tell 'em to bring me a glass."

Walter walked slowly over to the butler who was passing a tray covered with glasses of champagne. As he reached him, he saw that the lady who was lifting a glass from the tray was his boss's wife. He blushed. Why, he didn't know.

"Come, have a drink with me, Mr. Haines," Eleanor said pleasantly.

"Thank you, Mrs. Locke," Walter said and took a glass of wine. He turned to the butler. "*Monsieur le Sénateur désire du champagne. Voulez-vous le servir?*"

"*Oui, Monsieur, tout de suite,*" the butler replied and carried the tray to the receiving line.

"I didn't know that you spoke French," Eleanor said.

Walter looked at the rising bubbles in his glass. He did not raise his eyes for fear of blushing again. "I really don't speak French. Only enough to order meals, or tell the maid what to do. School stuff, that's all."

"What school?" Eleanor asked. It was not just conversation. She wanted to know about him—about his background.

"Ohio State," he said flatly.

"Oh," she said, momentarily stuck for a rejoinder. Had he answered Harvard or Yale or Princeton, or even Virginia or Dartmouth or Penn, she could have made some knowing comment to put him at his ease. But Ohio State was separated from her experience by the Appalachians. It meant nothing to her architecturally or culturally. Not even Thurber's pieces in *The New Yorker* came to her rescue at that moment.

Walter sensed her discomfort of ignorance, having learned during the war of the gulf which separates the East Coast from the plains of the Central States. Had it been anyone else he would have resented that "Oh" and the silence which followed it. He was proud of his Alma Mater and eager to defend her, but he knew, or wanted to believe, that this Mrs. Locke standing beside him, sipping her champagne, had not exclaimed out of disapproval or disappointment, but simply because she had run into a blank wall, without any identifying marks that she could recognize and communicate. He knew that it was up to him to speak, to say something gay and trivial which would break the deadlock, but those were the sort of words which had never been at his command, and now, under the stress of urgency to say something, they were impossible to locate. A mild panic seized him. "It's a mighty good school," he mumbled, and drank his glass of champagne in one gulp.

"One of the best," she lied. "What brought you here, the

Senator?" It was the first time she had seen him at one of these official parties.

"Livy's orders," he said.

"Does he command your social life, too?" she asked in a tone of banter, seeing how ill at ease he was.

For the first time he raised his eyes and looked at her. "Is this social life?" he asked, quite seriously. "I thought it was duty."

Eleanor laughed. "Duty at the social level—where the wives take over."

"I see. Yes, of course. It never occurred to me," he stumbled along. "Being a bachelor . . . Tell me, Mrs. Locke, do you think that I, as a Foreign Service officer, should attend these affairs more often?"

At first she thought he was pulling her leg, but a glance at his face told her that he was in deadly earnest. He trusted her and wanted her advice. She would have liked to tell him that the use of the word "affair" to describe a social gathering was an unpardonable solecism, but that could wait. If she went at it tactfully, there would be much that she could do to polish his rough edges. Had not Sam told her that this young man could go far if only he were house-trained? "Of course you should go out—whenever you're asked. That's an important part of diplomacy. Don't you know that more history has been made over brandy and cigars than ever was in chanceries and foreign offices?"

Walter revolved that thought in his mind. "I've read things like that," he said, pondering, "but I always thought it was just a romantic idea promoted by journalists for public consumption."

"Not at all," Eleanor said. "It's Gospel truth. I'm surprised that the Department hasn't told you that to get ahead you have to get around—in a black tie, with a glass in your hand."

"How do you know all this, Mrs. Locke?" Walter asked. "Livy isn't a career man."

"I've seen it going on ever since I've been here," she answered, smiling to give the impression that the discovery had proved enjoyable. "So has Sam. That's why we rarely have an evening at home alone."

It was Walter's turn to comment with a simple "Oh." There was nothing else he could say, for he found the thought infinitely depressing.

The Senator, released finally from his duties at the door, spotted Eleanor and came trotting over. The cigar had gone out, but it was still clutched in his fat fingers. "You haven't forgotten our date, have you?" he asked her.

"I should think not!" Eleanor said. "Imagine any girl forgetting that!" She turned to Walter. "The Senator has courage, hasn't he, Mr. Haines, to be seen strolling on the rue du Faubourg St. Honoré with Mrs. Livingston Locke?"

"More courage than I have," Walter mumbled.

The Senator glanced at Walter. "You're the Lausche Democrat, aren't you? Well, let me tell you something, son. When you've got no boss, it doesn't take much courage to do what you please."

"Have you forgotten those voters back home?" Eleanor asked with a sly smile.

"Them! Why, they kinda like me the way I am—a maverick," Donegan said boastfully. "If I was to be seen picking the fans off Sally Rand they'd give me a vote of confidence."

"Mercy, Senator, you frighten me," Eleanor said. "I shall keep my promise and be at the Crillon at two-thirty sharp, but I'll take the precaution of wearing sturdy tweeds. Now I must run off and help Peggy Carroway with her non-English-speaking guests."

There was a silence as the Senator watched her move across the room and join a group of guests who, from their appearance, were obviously not Americans. Walter saw that one or two of the men—Delvaux among them—were eyeing Donegan with a view to buttonholing him. He felt that this was the perfect moment to effect his escape.

"Well, Senator," he said firmly (his equilibrium having returned with the departure of Eleanor), "I think I'll be running along. I have a busy day ahead of me."

"Eh? What's that?" the Senator said, pulling his mind back to current events. "You going home? Good idea. I'll go with you. I've had enough of this. Come on, let's make a break before one of those Frenchmen grabs me." His big hand closed on Walter's elbow with a firm grip—like a cop making an arrest—and pushed him forward toward the door.

Peggy Carroway saw them and darted away from a group near the chimney. "You're not going, are you, Senator?" she asked as she caught up with them.

"Time to get to bed," Donegan replied. "I'm not one of your diplomats who can burn the candle at both ends."

"They are all going to be frightfully disappointed," Peggy said feelingly. "Jim tells me that many of them were very anxious to talk to you."

The Senator held out his hand and Peggy was forced to take it. "Talking to me won't help them," he said. "That's the Ambassador's job. Good night, Mrs. Carroway, and thanks for a good dinner."

Jim Carroway had noticed what was going on and rushed over to join them. "Sorry you have to leave, Senator. I was just saying to Monsieur—"

"See you at ten-thirty tomorrow," Donegan said brusquely and walked out into the foyer, where the butler was already waiting with his coat and hat.

"I'm taking Senator Donegan to his hotel, sir," Walter said to Carroway. "Good night and thank you."

As they walked through the iron-grilled gates of the little courtyard, one of the official Citroëns of O.S.R., with its bright-yellow CD license plates, drew up. The chauffeur jumped out and opened the door to the rear seat.

"We won't need this," Walter said. "I have my own car."

"Much better," Donegan said. "Tell this fellow to run along home."

Walter dismissed the chauffeur and signed the trip voucher with the Senator's name. Then they both crossed the street and got into Walter's Chevrolet.

"What hotel are you at?" Walter asked as he started off toward the rue de Varenne.

"Do you know any good spot where we can get a drink?" Donegan countered.

"What kind of a spot? Music? Or just a bar?"

"A floor show. Something snappy and Parisian."

"Let me think, now," Walter said, trying to recall the names of cabarets he had heard discussed at the office. "I'm afraid I'm not much of a guide to Paris night life."

"Look, Haines, you don't have to give me that stuff," the Senator said. "You're a bachelor, aren't you?"

"How about the Lido on the Champs Elysées?" Walter asked in a sudden flash of inspiration. "I hear they've got a new show."

"You name it," the Senator said. "You live here. I don't. They're all new to me."

CHAPTER EIGHT

SENATOR DONEGAN told Walter to order a bottle of champagne as the waiter hovered about the table. "What goes on here, anyway?" he asked when the waiter had left, his beady eyes taking in the dance floor crowded with couples. "Just dancing?"

"Oh, there's a show, too," Walter reassured him.

"A good one? You know, Parisian?"

"I hear that it's the best in town."

"Haven't you seen it?" Donegan asked.

"Not this one," Walter hedged. He had never been inside the place before. "They change it about every month or so."

"We ought to get some girls," the Senator said. "I feel like dancing."

"I'm afraid that's not possible here," Walter said hastily. "Of course, maybe after the show . . ."

The Senator laughed. "Don't worry, I'm not going to disgrace you in public." He nudged Walter's elbow. "Now that one over there, dancing with the boy with the patent-leather hair, she dances my style."

Walter was far from being pleased with his role of night-life guide to an important senator. He was intellectually aware that he should regard the invitation as flattering, knowing that many of his colleagues would have considered the opportunity to spend an hour or two alone with Sentaor Donegan as "golden," but this attitude did not impress him. He felt, with some degree of justification, that he had been chosen merely for the fact that he had been immediately available. He doubted that the burly senator wanted to talk about E.R.P. and European affairs. He had been in government long enough to learn that the majority of legislators (there were a few earnest and noble exceptions) relied on their committee experts to perform the analyses and draw the conclusions for them. Donegan, he felt sure, was one of those who would justify this trip abroad by bringing home a mass of documents which he would hand over to his legman, demanding in a whispered voice, as he did so, a brief résumé within twenty-four hours. All that the Senator wanted at the moment was a floor show of such dazzling nudity that he could describe it to the boys back home in the congenial atmosphere of his home-town Democratic Club. Walter was along as a convenient interpreter who, being dependent for his pay check on Congress, had no choice but to do as he was told. This thought was depressing enough, but added to it was the realization that he had to prepare Livy's briefing paper before ten o'clock the next morning. He knew from bitter experience that his was a brain which only functioned smoothly on eight hours of sleep. He asked the waiter, who was pouring the champagne, when the show went on.

"A onze heures, Monsieur, et puis encore à une heure du matin," was the answer.

Eleven o'clock. He glanced surreptitiously at his wrist watch. It was ten minutes to eleven. If the show lasted an hour they could get away at midnight.

"What was that?" the Senator asked.

"He says the show goes on at eleven."

The Senator turned his head and looked at Walter with

objective appraisal. "What's your job over here?" he asked abruptly.

"I'm with O.S.R."

"What's that?"

"Ambassador Sherrill's office—the Office of the Special Representative of E.C.A."

"That's what they call it, eh?" Donegan said scornfully. "Why don't they call it E.C.A. and not try to confuse people?"

"It might confuse people more if they did," Walter said patiently. "The E.C.A. Mission to France is only two blocks away. We want the French to think of that as E.C.A. We are merely the headquarters for all country missions."

The Senator was pleased with the answer. He had known it already, but he was trying out his method of putting the man he was talking to off balance. It had not worked yet with Walter, and his opinion of the young man had risen accordingly. "What's your particular job?" he asked.

"Assistant chief of the Fiscal and Payments Branch. The chief is Livingston Locke," Walter answered simply.

"Yeah, I met him at dinner. What do you think of him?"

"A very clear-thinking banker."

"Are we doing any good with all this handout money?" He was using the sharp, inquisitive tone of a committee hearing.

"In terms of our objective I should think we are doing very well indeed," Walter replied. He was puzzled by the question, not being sure whether it stemmed from ignorance or guile.

"And what, in your opinion, are our objectives?"

Now Walter knew where he was. No senator, least of all the flamboyant Donegan of the Appropriations Committee, could possibly be ignorant of the objectives of the Economic Cooperation Act after all those months of hearings and debate. The question was patently designed to enlighten the Senator on Walter's knowledge of his job. It was the examiner quizzing the pupil. Walter smiled. This was old stuff for him. He knew you had nothing to fear when you had learned your lesson thoroughly. He picked up a wooden swizzle stick and unwrapped the cellophane cover. "The first objective was to revive the tottering economies of the nations of Western Europe so that by increased employment and higher wages they could lessen the appeal of Communism as an internal political threat. The second objective is to increase the national production in goods and services to the point where these countries will be able to add a major burden of defense spending without causing an inflationary spiral which would nullify the first objective. The third objective, which is a corollary of the second, is to achieve an economic unity among these countries which should tend to raise the general standard of living and, with it, allow a unified defense effort against an external threat of Soviet aggression. That's putting it in the briefest terms."

"And you think we've done all that?" Donegan asked sarcastically.

"I didn't say we had, and I don't think we have," Walter said calmly, spinning the bubbles out of his champagne. "I think we have pretty well accomplished the first objective, which means that the second has a good chance. As for the third, well, I'll admit it isn't going to be easy, but I'm convinced it can be done."

"Why do you do that to your champagne?" the Senator asked.

Walter looked up in surprise. The sudden change of topic threw him for a second. "Oh, to get the bubbles out," he said meekly.

Donegan laughed loudly and heartily. "Damnedest thing

I ever heard. Hell, son, what do you think I buy champagne for? It's the bubbles that give it class."

"They say it's more digestible . . ."

"What have you got to worry about with digestion? Look at me. I'm sixty-four and those bubbles just tickle my gut. All right, you and your indigestion, what makes you think these Europeans have any mind to unite?"

Back on the other track. God, how the man could toss you around. Walter took a drink before answering. "I think they have very little mind to, but force of circumstance may bring it about."

"Circumstance? What circumstance? *Our* needling, with *our* dollars?"

"No," Walter said thoughtfully, "that, in my opinion, would never do it. They've got to come to it in their own way, and there's only one motive that will make sense to them —self-protection from a common fear."

"Then they'll never get together," the Senator said with finality. "They're less afraid of the Russians than we are. Look, I've talked to some of them. They think we're in a panic. They're convinced Uncle Joe Stalin is never going to invade Western Europe."

"That's right. They don't think Russia will invade. Maybe they're right. But there are other fears which are very real to them—economic fears. Since I've been here I've come to the conclusion that these people over here are inclined to think further ahead than we do. They are already worried about markets big enough to absorb all the products of Western Europe when the West German industry gets really going. With respect to steel alone—"

"Okay, okay," the Senator interrupted. "You can let me have that in writing tomorrow." The lights were dimming and the orchestra was blaring a fanfare. "Drink up, son, we're going to have the show. Tell the waiter to bring another bottle. Don't worry, it's on me."

"Bonsoir Messieurs, Mesdames. Nous présentons pour vos délices . . ." It was the *compère* speaking, that Gallic character who explains the plot and from whom we derive our master of ceremonies. A spotlight had flashed on the curtains at the far end of the dance floor, and he had emerged, a sleek young man in a dress suit, his hair perfectly marcelled, smiling a condescending smile. He went on to describe, in terms of hyperbole that would have made a huckster blush, the wonders and delights of the acts and numbers which were about to be performed. As he talked, he pranced around the dance floor in time to the soft accompaniment which the orchestra gave to his exegesis. Without breaking the flow of words he shifted easily from French to English to Spanish to German, peacock-proud of his linguistic ability.

At the precise moment when he had completed the circuit of the floor and returned to the curtain, the orchestra swelled to a full crescendo and the lights went out. Gradually a series of blue spots, growing slowly in intensity, picked out a tableau in the center of the floor. It was one of those dainty, highly artificial pastoral scenes so favored by Boucher and the eighteenth-century molders of porcelain. A group of shepherdesses in taffeta pannier skirts were seated on the floor, cuddling imitation woolly lambs. They surrounded a moss-covered mound on which there reclined a very beautiful and completely nude young lady. Had her smile been less provocative the whole effect might have charmed the ladies sewing circle of the Baptist Church. As it was, her dimpled cheeks evoked a grunt of approval from the Senator. Paris had not let him down and he was as pleased as he was titillated.

The lights dimmed again to another fanfare from the band and the applause of the tourists. The room stayed dark long enough for the props to be removed. When the lights came on again, yellow this time, the shepherdesses were standing at intervals around the edge of the floor, and the smiling nude, who had compromised with the brighter spots by putting on a great bouffant skirt of lavender brocade embroidered with garlands of flowers, was standing where her perch had been, singing a *bergerette* about the charms of springtime love. Walter, as an exercise in the language, made an effort to follow the meaning of the words. He thought them rather stupid, which they were unless one's French was colloquial enough to understand the dirty double meanings. His was not.

The Senator, unconsciously reacting to the music, was tapping out the rhythm on the table with a swizzle stick, but his mind was on the prima donna. His beady blue eyes were intently focused on her small but perfectly formed breasts, which she had sensibly not covered, so that the customers could continue to admire.

The acts continued without interruption—jugglers, acrobats, ballroom dancers, interspersed with production numbers which became progressively more nude. The Senator drank steadily, with the champagne having no apparent effect. Although he was silent, it was obvious to Walter that he was enjoying himself. His eyes never left the performers, as if he were endeavoring to capture every detail so that he could describe it accurately to his colleagues back home. When the finale came, with all the performers, hand in hand, singing the theme refrain of the review, Donegan clapped loudly and long, smiling at the chorus girl who faced in his direction.

"That was something," he said to Walter as the curtain closed and the lights went up for general dancing. "Better than anything on Broadway." He chuckled to himself, his whole body bouncing. "There's some boys I know ought to see this. Why, they'd leave home and mother."

"Yes, it was really good," Walter said. He, too, had been impressed, though not in the same way. The show had struck him as opulent, graceful, and in better taste than he had expected. It was his first experience with a French cabaret designed to attract the tourist trade, and he was surprised at himself for having enjoyed it.

"Good?" the Senator said. "It was terrific. You sure know your way around. Trying to kid me that you didn't know any good spots. Hah! That was a hot one. I understand. I get it all the time. Afraid the Senate might get the wrong impression and cut appropriations. Don't worry, Haines, we're as human as the next man. It's not the fellow who likes a little fun now and then whom I distrust. It's the psalm-singing bastards who don't know what life is all about. They're the ones to keep an eye on. They're the ones who get ideas—subversive ideas. Maybe you know what I mean."

"I think I know exactly whom you mean—the frustrated introvert with an unhappy past who hates sex and—"

"That's the fellow!" Donegan said enthusiastically. "You got me right away. The pimply-faced grind who wears thick glasses. Beware of him, son. The government is full of his kind. They're up to no good."

Walter was beginning to feel sick to his stomach. It was the sort of generalized attack on the studious which he loathed and resented. His own statement had been headed in another direction, but the Senator had not let him finish. He knew it was useless to go on now. Whatever he said would be misconstrued and he would be compromised. He felt a sudden hatred surging up from his stomach. Here he was, a civil servant doing his best to keep the economic policies of E.C.A. in tune with the broader lines of his government's foreign policy, suddenly performing the extracurricular duty of chaperoning an extrovert Senator on a tour of the fleshpots of

Paris. There was something immoral about it—not the flesh-pots, they served their purpose—, about the degrading character of his role. For the first time he understood the fundamental disharmony between the executive and the legislative branches. For the moment, at least, he and the Senator appeared to have nothing in common.

"Ask for the check," Donegan commanded. "It's time we were moving on."

With abundant relief Walter turned in his chair and snapped his fingers until he had caught the eye of one of the waiters. Thank God, he thought, that I can get rid of this man now. Not that he felt sleepy or had any particular inclination to go home to his flat. On the contrary, had he been alone he would probably have gone to Mme. Nicole's, such had been the stimulus of the wine and the floor show.

"You scored a bull's eye on this one, Haines," Donegan went on. "Now let's see if your favorite cat house is in the same class."

Walter was really thrown this time. Had the evil old man read his thoughts? He was so confused that he could not form a proper reply. Before he knew it, he was saying the wrong thing. "Why—er—I haven't got one."

Donegan chuckled and slapped him on the knee. "So that's it, eh? No favorites. You like 'em all."

"What I meant to say is that I don't know any."

The Senator stopped smiling and regarded him with suspicion. "What do you do for your nooky—or don't you?" he asked.

Walter knew what Donegan was implying. It was the old story about Foreign Service pansies. He couldn't let that one pass. "Look, Senator," he said, "you may not know it, but houses of that kind have been illegal in France since 1946. I know one, sure, a very high-class one at that, with a limited, trusted clientele. It's harder to get into than the United States Senate. I've never told a soul about it. I don't want to spoil a good thing."

Donegan's eyes narrowed. "You're not kidding me, are you?"

"I'm not dumb enough to try that," Walter said frankly. "I'll take you there, but on one condition."

"What's that?" the Senator snapped.

"That you keep the information to yourself. They let me go there because the madam trusts my discretion. If a lot of Americans start ringing her bell, the police will close it, and, what's more, she'll tell them who gave the place away. You can imagine what would happen to me if our security officer found that out."

The Senator did not appear to be listening. He was examining the bill and peeling off thousand-franc notes from a roll. When he had finished he turned to Walter. "Tell him the change is his." But there was no need. The waiter had understood.

On the way to the door the Senator took Walter's arm. He was chuckling to himself. "I suppose you thought I was too old. Well, see here . . . What's your first name, anyway?"

"Walter."

"Call me Mike. Yes, Walter, there ain't many as good as I am at sixty-four," and he went on chuckling until they reached Walter's car.

CHAPTER NINE

IT WAS clear that Mme. Nicole was annoyed. Walter assumed that it was because he had brought the Senator, but he was only partially correct. It was true that she was loath to take on any new clients, particularly Americans, who, she had discovered from long experience, were, as a race, incapable of keeping a good thing from their friends, and their friends were regimental in number; but she was really annoyed to have Walter arrive at this hour. Here it was past midnight and she had told them that he always came between ten and eleven. More than likely Germaine had already left the White Dove and was sound asleep at home. That meant that she would have to wait for his next visit, which might not occur for another three weeks. The chief would be furious and blame it on her. It was all very provoking, but she must hurry to the telephone at once in the vain hope that Germaine was still waiting.

"*Entrez donc, Messieurs,*" she said with an artificial smile, indicating the salon at the left of the small entrance foyer. "*Je vous enverrai des filles tout de suite.*"

They heard her run upstairs, calling "Loulou" as she went. There were muffled voices in the upper corridor and then the sound of footsteps descending the stair. The Senator sat down in an armchair and surveyed the surroundings. It was certainly like no brothel he had been in before. Although he could not have identified it, the décor was in the best tradition of the Empire. The satin brocade curtains were in royal crimson, embroidered with golden bees. The furniture, upholstered in the same material, with its claw feet, swan-neck arms and pedestals, and simple garlands of gilt, was copied from the best examples of the full Napoleonic period. The walls, with their precise and classic Pompeian panels against a dark-red background, added to the effect of antique opulence. Donegan was convinced that Walter had hit another bull's eye.

A thin middle-aged woman, dressed severely in black, came in and greeted Walter. He recognized her as Loulou, Mme. Nicole's second-in-command. She asked if they would care for a bottle of champagne, adding that the girls would be down in a minute. Without consulting the Senator, Walter told her to bring a bottle of the best brut.

"What was that all about?" Donegan asked after Loulou had vanished.

"I told her to bring a bottle of champagne," Walter replied. "She said the girls would be down in a minute."

"They better be good in this setup," the Senator grunted.

There was a titter of whispering voices behind the portieres which separated the salon from another similar room in the rear, and then the curtains parted and three girls came in single file, all smiling demurely. They advanced to where Walter and the Senator were sitting, not brazenly in the manner of seasoned tarts, but hesitatingly, almost shyly. They were all dressed alike in chiffon robes cut in the classic style of the Empire—off the shoulders, with the waistline under the breasts and the skirt falling in straight Grecian folds. They might have been debutantes about to appear at a charity bazaar in a tableau of the Three Graces, except for the fact that every detail of their young, pink, perfectly formed bodies was clearly visible under the sheer fabric of their gowns. The first to enter was a golden blonde whose hair was cut short in a mass of ringlets. She was plumper than the others, her firm breasts set high and wide apart, so appropriate to her costume of 1820 that she looked like a portrait by David. The second had masses of dark-brown hair, drawn up tightly to the top of her head and bound with a purple ribbon. Her smile was less animate, as if it were a faint pretense, hiding a thoughtful nature. The third, if there were any choice at all other than that of the individual taste of the observer, was the most beautiful. She was perhaps two inches taller than her stablemates, with the slender, lithe figure of a thoroughbred. Her breasts were small, but so were her hips. Her brown hair was parted in the middle and the coils over her brow each had a streak of blond, giving a piebald effect which accentuated her green, mischievous eyes.

They all greeted Walter, whom they knew to be a patron; then, as they turned to the Senator, the blonde asked, *"Votre ami, est-ce qu'il parle le français?"*

"Not a word," Walter replied and turned to Donegan. "What name shall I give you?"

The Senator was smiling so broadly in his happy appraisal of the trio that he did not even look at Walter. "They can call me Jim," he said.

"This is my old friend Jim," Walter said, introducing him to the girls.

"Bonsoir, Monsieur Jeem," they chorused before sitting down. Each one selected a chair and immediately crossed her legs and straightened the folds of her tunic. It was all as proper as the reception room of a young ladies' boarding school, that is, if one could forget those pink bodies shining through the chiffon, which, of course, one could not. They all looked at the Senator, perhaps because they knew that

Walter always had his own girl, Jeannette, but perhaps because they found him a new and interesting type. To their eyes he was unusual, to say the least. Most of the men past middle life who came to Mme. Nicole's were worn-out roués who demanded strange and unattractive stimuli for their fading appetites. This one, so big, so strong, so plump, so florid, with such an avid twinkle in his blue eyes, they knew instinctively would heartily enjoy his vigorous love-making. They liked that. It was their chosen profession, to be sure, but that did not deter them from considering it a sport which should be thoroughly enjoyed. When it was, they were happy and slept well, content in the knowledge of a task well done.

The blonde was sitting next to the Senator. They kept smiling at each other, smiles that soon developed into broad grins. "Ask her what her name is?" he said, without altering the grin.

"Jim would like to know your names," Walter said, tactfully including all three.

"I am called Hélène," the blonde said promptly.

"And I am Méduse," the dark girl with the hair on top of her head said.

"And I, Coryphée," the piebald beauty whispered.

"Her name is Hélène," Walter translated for Donegan. He did not bother to repeat the other two names, as it was obvious that the Senator had made his choice.

Loulou came bustling in with a champagne bucket, followed by Mme. Nicole who carried a tray with six glasses, which she placed on the marble-top table in the center of the room. Loulou poured the wine while the madam took a chair and sat down next to Walter.

"Where is Jeannette?" Walter asked her in French.

Mme. Nicole straightened herself in her tight corset and scowled. She was a big woman whose great bosom was encased in a white satin blouse, upon which hung a gold watch with a single brilliant set in the center of its case. At her throat was a cameo brooch, appropriately engraved with a figure of Aphrodite. Her hair, which was dyed a deep Venetian red, was coiled neatly in a chignon on her head. Her face was heavily powdered and rouged. The only clue to her original coloring was her shrewd, beady black eyes. "Ah, Jeannette, that ungrateful one," she snorted. "She has left me—after all that I have done for her. When she came to me a year ago she was nothing but an ignorant peasant who had scarcely ever worn shoes. I made her into a little lady. With that you will agree, I am sure. She was just that—a little lady, worthy to associate with my clientele. And what does she do? She dances off to Algiers. And as if that were not enough, she takes with her one of my most faithful clients. There! I lose a good client and a useful girl all in one night! What ingratitude!"

"I shall miss her," Walter said, quite truthfully. "She was a nice girl." He lowered his voice to a whisper. "Under the circumstances I think I shall try the girl who calls herself Coryphée."

Mme. Nicole raised her hands in a gesture of horror. "Oh, no. Surely no. I have something much better for you. A new girl of the utmost refinement. When Jeannette ran out on me last week I was lucky to find this child—something very special —and I said to myself at once, I shall save her for Monsieur Valtaire. She is his type." She shook her finger at him. "But take care, don't you run off with her as Monsieur Robert did with Jeannette."

"Where is she?" Walter asked, seeing that the Senator and Hélène, having finished their champagne, had risen and started out of the door.

"See you later," Donegan said as he left the room, hurrying impatiently after his plump blonde.

"She will be here shortly," Mme. Nicole replied to Walter, beaming with satisfaction. "When you came this evening it was a great surprise. So late for you who are usually here by ten-thirty. She has not yet been at my establishment. I told her that I would call her when you came. As I told you, I wanted you to be the first to have her."

"My God!" Walter said in astonishment, "She's not a virgin, is she?"

The madam laughed, her bosom shaking. "Alas, my friend, they are impossible to find these days."

Walter was not happy. Everything he had done all evening, beginning with the reception at the Carroways', was contrary to his established pattern of behavior. He considered himself a serious economist, charged with an important role, not one that made him an object of public view, but an anonymous role, the prompter behind the scenes who supplied the actors with the words which were designed to bolster the combined strength of the Atlantic community. The weight of this responsibility never ceased to press on him. He was keenly aware of the trust which had been placed on his shoulders. He also realized that the future of his career depended not alone on the quality of his work but on the dignity of his deportment. Livy was not the sort of man to look with favor on an assistant who spent his nights in cabarets and whorehouses, entertaining visiting firemen, and it was Livy who would furnish the Department with his next qualification report. Yet here he was, drinking champagne at midnight with the madam of a brothel, awaiting the arrival of a new specimen reserved for his special delectation. It was all wrong, and the Senator—the preposterous, earthy Mike—was to blame.

While his annoyance expanded, Mme. Nicole kept up a running fire of conversation to which he listened only partially. Vaguely he gathered that it concerned the high quality of her clientele. The snobbery of it made him smile to himself. She prided herself on catering to men of distinction. How pleased she would be to know that Donegan was a real, live Senator. Had he not been a civil servant, he would have told her, just for the pleasure of hearing her purr.

A bell sounded faintly in the rear of the house and Mme. Nicole jumped to her feet. "*Violà! Elle arrive.*" She motioned to Méduse and Coryphée, who had been silently sipping their champagne, to leave the room, and then she swept out into the foyer. The girls put their glasses on the tray and went out through the portieres, Coryphée going last, turning to give him a seductive smile as she disappeared.

"Germaine, I wish to present Monsieur Valtaire, one of my most distinguished clients," he heard Mme. Nicole say. He turned in his chair and what he saw made him rise instinctively to his feet. He was at once annoyed with himself for having done so. He was well aware that protocol forbade a man from rising when introduced to a girl in a brothel. It was her appearance that had caused the unconscious reaction. He had expected another girl draped in diaphanous chiffon. What confronted him was a handsome young lady in a well-fitted gray worsted suit, with waves of short, unruly chestnut hair and a pair of large, intense, rebellious gray eyes that looked into his without wavering. She was undoubtedly good-looking, but he saw little beyond the eyes.

He held out his hand (another ridiculous *faux pas*), and she gave it a quick pump-handle shake. "It's a pleasure to meet you," he said. (He was behaving like an ass.)

Mme. Nicole beamed on them both, as if she sensed an instantaneous conquest which justified her judgment. "Now run along, my dears. Take the room at the right, at the head of the stairs. Shall Loulou bring you some champagne? It always helps to cement new friendships."

Walter was astonished. He had never seen the madam behave like this before. She was usually so imperious and businesslike.

"Yes, we will have champagne," the girl named Germaine said, without consulting him. "I need it. It is late and I had almost fallen asleep."

"*Bon!*" Mme. Nicole said cheerfully. She made the gesture of shooing chickens. "*Allez-vous en, mes enfants, et amusez-vous bien.*"

When the door to the bedroom was closed, Walter walked over to the dresser and took off his jacket, which he hung methodically on the back of a chair. Then he unknotted his tie and began to unbutton his shirt, when he saw in the mirror that the girl was sitting on the bed but making no effort to undress. Her head was lowered so that the waves of chestnut hair covered her face. She was rubbing the palms of her hands together.

Walter turned. "Aren't you going to undress?" he asked.

"As soon as Loulou brings brings the champagne," she said.

Walter almost laughed. Jeannette had never minded if Loulou saw her naked. Loulou was impervious to nudity—more impervious than he was by a long shot. Was it true, then, what Mme. Nicole had said about this being the girl's first experience as a whore? "Loulou does not mind if you are not dressed," he said.

"But I do," she said in English.

"You're English?" Walter asked in surprise.

"No, I'm French, but I speak English better than you speak French."

"That isn't difficult."

"Oh, you do very well. Better than most Americans."

The door swung open and Loulou barged in with a bottle of champagne and two glasses on a tray. "*Ne vous dérangez pas,*" she sang as she put the tray on the dresser and went out. Walter filled the glasses and brought them over to the bed. The girl took one and raised it to him, looking at him intently again with her big gray eyes. "Cheerio," she said, and emptied the glass in one swallow. Walter watched her, forgetting to drink. She looked at him again, a little defiantly.

"What's the matter?" she asked. "Don't I suit you?"

"I was wondering."

"What about?"

"About you."

"Don't do it. It's a waste of time. Never wonder about girls you meet in a place like this. It's always the same story. It never varies." She got up, put the glass on the tray, and started taking off her jacket. "Let's get on with this."

"Do you want to?"

"No, of course not."

"Then, why should you?"

"Because I'm hired by Mme. Nicole to satisfy your desire." She threw the jacket on a chair and unzipped the placket of her skirt. "Come on, drink your champagne. It's late."

Walter sat down on the bed, still holding his untouched glass of wine. "Sit down a minute. I want to talk to you."

She swung her head around sharply and looked at him, her eyes more defiant than ever. The movement caused her skirt to fall to the floor, disclosing a cheap cotton slip. It was clean. That was all you could say for it, lacking, as it did, the seductiveness Walter expected of the underwear of a courtesan.

"Talk is not part of the bargain," she said curtly.

"Do you mind if . . ." He was buttoning up his shirt.

"If you demand one of the other girls instead of me? Yes, I do mind."

"That's not what I was going to say. But suppose it was. Why should you mind?"

"Because I should probably lose my job. This is my first time here. Mme. Nicole would not like it if I failed to please the first customer, particularly as it is . . ." She shifted her big eyes from him and regarded herself in the mirror.

"As it is what?"

"You."

"Am I that important?" he asked.

"Apparently—in her eyes. I was being saved for you. Aren't you flattered?"

"It depends. Was it because you speak English?"

"Perhaps. That, and the fact that it is, I believe, considered a special privilege to initiate a girl into whoredom."

"Where did you learn your English?'

"From an Englishman."

"Your lover?"

"He was."

"Where is he now?"

"Where all Englishmen end up—in England."

"Would you mind filling my glass?" he asked, holding it out toward her.

She took the bottle and poured the champagne, first for him and then for herself. Lifting the glass to her lips, she looked at him. "Well, are we or aren't we?"

Walter smiled. The girl fascinated him. Her mind was not only alert, it was cultivated. Not that he had had any clue from anything she had said. It was more subtle than that, a manner of phrasing, things like "a special privilege to initiate a girl into whoredom." A foreigner doesn't learn phrases like that by sleeping with an Englishman, not even though he be an Oxford don. "Let's don't and say we did," he replied. He thought he detected a faint smile on her lips as she drank her champagne.

"Then you don't find me attractive," she said finally.

"Oh, yes," Walter said quickly. He was embarrassed and not quite able to explain exactly what his feelings were. "It's this room." He looked around at the stuffy bourgeois opulence of heavy red curtains drawn securely across the window, imitation flowered Savonnerie carpet on the floor, the golden oak dresser with its big oval mirror, the low double bed without footboard—the kind they called "Hollywood" at home—and the *bidet* in the corner with two towels folded neatly across it, on each of which was a small, hotel-size cake of soap. "You don't seem to fit the picture."

"Perhaps if I took my clothes off . . ." She made a gesture as if she would unbutton her blouse.

"No, please don't," he said hastily. "It would only make it more incongruous. It's difficult to explain. You're as good-looking as any of these girls. I can see that. But it isn't the point. Maybe it's the way you talk. Whatever it is, you're not —to me at least—the kind of girl one goes upstairs to bed with the moment one meets her."

"Aren't all women the same?"

"No, of course not, and you know it. Tell me, what made you start this sort of thing?"

"One has to eat."

"Money?" Walter said indignantly. "There are plenty of ways to earn it without doing this."

She shrugged her shoulders. "I can put on my *tailleur*?"

"Sit down here first. I want to know the story."

"Why? Are you a writer looking for atmosphere?"

"I'm curious."

She sat down on the bed beside him, still holding the glass in her hand, and turned her big eyes slowly on him. "You are strangely contradictory, you Americans. You say I am not the sort of girl one makes love to at first meeting. *Tant mieux pour moi.* Would you, then, ask the same girl the story of her life out of pure curiosity when you have known her for only five minutes?"

Walter smiled at her. It was a good question. His mind was alert again, now that the business of love-making had been put aside. "It would depend," he said, "on the cause of the curiosity. Mine is not as *pure* as you think. As I said before, I can't fit you in here. You are—I hope you don't mind my saying so—a fish out of water."

"So you must find the answer to the riddle for your own satisfaction," she said.

"If I didn't find you attractive, I wouldn't care."

She gave a short laugh, which sounded more bitter than amused. "You wish to rescue the damsel in distress. That is very American."

"Uh-huh, I suppose it is. We are very sentimental about our women."

"Do I look as if I wished to be rescued?" she asked with a hard smile.

He looked at her before answering. Her big gray eyes did not flinch. They were opaque, unfathomable, giving off nothing but his own reflection. "Yes," he said gently, "I rather think you do."

The opalescence of her eyes dissolved, the gray deepening in color, becoming gradually liquid. She put a hand on his arm. "*Vous avez raison, cher ami,*" she said in a whisper, and Walter was strangely stirred by this admission that he had sensed the truth.

They sat for a while, silent and without moving. Walter's mind was in a turmoil, ceasing to function with its normal precision, returning to that state of euphoria, not champagne-induced this time, but stimulated by a new and, to him, strange emotion, a sudden glow of strength, of power to protect. The fingers of her hand on his arm had tightened imperceptibly, but he felt it, as if it were a plea. He liked this sensation, the fingers, the faint odor that came to him from her hair, her body, scented, but only faintly, not like the heavy, sickening musk in which Jeannette and the other girls were bathed. This drowning girl was counting on him to bring her to shore. The fingers tightened. They were desperate, he was sure.

The silence was broken by a deep bass laugh in the hall outside their door, followed by a feminine giggle. It was the Senator, Walter knew, as he heard the heavy steps descending the stairs. An involuntary contraction of his muscles made Germaine remove her hand from his arm.

"You will be going now?" she asked.

"Yes," he answered, "I must take my friend to his hotel."

She got up from the bed, picked up her skirt from the floor, and slipped it on. "And don't forget," she said, "we are telling Mme. Nicole that we did."

"When am I going to see you?" Walter asked without moving from the bed.

She shrugged her shoulders. "On your next visit, I suppose."

"Not here. I don't want to see you here."

"Where, then?"

"Tomorrow evening. Any place you say."

She was putting on her jacket before the mirror, straightening her blouse and fluffing out her hair. "Hurry," she said, "put on your tie and coat."

He got up and started knotting his tie. "Where will it be?"

"Do you mean it?"

"I wouldn't have asked you if I didn't."

She hesitated. "There is a bar in the rue Condé . . ."

"Where is that?"

"Near the Odéon. It is called the Bar Condé. It is on the corner of the rue des Quatre Vents. A small place, not very chic. If you like, I could meet you there. What time?"

"Seven thirty."

She looked surprised. "Oh, for an *apéritif*."

"And dinner after." He took a wallet out of his coat pocket, picked out three thousand-franc notes, folded them, and reached out to stick them in the pocket of her jacket.

She caught his hand. "No," she said, "you can't do that. I haven't earned it."

"I thought it was money that you needed."

"You pay Mme. Nicole. I will get my percentage from her." She started for the door, stopped suddenly, said, "*O-la-la, il faut déranger le bidet,*" and darted into the corner, where she tore the wrappers of the cakes of soap, rumpled the towels, and sprinkled them with water. She turned to him and smiled. "Our alibi."

The only light in the narrow Cité Pigalle was a lamp, mounted on a bracket which extended from the wall of a little house opposite. The noise of motors and horns from the boulevards sounded only faintly. A cat scuttled across their path, disappearing into the gloom, as Walter and the Senator, putting their coat collars up, hurried into the rue Pigalle, where Walter had parked his car. There was a chill dampness in the night air. It was not raining, but the pavement was wet.

"By God, that was something," the Senator said.

Walter said nothing. He was disturbed by Germaine and by his own behavior.

"It's a good thing I'm leaving town," Donegan went on. "A kid like that Helen could turn an old man's head. Jesus, what a girl! I'll bet she's not more than eighteen."

CHAPTER TEN

LIVY LOCKE pushed the red button on the edge of his desk and waited. A minute passed before Janice Callery opened the door and came in, dictation book and two pencils in hand.

"Get me the *Congressional Year Book*," he ordered without looking at her. He sat motionless, staring at the window, his face clouded by the excessive concentration of his thoughts.

Miss Callery returned briskly and put the book on the desk in front of him. "Is that all?" she asked.

"Wait a minute." He flipped the pages over quickly until he found the one he wanted, then ran his forefinger down the column of names until it rested below Michael J. Donegan. He noted with satisfaction that the Senator was up for reelection in 1950. Snapping the book shut, he handed it to his secretary. "The briefing has been called off. Senator Donegan is downstairs with the Ambassador. He is coming up to see me in five or ten minutes. Show him right in."

"Very good, Mr. Locke."

"And no calls or interruptions while he's here."

"I understand." She said it purposely, to let him know that she was wise to the fact that he would seek the Senator's help.

Livy glanced up at her sharply, but she smiled sweetly at

him before turning and mincing out of the room with a special walk she used when she wanted her cute little Irish behind to wiggle.

Livy picked up a report and tried to read it, but his mind kept jumping off the page and practicing sentences to be employed in the forthcoming conversation. Finally he gave up all pretense of trying to read, letting his thoughts experiment while he looked into the top left-hand drawer of his desk to be sure the box of outsize Punch cigars was there and ready.

When the door opened, he jumped to his feet and strode out into the room. "Good morning, Senator," he said, with his most charming smile, shaking the fat red hand. "Do sit down."

The Senator plumped himself down in a chair by the desk and yawned. It was such a big, powerful yawn that he was forced to slap his mouth to get it shut. Livy noted that the hand he slapped with held an unsmoked Upmann with its band still on. He recognized it as one of Sherrill's.

"Where's Walter?" Donegan asked. "Did he show up this morning?"

"You mean . . ."

"Walter, your assistant."

"Why, yes, of course."

The Senator chuckled. "That's youth for you. They can take it."

"I don't understand."

"You wouldn't. He's not the kind to go shooting his face off." Then he smiled, not at Livy, but to himself, with a look of rich memories crinkling the corners of his eyes. "He showed me the town last night after leaving that party, and, boy, does he know it."

"Walter Haines?" Livy asked stupidly. The whole thing sounded so unlikely.

"Yeah, and what do you know? I slept right through the briefing. Never got here at all. Well, I guess I didn't miss much."

"Where did he take you?" Livy asked, still incredulous.

"Don't ask me the names or addresses, but they were high-class. Nothing but the best."

"I would never have thought of Walter as a playboy," Livy said guardedly. "He's so—"

"He's no playboy," Donegan said defensively. "He's human. That's what I like about him, he can turn in a job of work without being a Christer."

"You knew him before, then."

"Never laid eyes on him until last night. He offered to give me a lift, so Uncle Mike repaid the kindness by buying him a few bottles of champagne." The Senator rubbed his forehead with the fat hand that held the Upmann. "The way my head feels we must have overdid it. By God, I'll bet we killed a half-dozen quarts between us."

"No doubt it was worth it," Livy said, trying to put a note of good-fellowship into the statement.

Donegan smiled again, the smile of inner pride and satisfaction. "Oh boy, you're telling me! I'm going to nurse this head all across the Atlantic, just for the fun of thinking about it."

"Did you get the reports you asked for?" Livy asked. "I had my secretary leave them at your hotel."

"Yeah," the Senator replied dreamily. He had not been listening. "What? What's that?"

"The reports you wanted. I sent them to your hotel."

"There was a bunch of big envelopes there. I stuffed them in my briefcase." He said it in a tone of extreme boredom.

"I think you'll find them interesting. They contain the

essentials of the structure and purposes of the European Payments Union."

"Did you write 'em?" the Senator asked.

"Yes," Livy said, then added, "that is, Walter and I collaborated."

"He's on the ball, that Walter."

"Good on detail," Livy said stuffily. He suspected that Walter, over his champagne, had told the Senator that he was the author of Livy's reports. This annoyed him acutely.

"He gave me some good slants last night," Donegan went on, ignoring Livy's comment. "In a few words he gave me more real dope on the reasons for all this foreign-aid spending than you can find in a dozen reports. He's the first one to explain it to me in a way I can go out and tell the folks back home so they will understand what it's all about."

"Well, that's fine. I'm glad . . ."

"That's what I mean when I say the boy's on the ball. Yeah, and he said you knew your stuff. Said he liked working for you."

"That's very kind of him," Livy said, without conviction.

"Look here, Locke, what's the use of you and I kidding each other. We swing the ax, sign the papers, and make the speeches. But who does the work, who reads all the stuff and pulls out the nuts, who writes the reports and the speeches? Why, these smart kids like Walter and my assistant, Jimmy Clancy. So where do we figure? Well, I'll tell you—not that you don't know already, because you were smart enough to head up a big bank in Wall Street. If they were to put down all they know, who would read it, who would listen? No one. But let those same words come from Senator Donegan or Mr. Livingston Locke, and right away they're headlines."

Livy smiled. The truth of it was obvious, though he, being less of an extrovert than the Senator, would never have acknowledged it, even to himself. "Also, you have to admit, Senator, that we, the wiser, older heads, guide the policies and exercise the final editorial judgments."

Donegan winked at him. "Okay. Have it your own way."

"When are you flying back to the States?" Livy asked, more to change the subect than out of any particular interest.

The Senator looked at his watch. "Sherrill is sending a car to the hotel for me at four thirty. The plane takes off at six thirty."

"You'll be having a busy time back home."

"The way the Senate has been horsing around it looks as if we'll be in session all summer."

"And you'll have a campaign on your hands," Livy added.

"Yes, and that might turn out to be tougher than you think."

"If I can be of any help . . ."

"I'll let you know."

"You can count on me."

The Senator's eyes narrowed. He looked at Livy appraisingly. "You got ambitions?" he asked.

The question was too direct. It disturbed Livy. "If they are looking for someone for a post . . ."

"Have you got one in mind?"

"Nothing specific. . . ."

"Look, when you've figured out what you want, drop me a line."

"Thank you, Senator, you're very kind."

"You can save the thanks until I need it."

"I told you, you can count on me, Senator."

"Good. That's settled. Now, no more of this Senator stuff. Call me Mike." He got up out of his chair heavily; the spryness of the day before had vanished from his knees. "How do you call yourself?"

"They call me Livy."

Donegan held out his hand. "Okay, Livy, I'll be seeing you."

"There's some talk about my going to Washington for the Senate hearings. If I do, I'll look you up, Mike." Livy's voice was full of friendliness. All fear and disquiet had vanished. The interview had finally turned out better than he had hoped.

They walked toward the door, but the Senator stopped suddenly. "By God, where's Walter? I want to see him."

Livy opened the door and stepped out into the anteroom. "Ask Mr. Haines to come here," he said to Janice Callery, and turned to go back, only to find that Donegan had followed him out.

Janice walked across the room to the door of Walter's office, using, for the second time that morning, her special walk. The Senator watched her behind gyrate with fascination. He nudged Livy and gave him a big wink. Livy was unaware of what it was all about, but to show his good fellowship, he smiled at Donegan knowingly.

When Walter saw that the Senator was with Livy, he felt a cold chill run up his spine. It flashed through his mind that the Senator had been boasting of their exploits of the night before. He knew Livy well enough to realize that he would not be amused. He must have turned pale, because Donegan looked at him and started to chuckle.

"What's the matter?" the Senator asked. "The old head not feeling so hot?"

Walter smiled back at him wanly. He was very unhappy, particularly as he could not fail to observe that both Livy and Janice Callery were looking at him in a sort of wonderment. "Not too bad, considering the hour I got to bed," he said, but his voice came out an octave lower than normal.

Mike laughed. "Well, if it's any comfort, I feel like hell, too."

Livy was in no mood to be critical. In fact, he attributed his success with the usually dour and snappish Senator to Walter's sagacity in taking him out on the town and filling him with champagne. It was a gambit which would never have occurred to him. Walter deserved good marks. He had not only prepared a sound report but had softened the old brute up to the point where he would be useful. "You fellows have me envious," he said jovially. "The next time you'll have to take me along."

Donegan gave Walter a big wink. "What do you say, Walter? Shall we?"

Walter blushed. "I'm afraid that Livy . . ."

"You think I'd be shocked by places like Eve and the Bal Tabarin?" Livy asked, in an effort to appear the good fellow.

Janice, who had been standing by the door to Walter's office, listening, burst into a giggle which she tried vainly to make sound like a cough. The picture of her boss, the dignified Mr. Locke, looking with hungry eyes at the naked girls of the Bal Tabarin had been too much for her. It was so incongruous that the laugh had bubbled up before she could stop it.

When the Senator saw her, choking back the laughter, leaning against the door jamb, red in the face, he suddenly burst into a great guffaw. The champagne of the night before was still tingling in his brain and this was all that was needed to release it. Then Walter, not knowing why, but suffering also from bubbles in the head, added his laughter to the Senator's. The effect was to release Janice from any compulsion of restraint. She wiped her eyes, giggling so hard that she had to clutch her side. Livy looked at them all in wonder before he smiled and chuckled softly just to please the Senator.

Poor Miss Kleinholz, who had been concentrating on her typing, looked up with surprise. She could not believe her eyes or ears. For an instant she thought that either she or they had gone mad—stark, staring crazy. The shock translated itself into an acute desire to escape; so she jumped up from her desk and darted out into the corridor in a race for the ladies' room.

The suddenness of her exit stopped their laughter for a brief second.

"My God, what's happened to her?" the Senator asked.

"She's gone for help," Janice managed to gasp. Then they were off again, laughing louder than ever.

Livy was the first to stop. "I don't want you to go back to Washington thinking this is the way we usually carry on," he said, trying to be serious and light at the same time.

"You pick me up at four thirty, Walter," the Senator said, ignoring Livy's comment.

"Where are we going?" Walter asked with a mystified air, looking at Livy.

"You're going to Orly with me," Donegan replied.

"I think that Sherrill has arranged to have Lambert Charlton accompany you," Livy said.

"I canceled that," the Senator said brusquely. "I told him Walter was to come." He glanced at his wrist watch. "I've got a date with Mrs. Locke. Don't forget, Walter, four thirty."

While Walter, still in a daze, repeated "four thirty" mechanically, Donegan walked over to Janice and held out his hand. "I don't think we've met," he said.

"That is Miss Callery," Livy said.

"Glad to meet you, Miss Callery." He looked her up and down, without letting go of her hand. "A good Irish name. Where are you from?"

"From Worcester, originally," Janice answered, looking straight into his blue eyes without embarrassment.

"Good girl. Now mind, if this Livy Locke don't treat you right, let me know." He gave her cheek a pat.

"He's a very good boss," Janice announced loyally.

"He'd better be. And wherever he goes, he ought to take you with him. There's nothing like a bright Irish colleen to help keep a man on the tracks."

"I hope he's not leaving," Janice said with feigned surprise.

Walter cleared his throat as if the command had just penetrated. "That will be four thirty at the Crillon," he said.

Livy put his hand on the Senator's shoulder. "The best of luck to you on the campaign, Mike," he said cordially.

"I'll take a little of your luck, Livy," Donegan said. "Good-bye now."

Livy walked slowly back to his office. He was very pleased with himself, having momentarily forgotten about the undignified laughter.

CHAPTER ELEVEN

"WE are with Mr. Warren's party," Sam said to the maître d'hôtel as he handed his hat and coat to the *vestiaire*.

The maître d'hôtel looked puzzled and consulted his little *cahier des réservations*. "Warren? Warren? I do not recall the name. You are sure it is at Lapérouse?"

"It's probably under the name of his lawyer," Eleanor suggested. "You said it was he who was arranging the party."

"That's right." Sam looked in his notebook. "I wrote it down. Here it is. Maître Peyraud. Is there a reservation for—"

"Certainly, certainly," the maître d'hôtel said, beaming. "*Bien entendu*. This way, please." He led them to a small staircase which curved upward steeply to the first floor. At the top of the stairs the maître d'hôtel stood aside and motioned, with a sweeping gesture, to the room on the left. It was a small dining room, facing the quay, which had been closed to the regular clients for the evening, the small tables having been removed and replaced by a single large table dominating the center of the room.

As they entered, Percy and Sally Warren stepped forward to greet them and introduce them to Maître Peyraud.

The lawyer was a little man, neatly dressed in a well-cut double-breasted dinner jacket. He appeared to be in his early fifties, almost bald and wearing horn-rimmed spectacles with very thick lenses. His manner was courteous but reserved. "I should like you to meet some old friends of mine," he said to the Lockes in excellent English, and led them over to a group of four people who were talking animatedly at the far end of the room, near the window.

As they approached the group one of its members, a tall, emaciated, elderly man with gray hair, gray drooping mustaches, and a pallid complexion, having only the rosette of the grand cross of the Legion of Honor in the buttonhole of his loose-fitting dinner jacket to lend him any color, lifted his head as a gesture to tell the others that their attention was demanded.

Maître Peyraud acknowledged the look with a smile of thanks and began his introductions. "I wish to present the Honorable Mr. Locke and Madame Lock of the E.C.A. [he pronounced it "aykah"] Mission to Europe, Monsieur le Marquis de Tonville [it was the tall gray man], Madame la Marquise, Lady Lettice Burnham, and Monsieur le Comte de St. Avit."

When they had all shaken hands, Lady Lettice, who had masses of thick chestnut hair, and a face and neck dotted with freckles which she patently made no effort to cover with paint or powder, turned to Sam and said in a shrill, high-pitched voice, "How jolly having Americans with us. Quite a treat, I assure you. One never meets them, though I am told there are absolute masses of them in Paris. You stick to yourselves, no doubt."

"We have a job to do here," Sam said stiffly.

"Evenings, too?"

"Evenings, too."

"How frightfully dull."

Mme. de Tonville stepped out of the group in order to

speak to Eleanor. She was a pale woman who looked twenty years younger than her husband. Her black hair was beautifully coiffed and she wore a very simple but perfectly fitted black taffeta dinner dress with flaring skirt. Her features were delicate and finely chiseled. She looked as if she had been raised in a hothouse and had never been taken out of doors. "I regret," she said slowly, "that I cannot speak English as well as my husband."

"*Alors, parlons en français,*" Eleanor said with a smile.

"Ah, thank God, you have saved me," Mme. de Tonville said in French, raising her eyes to the ceiling in relief. "I dread those evenings when I have to struggle with a strange language. It reduces conversation to the dull essentials—weather, food, and the state of one's family. If one can only speak of the obvious one had better shut up."

"Perhaps it is I who should thank God," Eleanor said. "Since coming to Paris I have lunched and dined on nothing but the obvious."

"But what people do you see?"

"Government functionaries and their wives—from every country of Western Europe."

"Ah, then I understand. They are a race of men who classify all wives as domestic animals. When they talk to a woman they can only think in terms of kitchen utensils and diapers." She suddenly raised her head and looked past Eleanor, squinting her eyes as if her vision were none too good.

Eleanor recognized it as the same sign the marquis had given—the sign of an approaching newcomer. She turned and what she saw made her heart skip a beat. Maître Peyraud was leading a new guest to her end of the room. He was a big, florid man with sandy hair turning gray, and a bristling sandy mustache which was carefully brushed upward, disclosing a pink, sensual mouth. It was Derek Dunglass.

When he saw her he rushed forward, not waiting for Peyraud, and took both her hands in his. "My God, fancy meeting you here! In a *salle privée* in Paris, of all unlikely places."

"You haven't changed, Derek," she said, smiling into his china-blue eyes.

"Not in spirit—er—my dear . . ."

"Eleanor is the name."

"Quite. Eleanor. I've sung it to myself for years, yet the first sight of you drove it clean out of my head."

Mme. de Tonville watched the byplay of this meeting with an amused smile. She knew at once, with the instinct of her race, that it was a reunion of old lovers. Her opinion of Eleanor heightened. Obviously she knew more of French living than the mere language.

Derek suddenly realized that Mme. de Tonville was standing beside them. His ordinarily red face became crimson. "My excuses, my dear Jacqueline," he said in French, making a deep bow. "It was this charming lady who blinded me."

"It is nice to meet old friends," Mme. de Tonville said. "When was it you saw each other last?"

"Oh, I say," Derek blustered, still confused. "It must have been in 1938."

"April, 1937," Eleanor corrected him.

"Was it really?" he asked.

"Trust a woman's memory," the marquise said, with a sly smile at Eleanor.

Eleanor noted that Peyraud introduced him to Sam as Brigadier Dunglass, but he was not introduced to the others, with whom he seemed to be on easy terms of intimacy.

"Nice meeting you at last," Derek said to Sam. "When I

met your wife in New York some years ago, you were off on a trip."

Sam was greatly puzzled by the greeting which he had witnessed between his wife and this British officer. He tried to recall if she had ever mentioned anyone by the name of Dunglass, or even a nameless Englishman, but he drew a blank. And that was what disturbed him, for she had a habit of describing in detail any new person she met who had impressed her. The expression of her face as she had been held by both hands by this chap seemed to indicate that she had once been very impressed. He made a mental note to question her about this. In the meantime he would get in a word with Percy Warren and explain why he had had to break the date on Wednesday. He wondered whether it was out of pique that Percy had changed the plans from a little dinner of four at the Ritz to this oddly mixed affair in a little Left Bank restaurant with a group he neither knew nor fancied.

Eleanor sat between Maître Peyraud and the Comte de St. Avit. She liked the party. She had been aware from the beginning that Peyraud had selected the guests for their urbanity and knowledge of English. She leaned toward him. "Tell me," she said in a low voice, "about each one of Percy's guests."

Peyraud smiled. "You are asking for a great deal. First, they are my dearest friends. Second, they are as different from each other as it is possible for people to be. Let us start with Jacqueline de Tonville. She is a critic of literature and art, a brilliant woman who writes *feuilletons*— Now, how would you say that in English—'essays,' perhaps?"

"We would call her a columnist," Eleanor said.

"That is the word. She is a columnist who is often a calumnist. She wields a bitter pen when she dislikes."

"And her husband?" Eleanor asked.

"He also writes, but in a different vein. He is a philosophic historian—a medievalist."

"He seems much older than his wife."

"In years only."

"And the man on my right?" she whispered.

"Ah, there is a paradox! How can one describe Christian de St. Avit? To each of his friends he is a different being. What you see in Christian is a commentary on your own character. I see him as a patriot, as a symbol of the true spirit of France. . . ."

"What does he do?"

Peyraud smiled at her again. "In the sense that one is employed at a regular job, nothing. He thinks and he talks."

"And writes?"

"Not yet. He may some day. All Frenchmen of cultivation do eventually. Now he is young and wisely allows his thoughts to cook slowly on the back of the stove."

Eleanor tasted the *quenelles de brochet* which the waiter had placed before her. Their consistency was as airy as down and the flavor of pike was mellowed by a sauce which only a master chef could have devised. Then she sipped the cold Mersault, with its perfume of flowers as wedded to the fish as iris to the water's edge. She listened while Peyraud told her about Lettice Burnham, the defiant daughter of an eccentric earl, who preferred Paris to the family seat in Gloucestershire and who, when the spirit moved her, wrote malicious novels about her county upbringing in which the heroine was always escaping across the Channel with some elegant bounder of a foreigner. Eleanor could not prevent the evil thought from rising to the surface of her mind that Sam and the Warrens were miserably out of place in this company, and that Peyraud had invited his friends for the purpose of proving something —something derogatory to Americans. *Tant pis*, she thought, at least I am enjoying it, and she let her eyes take in the setting: the low-ceilinged room with its mirrored walls which reflected the long table with its center a cascade of daffodils.

Peyraud was about to launch into a brief biography of Derek Dunglass when St. Avit turned to her. "I have just said to Lettice," he announced, "that English is a language which should be spoken only by the English and written only by Americans. I think she is angry with me, so I must steal you from René Peyraud."

"Being an American, I, too, should be offended," Eleanor said in French.

"You are not, however," he said, continuing in English, "because you Americans value the written word far more than the spoken one. Compare the *Congressional Record* with *Hansard* and you will see what I mean."

"What about the speeches of Roosevelt?" she asked, not that she really disagreed, but to draw the young man out.

"He rarely spoke extempore as Churchill does," St. Avit replied. "He read, in a rather flat but melodious voice, the beautiful phrases that were written for him by a craftsman. By mentioning Roosevelt you have fortified my argument. The pleasures of rhetoric, which is our Latin heritage, and which the English have continued to emulate, are no longer enjoyed in your country, though they were in the eighteenth century when you were still a colonial by-product of Europe. Perhaps it is because you have taken in so many other races with other mother tongues that speech has become slovenly and limited. Your spoken language is a sort of pidgin English of scant vocabulary which relies on inflection to convey meaning."

"You have been in the United States?" Eleanor asked.

"Never."

"Then how do you know so much about our speech?"

"You forget that your invasion of France, which began in 1917, has continued with ever increasing force until now. What with the tourists, the NATO, the USIS, the Marshall Plan, and God knows what other agencies, there are large areas of Paris where one hears nothing but 'hi,' 'hey,' and 'what-the-hell.'" As he spoke, his blue eyes scrutinized her appraisingly. She was aware of this, aware that his words, as he had said, were the mere pleasure of rhetoric and therefore totally removed from emotion.

"Do you resent the invasion?" she asked, turning to catch him calmly observing the back of her neck.

"Not at all," he said, without interrupting his study. "On the contrary, I find it amusing and exhilarating. Nothing delights me more than the sight of masses of earnest people busily engaged in doing good."

"You concede, then, that we are doing good."

"Unquestionably—you are saving us."

"From the Russians."

He shrugged his shoulders while he sniffed the Richebourg 1935 which the sommelier had just poured. "Perhaps; but chiefly you are saving us from ourselves."

"You make us sound like missionaries."

He looked at her in surprise. "But of course! That is what you are, are you not?"

Eleanor laughed. "Even supposing it were true, do you like being converted?"

"Not in the least. In fact, I never shall be. But then, I am not a typical example. I observe, but I do not join in." He tasted the duck—Caneton Colette—which was a specialty of the house, then broke a piece of bread and put it in his mouth. "Now you must tell me, dear madame, what you do here in Paris while your husband supports the franc on his capable shoulders."

"I play the part of a good wife," Eleanor said, hoping that the truth would disconcert him. There was something so assured and didactic about him that she could feel her feathers ruffling. No young man as good-looking as he was, she felt, had the right to hit the nail so squarely on the head. He was having fun with her, being naughty on purpose to demonstrate that he, at least, felt no gratitude toward her country. "I look after my children and my ménage, and when not doing that, I read and, like you, observe without joining in."

"Very interesting," he said, suddenly turning his face to her with a smile, "and quite unlike the accepted picture of the American wife."

"You mean the pampered lady who spends her mornings shopping and her afternoons at the cinema?"

"Exactly—the beautiful, spoiled creature to whom the advertisers sing their praises on bended knee. When she is old and no longer beautiful, I am told she joins a club where she wears orchids on her enormous bosom and makes speeches about the evils of sex."

Eleanor laughed. "I can hardly wait for my moment to come."

"Your speech is already prepared?" he asked.

"I am gathering the material."

"You have come to the proper place."

At the other side of the table, Derek Dunglass was talking animatedly in French with Mme. de Tonville, but his eyes were constantly darting across to Eleanor. Once or twice their eyes met and she saw his wrinkle at the corners in a signal of secret understanding which she remembered. What a strange coincidence, she thought, that he should have reentered her mind on that morning only three days ago. What psychic influence had brought Derek back after all these years? It was as if that recall had been a warning that he was in Paris and they were destined to meet again. She could feel the fingers of the old emotion tickling her throat. She had loved him once, and she wondered now as she watched him eating, drinking, talking, laughing in his hearty, extrovert British way whether love ever finally faded, whether or not that special compartment of her heart which had been his might open again. Looking down the table at Sam, her husband, the father of her children, she saw that he was holding forth pompously, not to anyone in particular, but to everybody at his end of the table. The missionary, she thought.

When the coffee and the *fine champagne* arrived, Derek picked up his cup and *ballon* and motioned to the waiter to bring his chair to the opposite side of the table, at the same time apologizing to Mme. de Tonville, who, having already sensed the situation, urged him to go and sit by Eleanor. He had the chair placed between her and St. Avit.

"Old man, you'll have to excuse me for separating you from this charming lady," he said to Christian in French, "but I have not seen her for many years and we have much to talk about."

"I quite understand," St. Avit said. "Even I, who have only known her for an hour, find talking to her a particular pleasure."

"I hear that you are living here," Derek said to Eleanor in English. "Your husband's one of the Marshall Aid chaps."

"That's right, Derek," Eleanor said. "We have a house in Neuilly. You must come and see us. And you—just here on a visit?"

"I'm a commuter—work in Paris and week-end in Kent."

"Married?"

"Just after my trip to the States in nineteen thirty . . ."

"Seven."

"Got caught on the rebound."

She smiled. It was so like him to include her among the reasons for his marriage. "Children?"

"Three. And you?"

"Two. Your wife doesn't mind that you spend your weeks in Paris?"

"She's furious with me. Can't say I blame her. If you could see what little she has to feed herself and the children, while I wallow about in places like this, gorging on caneton, filet mignon, and crêpes suzettes. She's a jolly good girl, though, keeps a stiff upper lip. I think she'd chuck me if it were not for my smuggling."

"Smuggling?"

"Shsh! Not so loud," he whispered. "It's strictly against the rules, but how can I tell her about these meals without bringing the old girl a morsel or two—a bit of cheese, a ham, a roast of veal—wrapped up in my soiled linen."

"Good for you," Eleanor said feelingly. "It must be hard on her."

"Oh, she manages to bear up without me," Derek said lightly. "She has the kids and her garden. She's an absolutely mad gardener." He stopped smiling and looked at her pensively. "You know, Eleanor, I believe you're more beautiful than ever."

"Don't be silly, Derek, I'm nothing but an overfed matron."

"Just my dish."

She smiled at him. "That's what you used to say."

"And I say it again, with the same emphasis."

"What do you do here?" she asked, trying to get him on safer ground.

"Oh, staff rot. You know, military committee of NATO. What day next week will you lunch with me?"

"I'll have to ask Sam what his engagements are."

"Sam's not in this. Just us two—tête à tête—to talk over old times."

"Should we, Derek?"

"Why on earth not? I know a lovely little place."

"You always know 'a lovely little place,' don't you?"

"My hobby. How about Tuesday?"

"No good. It's the hairdresser's day."

"Wednesday?"

"I'll think it over. Give me a ring when you get back from Kent."

"Righto."

Sam had risen and was saying goodbye to Sally Warren. He moved down the table, shaking hands with everyone, a frozen smile on his face which Eleanor recognized as the expression of polite boredom. She got up from her chair as Sam neared her. As she did so, St. Avit jumped to his feet and kissed her hand.

"I am at your service, madame," he said, "if you should need help in gathering your material."

Eleanor smiled at him pleasantly. He was a strange young man, so attractive, yet so annoying.

"What's your telephone number?" Derek asked.

"Neuilly 32-76. Au revoir, Derek."

"I'll give you a ring on Monday," he said, giving her hand an extra squeeze.

"Good God!" Sam said when they were seated in the car. "Whatever made Percy do a thing like that?"

"Like what?" Eleanor said.

"Like that party. Who were those people, anyway? Incredible lot."

"I thought they were rather fun."

Sam grunted. "You would. A lot of half-baked writers and dilettantes. Just a waste of time. If I were Percy, I'd fire that fellow Peyraud tomorrow. Never catch me putting any business his way. He's a lightweight." He turned his head and looked at her sharply. "Who was the Britisher you seemed to know so well?"

"Brigadier Dunglass. He's with NATO."

"Where did you know him?"

"In New York, years ago."

"Never heard you mention his name."

She shrugged her shoulders. "That's possible."

Eleanor had no desire to prolong the conversation. She wanted to unravel with care all of the thoughts and impressions which had been weaving a squirming tangle in her mind during the course of the evening. Each one of the strands had to be separated, examined, and placed in its proper category of truth or falsity, of wisdom or ignorance. The effect of the crazy pattern had been attractive to her. Whatever the final analysis, the afterthoughts, the tingling pleasure of the evening would not be erased. They had been her kind of people, the company towards which, left alone, she would gravitate. Of course there had been Derek, but she must avoid pigeonholing the pleasure on that plane. And young St. Avit had scrutinized her face, her eyes, her hair, her *nuque,* as if he were a judge deciding whether this filly deserved the blue rosette; but, again, that was reducing a single effect to a level below the merit of the whole, like examining the nudity of a figure by Ingres instead of seeing the perfection of the canvas as unity of art. It had been a good evening, one she would not forget, but without Sam and the Warrens it would have been brilliant.

For his part, Sam was irritated on three counts. He tossed his cigarette out the car window and settled back in his corner to enumerate them to himself. They were crossing the Pont de la Concorde, and the lights on the bridge and on the great oblong plaza in front of them were ringed with halos in the gathering mist. The pinnacle of the obelisk was lost in infinity, and Gabriel's massive monuments, housing now the Crillon, the Automobile Club, the Guaranty Trust Company, and the Ministry of Marine, were but dim outlines, bisected by the faint lights of the rue Royale.

But Sam was unaware of this incomparable Whistler-like nocturne. All that his eyes took in were the lights in the windows of the Ambassador's room in the Hôtel Talleyrand. That meant that Sherrill must have returned. Only Sherrill would be working, driving himself in an orgy of dedication while everyone else was on his way to bed. For some reason this added to his irritation. It raised the count to four. The car swung up the Champs Elysées as he began to catalogue them in order. Number one: a quiet, comfortable, sensible evening, during which he would learn enough of Ulysses profit forecast to make the proper adjustments in his block of common and would be able to suggest, imply, subtly plant the notion that he, Livy Locke, was available if the White House was looking for a capable diplomat, had been ruined by the introduction of a group of extraneous, volatile, inconsequential foreigners, shabby aristocrats posing as intellectuals, a second-rate menagerie gathered together as a side show by a popinjay of a lawyer who wanted to show the visiting firemen Paris, in quotes. Number two: Eleanor had swallowed the bait, hook, line, and sinker, falling for the notion, carefully planted by Peyraud (he had seen them with their heads together and guessed that the lawyer had been dishing out highly colored biographies) that she was being accorded the enviable opportunity of meeting the most select coterie of wits, which was clear proof that she was still socially irresponsible and, in spite of appearances, had never changed. Number three: the evening had been a complete waste, and he had no evenings to waste from now on out. Number four: why should Sherrill rush from Orly Field to the office instead of waiting until morning, when the whole staff would be there and he could carry out his new instructions with some degree of order?

"What's the matter, darling, don't you feel well?"

"Nothing the matter with my health, if that's what you mean," Sam grunted.

"You left so early."

"I've got a heavy day tomorrow."

"Even so . . ."

"Skip it."

Eleanor looked out at the misty Avenue de Neuilly, finding the reflections of the street lights on the glistening pavement a solace.

CHAPTER TWELVE

WALTER parked his car around the corner in the rue St. Sulpice and walked back to the bar. Although it was seven o'clock, the light of the cloudless spring evening was still strong enough to show up the newly painted mustard trim with its large red letters saying, "Bar Condé." Inside, the bar itself, high and zinc-covered, dominated the narrow interior, and Walter wondered if they would have to take their drinks standing up, like the workmen and the clerks now there, sipping their wine and *apéritifs*. It was only when he entered the open door and looked around that he saw the little tables in the right-hand corner, at one of which Germaine was sitting. She stood up to greet him.

"*Ça vous gêne de parler en français?*" she asked.

"*Du tout,*" he answered, and they sat down.

"I think it is better to speak French here," she said, continuing in her own tongue. "You see, I am known in the *quartier*, and it might cause talk if I were heard speaking English with an American."

"You mean that you are known here as—how do you call it? —an honest girl?"

"'Serious' would perhaps be a better word."

Walter was pleased to find that she was just as good-looking as the picture retained by his champagne-clouded memory. If anything, here in the daylight, against the drab background of the rue des Quatre Vents as seen through the glass front, she was more than handsome, with her unruly, yet ruled, waves of chestnut hair, her large, somber gray eyes, her clear complexion, unaided by makeup, like the smooth skin of a nectarine. Wearing the same gray worsted suit and a simple cotton blouse, she looked what the French would call "*convenable.*" Yet, appealing and eminently respectable as the picture appeared, he was not happy. He had regretted the impulsiveness, champagne-induced, which had prompted him to make this date. Sober reflection had told him that there was, there must be, a hitch in it. Either she was no better than the other girls in Mme. Nicole's establishment, except for an ability to speak English and act a role with credible conviction, or she was engaged in some kind of confidence game, probably in cahoots with the madam, in the belief that he was a rich, guileless young American who could be played for a sucker. He should, of course, not have shown up here at all. Maybe this was the gang's hangout. Why had he been fool enough to meet her? Curiosity, perhaps, and perhaps plain loneliness. Well, he was here, and he might as well play it through and mark it off to education; after all, he was poor pickings.

The man behind the bar leaned over and asked them what they wanted. She ordered a Bourin, and Walter, after some hesitation, said he would take a Cinzano. He did not like these sweet French *apéritifs* much, but he felt that ordering a martini or a whiskey would have marked him too readily.

"You live near here?" he asked her.

"I used to."

"With your parents?"

She hesitated. "No, when I was a student."

"After the war?"

"During the war and after for a short time."

"At the Sorbonne?"

"Yes, in English literature and in history."

"Ah," Walter said, "then you knew English before you met the Englishman."

"Enough to read and write. With him I learned to speak. And you, where did you learn French?"

"I work here. I speak very badly."

"Not badly. You are in business?"

Here it comes, Walter thought. This is the size-up of my economic potential. Better nip this one quickly. "I'm just a government functionary, not even a big one."

She smiled at him. "And even the little ones have automobiles?" she asked.

"How did you know I had an automobile?"

"I watched you pass by in your beautiful machine and go into the rue St. Sulpice."

"They don't cost much in the United States," he said in defense.

"So everyone has one there."

"Yes, everyone, even the factory workers."

"Even the little girls who work in houses like that of Mme. Nicole?" she asked, with the suspicion of a smile at the corners of her eyes.

"We don't have houses like that. They are forbidden."

"But they are forbidden here, too."

"Well, maybe there are a few," Walter conceded, "but I've never been in one."

"You had your little friend?"

"Not a regular one. Just from time to time, when I felt like it. It's difficult to explain. Everything is different over there."

"Love is different in the United States?" she asked.

"We don't call that love," Walter said sternly. "With us love is something serious."

"Interesting," she said. "You must explain this to me when we can speak English."

"Let us eat now. I am very hungry." The conversation was getting very boring and out of hand. The comparative mores of France and the United States was a subject he had no wish to discuss, chiefly because he was acutely conscious of his own ignorance; besides, it was far too complex for his meager French.

"Good. As you wish," she said pleasantly, as if she fully expected him to make the decisions. "There is a nice little restaurant quite near here."

This time he was not going to get caught in a joint of her choosing. "We are near the Odéon, aren't we?" he asked.

"Yes, it is only two steps."

"Then we shall go to La Méditerranée," Walter announced with finality.

She looked surprised. "But that is a gunshot."

"What do you mean?"

"It is an expression. It means it is very expensive."

"Never mind for once," he said, determined to go there. He had heard his colleagues in O.E.E.C. speak of it as one of the best restaurants in Paris and he was curious to try it, and, above all, he did not want to go to one of her hangouts.

Germaine shrugged her shoulders. "As you wish," she said amiably.

They paid the barman and walked out. While they stood waiting for their change, Walter had taken pains to observe if any of the customers made sign of recognition. But they ignored them.

"The car is in the rue St. Sulpice," Walter said in English as soon as they were in the street, out of earshot.

"It is better to leave it there," Germaine said. "If you take it to the Place de l'Odéon, the *chasseur* will send word to the maître d'hôtel and the prices will go up."

"How far is it?" Walter asked.

"As I told you, only *deux pas*. Just up there." She pointed to where the rue Crébillon angled off to the left about a block away.

They walked up the rue Condé in silence. Dusk had fallen, deepening the gray of the buildings. The street was virtually empty. The only shops in this section dealt in surgical supplies and they were closed for the day, the writhing forceps and scissors hanging in their windows reflecting the light from the street lamps. There was something eerie about these instruments of pain guarding their passage up the deserted street which made Walter shudder. When they reached the angle of the rue Crébillon, Walter took her arm and they crossed to the other side. He glanced down at her. Yes, he could get away with it if he were to be seen by an acquaintance. She looked respectable, even ladylike. They might even envy him, he thought, and that made him feel better. What he had not noticed was the police station on the corner, but Germaine had, and it had made her laugh to herself, thinking, "The poor *flics*, if they only knew!"

The entrance to La Méditerranée disappointed Walter, with its baskets of molluscs and shrimps next to the door, crowding the narrow passage. He had expected something imposing and slick, like the Café de Paris. The small foyer, with its high counter and desk for the cashier, with its paintings of St. Tropez by artists who deserved anonymity, was hardly impressive. It was all very small, cut up into little rooms with low ceilings, and everywhere the paintings of boats and fish and seminude bathers, like a stage set of a harbor hangout for artists on the Côte d'Azur. Not what he expected, not in the least.

The maître d'hôtel, or what seemed to be the maître d'hôtel, though it might have been the proprietor, as he was dressed in a brown business suit, came forward with an inquiring expression.

"A table for two," Walter said.

"Here, or upstairs?" the man asked. They were lucky to have the choice. Seven-thirty was early for this place, the regular clientele rarely arriving until eight-thirty.

"What do you say?" Walter asked Germaine.

"Upstairs is better," she answered softly.

The man understood English, for he said quickly, "Good. You have only to mount and take the table which pleases you."

They found a table by a window looking out on the Odéon. A waiter gave them each an enormous sheet of paper which was the menu. They studied it in silence.

"What would you like to start with—hors d'oeuvres, soup?" Walter asked.

"One comes here to eat fish," she said gently, as one might to a child who must learn about the world.

"That's right, I forgot. How about oysters?"

"Have you ever eaten bouillabaisse?" she asked.

"No. What's that?"

"It is a fish stew of the Mediterranean. Very good indeed. It is a specialty here."

"That's fine. Let's try it." Though far from being a gourmet, Walter had a keen desire to learn about French food. "And after that?"

"It is a meal in itself," she said modestly.

"We must have another course," he insisted. "How about a lobster?"

"That would be too much. Better we should have this."

She leaned over the table and pointed to an item on his menu. "Coquille St. Jacques Provençale."

"That's scallops, isn't it. All right, it suits me."

"You don't mind *ail*—garlic?"

He smiled. "Not if you eat it, too."

Walter gave the order to the hovering waiter; then the sommelier, a big man in a blue denim apron, handed him the wine card. Walter opened it, looking at her. "What shall it be? A Burgundy?"

"You don't mind if I suggest?" she asked hesitatingly.

"Go ahead. I don't know much about wines."

"With a bouillabaisse one should drink a very dry, pleasant wine that is not too heavy and is very, very cold." She looked at the sommelier and repeated the sentence in French, adding, "*N'est-ce pas?*"

"*Précisément, Mademoiselle,*" the sommelier agreed. "*Je vous recommande une bonne bouteille de Gewürztraminer de quarante-cinq, bien glacée.*"

"That is a wine of Alsace, very good with fish. Do you agree?" she asked Walter.

"Sure. Whatever you say. Is it red or white?"

Germaine could not suppress a look of pained surprise as the sommelier smiled. "But one does not drink red wine with fish," she exclaimed.

"Oh," Walter said, blushing. He would rather have learned this bit of information without the presence of the sommelier.

When they were alone again he looked at her. She was gazing out of the window at the classic columns of the Odéon, now showing almost white against the blackness of the portico. It was an off day—*jour de relâche*—for the Comédie Française, so the only lights on the building were the single bulbs which flickered like stars high up under the colonnade.

Her profile, he thought, was classic, too, like the Hellenic heads in the Louvre, except that her nose, unlike most of those marbles, was intact—straight, narrow, ending in a bevel which gave it an aristocratic air. Her mouth curved down slightly at the corner, a sad, unhappy mouth, almost wistful, and yet at the same time defensive, bitter. Where her neck met her chin there was a slight outward curve which lent her features a softness, a boneless quality, something pleasant to touch, amending the pity that the mouth inspired.

"I take it you've been here before," Walter said finally.

She turned quickly to him with a smile. "Once," she said.

"With the Englishman?"

"As a matter of fact it was."

"Tell me about him."

"There is nothing to tell. He was nice, a little brusque, perhaps, very demanding, but he was good to me."

"And then he left."

"Exactly."

"Just like that?"

"Just like that. He had to go to England. Said he would come back, but he never did. He left me some money, and when that was gone . . . well, you know."

"Does he write?"

"Never."

"Where did you meet him?" Walter asked.

"In the Résistance. He joined us by parachute."

"You worked in the Resistance?" He pronounced it as an English word.

"For four years."

The sommelier brought an ice bucket with the opened bottle of Traminer pointing out of it like an antiaircraft gun in an emplacement. Then the waiter brought two big soup plates, big enough for washbasins, brimming with liquid from which protruded claws and bits of fish. Walter tucked a napkin over the top button of his coat and took a taste of the broth. It was a medley of conflicting, harmonizing flavors, obvious, blatant, subtle, delicate, ranging from saffron to garlic, but never completely drowning the underlying aroma of fish.

"You like it?" Germaine asked.

"I can't tell yet, but I think so," Walter answered.

They ate in silence for a while. It is difficult for one not born in the Provence to eat bouillabaisse and talk. Halfway through, Walter put down his spoon and fork and took a long drink of cold Traminer to rest his palate.

"I still don't understand it," he said.

"What is it you do not understand?"

"Why you want to work in a place like Mme. Nicole's."

"I never said I *wanted* to," she said, frowning.

"But if you don't want to, you don't have to," he protested. "You can't make me believe that a girl of your education, who studied at the Sorbonne, who speaks English as well as I do—maybe better—who knows her way around in places like this—you know, knows what to order and what wine goes with it—can't get a decent, respectable job."

She looked out of the window again with the wistful-bitter expression at the curve of her mouth, still holding a spoonful of fish. "There are reasons why I cannot get such a job," she said, so quietly he could hardly hear her words. "Reasons which I cannot explain."

"Having to do with the war?"

She nodded ever so slightly, and went on eating.

Walter was confused. What could she have done to acquire a police record which prevented her from getting a job? Communism? No. Obviously that was no deterrent, not in postwar France, where the Party was accepted as a legal and political entity and took good care of its members. Besides, the last place one would find a Commy would be in a whorehouse. The smart ones, the agents, were intellectuals who found good jobs in high places. Collaboration? That was more likely. Maybe she had been tried and was a marked woman, with the facts inscribed on her identity card. He began to pity her. The suspicions about her playing him for a sucker had vanished. Why, he didn't know, except that there was nothing about her which even faintly resembled the scheming adventuress. Collaboration. That was it all right. That would be the brand on her, not Communism, which bothered no one, not even the police. In any event, there was no point in beating her over the head with an inquisition which patently made her unhappy. He would have to find a new subject, something more in keeping with the good food, the view of the Odéon, her pretty face.

"Do you like music?" he asked with an attempt at gaiety. He realized it was clumsy, but small talk was something he knew as little about as wine.

"Yes," she said, with an expression of surprise. "Yes, very much." Then, realizing he was an American, she became cautious. "What kind of music do you mean? Jazz?"

"No, I meant good music, music like Beethoven and Bach."

She looked relieved. "Yes, of that I am very fond."

"It's my hobby. Not that I know much about it, but I love it, I really do. I can listen to it by the hour."

"You go to the concerts?"

"Sometimes. But mostly I sit home and play the phonograph. I have a nice little collection of records."

"You have the Beethoven symphonies?"

"Only the Fifth and the Seventh, but I have a lot of other things you know, like Bartók and Stravinsky and Katchaturian. What do you like?"

"It is difficult to say," she said thoughtfully. "I like so many composers—Mozart, Ravel, Poulenc. . . . So, you sit in your hotel room and play your gramophone. That does not sound like an American."

"You say that because you met me at Mme. Nicole's after I had been to a night club with Sen—— that friend of mine. Well, I'll tell you something, believe it or not, that was the first time I've been to a night club since I've been in Paris. What's more, I don't live in a hotel. I have my own little apartment in the sweetest spot in Paris."

"And what do you call 'the sweetest spot in Paris'?" she asked with a smile.

"The Quai d'Orléans on the Ile St. Louis," he answered emphatically.

Her smile changed, brightening with warmth and understanding. "Perhaps you are right," she said. "It is the very heart of Paris."

"Where the Romans founded Lutetia," he added proudly.

"Maybe, but as one sees it today it is the Paris of Louis XIII, of his Italian mother, Marie de Médicis, and of those great scoundrels who were stronger than either of them, the Cardinal Richelieu and *son éminence grise*."

The chord had been struck. Without either of them being aware of it, something in an instant had broken through the suspicion, the distrust, the parrying, the watchful guile, as they wove it into invention and counterpoint. He, for his part, forgetting caution, no longer caring about her doubtful past, seized gratefully the welcome harmony, the safety of scholarship and history. At ease now, he dropped without knowing it all shyness, expanding, letting his thoughts flow from his tongue, listening, absorbing, accepting her corrections and amendments, feeling the excitement, the joy of discussing the subject which he had been secretly studying during these past months while his phonograph played and the faint sound of automobile horns on the Quai de la Tournelle echoed across the Seine—Paris, and its place in the history of France. Perhaps there were others among his French acquaintances who knew as much about it as this girl, but they were economists who, believing him to be the voice of the oracle, kept the talk firmly on the immediate, pressing plight. Until this moment he had kept it to himself, learning bit by bit from the books he had bought along the quays, slowly from the precise French sentences. It was a release, this, hearing her recite in her clipped Oxford English, telling him the little anecdotes, the human touches of triumph and disaster which his books had failed to give, knitting the whole together in a consequent tapestry, believable and bright, from the Merovingians to Henri IV.

With this stimulation of his mind came the accompanying excitement to his body as with each mouthful of the bouillabaisse, the Coquilles St. Jacques, the Traminer, a glow suffused him, heightening the color of the words, of what he saw; he did not know, of course, that what he was experiencing was an initiation into the secret of French civilization, its profundity of sensation, of subjectivity.

It was inevitable that, after the coffee and a *fine*, she would agree to go to his flat to listen to his record of "La Valse" by Ravel.

CHAPTER THIRTEEN

GERMAINE had seen him as they walked out of the door of La Méditerranée—Alexis de Breuil, with a chic, pretty girl, entering from the street. She had turned her head quickly, hoping he would not notice her, but when they had passed in the narrow doorway, he had said, "Still getting recruits, my captain?" The impertinence had stung her and she had whispered, looking at the girl, who might have been a *vedette* or a mannequin, "Yes, but not your kind, Alexis." She had hoped that Walter had not overheard.

She was feeling very smug, very pleased with herself, sitting next to Walter in his Chevrolet as they turned into the Quai St. Michel from the rue Danton. Patently she had played it flawlessly, keeping him guessing, suspicious, until she had found the note which made him echo, or rather—and this she considered the cleverest gambit—until he himself had disclosed the note. She had been worried in the beginning, at the Bar Condé and while they were ordering dinner. He had been so clearly ill at ease, so obviously suspecting the disparity between herself and the tarts at Mme. Nicole's. It had looked hopeless for a time, as if he had regretted making the engagement at all. For a moment, on the walk up the rue Condé, she had wondered if perhaps she should switch her cover, break down and confess that she was, in reality, nothing but a little whore trying to touch him for his bankroll and throw herself on his mercy. Thank God she had not succumbed to that idea. It would have been fatal, she knew now, now that she had had a chance to learn what he was really like—a child, an earnest little boy, happy with his new toys of culture. She was confident that if she played it as she had through dinner, with the same studentlike solemnity (so easy, in that she was merely reverting to a former self, an earlier, incandescent girl who was blinded by her own inner light), it would all come out, fall into place, according to plan. The thing to do was to keep it sweet, trusting, motherly, without a breath of sensuality. The story about being unable to get a decent job would, of course, have to be carefully embroidered. He would want to know it eventually, when he had, in his stupid, sentimental Anglo-Saxon way, fallen in love with her; but there was time yet to work out that design. For the moment she must keep up the pretense that it was a subject so distasteful and galling that it had better not be mentioned. Somehow that Englishman—should he be a lieutenant or a captain?—would have to be involved in it.

"What did that fellow mean when he asked you if you were still getting recruits?" Walter asked. They were crossing the river now, on the Pont de la Tournelle.

So he had heard after all. Germaine wondered if his original suspicions had returned. "He knew me from the Résistance. Recruiting used to be my job."

"Here, in Paris?"

"Yes, from among the university students."

"Why did he call you 'my captain'?"

"That was my rank."

"Was he being sarcastic?"

"I am afraid he was."

Walter glanced at her. She had purposely turned her head

away, assuming the wistful look. He seemed satisfied, for he said, "I should have poked him in the jaw."

"That would have been a very great mistake," she said sadly.

"I suppose so. No sense to that sort of thing. But he made me mad just the same, making a crack like that when we were all nicely in the mood for Ravel."

"The mood will return with the music," she said softly.

Walter turned the car left on the Quai d'Orléans and stopped in front of number 26. Switching off all but his parking light, he jumped out and raced around to her side, opening the door and waiting for her to descend. He pushed the doorbell twice and the door clicked open and lights went on in the entry and up the narrow stairway. They were timed to allow the fourth-floor tenant to mount the stairs and open his door before they went out automatically, thus giving Walter, who lived on the third floor, plenty of time to reach his flat without groping for the switch.

The apartment had obviously belonged to people of taste, for it was attractively decorated, not lavish but with a certain flair for combining old and new. The paneling of the small oblong foyer was painted in ivory white, which made a bright frame for a Venetian console, surmounted by a large Italianate mirror. Walter preceded the girl to the left in order to turn on the lights in the living room. It was a big room, with three tall windows looking out on the river, a couch and two low armchairs at the left, upholstered in mauve brocade, and a simple marble mantel of Empire design over the fireplace at the right. The curtains at the windows, which were of the same brocade as the couch and armchairs, were not drawn.

Germaine took it all in. She recognized in an instant the social category of the owner—a woman of the world who moved in a restricted circle of elegance and wit, with a limited income, just large enough to allow her to indulge in one good dress each season and one good suit every year, who probably now, on the rent she was getting from Walter, was living in a small but chic hotel on the Côte d'Azur, spending her days with the chattering pederasts, and her nights with her lover. It was a world she had renounced in disgust, yet she could not help smiling at the thought of this serious, awkward American settled in this environment so totally alien to anything he could possibly know.

She watched him as he switched on the lamps, with their huge parchment shades, and turned out the lights of the crystal chandelier, but when he started to draw the curtains at the windows she walked quickly over to him.

"I must see your view," she said, standing at the center window. He came to her side and they both looked out. The lights of the garden made the end of the Ile de la Cité look like the prow of a great liner cleaving the waters of the river, with the floodlit towers of Notre Dame as its stacks.

"I think it is probably the most beautiful view in the world," Walter said feelingly.

"The great ship moving forward," she murmured.

"It is like a ship, isn't it?"

"L'Ile de France."

"Yes, it might be."

"It is. That is its name—the Square de l'Ile de France."

"I can watch it by the hour."

She turned toward the room. "May I use your bathroom?" she asked.

"Certainly," Walter answered. "I'll light the lights for you."

He led her to the rear of the foyer and into his bedroom, which was even more incongruously feminine than the living room, with its satin-covered double bed, chaise longue, and dainty dressing table on which was an untidy pile of male toilet articles. He opened the door of the bathroom and switched on the lights.

When she returned to the living room she found that he had drawn the curtains and put out a tray of whiskey, soda, ice, and glasses on the coffee table in front of the couch.

"Can I pour you a drink?" he asked.

She hesitated, hating whiskey, but decided it was better to play along with him. "Just a drop," she said, "with a great deal of soda."

"I'll fix these first," he said, pouring two drinks. "Then we'll have the Ravel."

"But where is the gramophone?" she asked.

"Behind the screen," he answered, nodding toward a painted screen in the far corner which shielded the door to his small dining room.

Germaine settled in a corner of the couch while Walter searched among the records on the bottom shelf of a bookcase next to the fireplace, then disappeared behind the screen. As the music started, he came back, picked up his drink, and sat down in the chair next to her. For twenty minutes they listened in silence. She watched Walter pull a pipe and a tobacco pouch out of his pocket, fill the pipe, punching the tobacco down into the bowl with his long, flat thumb, carefully close the zipper of the pouch, put it back in his pocket, light a paper match, and put it over the bowl while he sucked until the whole top of the tobacco was an even glow of red. She could see that all these gestures were automatic, that his mind was neither with her nor with the pipe but deeply concentrated on the music. She listened, too, but lightly, with only half her mind. The other half was still speculating, alert for the next move, wondering what play he would make finally, after he had had his fill of music. She was convinced that nothing should be rushed, that he would be frightened off by any intimation of an advance on her part. He would have to do the leading, but she would have to sense each hesitant step forward and hold it, consolidate it, before shyness made him retreat. His pity for her was the winning card, and she could make him play it by dropping those hints of a cultivated upbringing from which she had been alienated by the war. The bits of history, the familiarity with the works of the good composers, the sad, faraway look, were the intimations which should be played adroitly, never blatantly. With the pity would come the soft, doting affection, the handholding, the sentimental companionship without which these slobbering Americans could not justify their zeal to capture and control the world.

The music ended and the phonograph clicked to a stop. Walter put down his pipe and beamed at her. "What do you think of that?" he asked proudly.

"Beautifully played. What orchestra was it?"

"L'Orchestre de la Suisse Romande, with Ansermet conducting." He got to his feet. "Now what would you like?"

Under normal circumstances, guided solely by her own taste, she would have suggested Béla Bartók, but she thought it wiser now to choose a background more romantic, more cloying, and, above all, French. "Have you anything of Jacques Ibert?" she asked.

He looked disappointed. "I'm afraid not," he said.

"Of Fauré?"

"Yes," he said brightly, "the Violin Sonata with Heifetz."

"I love it."

"So do I, in a way," he said, as he went over to the bookcase and searched, squatting down so he could read the names on the neatly stacked records. "I used to play it often, but I haven't lately."

"Maybe you would prefer something else."

"No, we shall have it. This is your concert tonight."

"You are very kind," she said sadly.

"Nonsense, I'm having the time of my life. This is what I really enjoy—listening to good music with a friend who appreciates it."

There it was, the word "friend." She must grab that one quickly before it was lost. "A friend," she said, seemingly revolving the word on her tongue, in her mind. "That is one of the nicest words in the English language, so gentle, so comforting. It is not '*ami.*' It is not '*copain.*' There is something stronger—shall I say, more loyal—in it. You must take care how you use it."

"You're right, you know," he said from behind the screen. "It's not a word that should be batted around recklessly. Friends are something you can't buy—they're priceless."

She did not answer, purposely. It seemed wiser to let him develop the thesis. He would interpret her silence as bitterness, disillusion.

His head appeared over the top of the screen. "You agree, don't you?"

"Of course, but that is why I warned you."

His head disappeared. She could hear the turntable revolving, then the music began and he came back to his chair, not sitting down, standing, looking at her. "You're afraid of friendship, aren't you?" he said earnestly.

"Yes," she said, looking up at him, then quickly lowering her eyes.

"Because of that Englishman."

"You can understand, can't you?"

"You loved him?"

For an answer she shrugged her shoulders.

"And you still love him."

She raised her eyes to him again, smiling this time, a smile that meant to convey gallant courage. "See here, Mr. Walter . . ."

"Cut out the 'mister,'" he said impatiently. "Call me Walter. That's my first name."

"Very good, I shall call you Walter—but please, let us not talk about that man. As far as I am concerned, he is dead, forgotten."

He put the pipe in his mouth and held out both hands. "*Entendu.* We'll expunge him from the record. He is officially buried to the music of Fauré."

She took his hands, gave them a slight squeeze, smiling at him gratefully. "Thank you," she said, managing to get a catch in her voice.

He wanted to go on holding her hands, she could tell that, but it was awkward, with him standing up in front of her and her having to stretch her arms to reach him at all, the couch was so low. Dropping her hands finally, he walked around the end of the coffee table and sat down beside her.

"This is a lovely bit here—this melody," he said, leaning his head back and waving the pipe in time with the music.

"Charming," she said, "and a little sad."

"I hadn't thought of that, but I suppose it is a little sad." He put the pipe back in his mouth and let his left hand fall casually, palm up, on her thigh.

She waited a moment or two before she placed her hand on his and felt his long, strong fingers twine themselves between hers. Her heart beat faster. The excitement, she thought, of seeing the trout come to the lure. How clever she had been to suggest Fauré. The sonata was working for her, reducing him to mush. Heifetz, with those honey-sweet tones, was weaving the spell which would, she knew now, bind him to her, a stupid, adoring slave. How Georges would rave if he could see her now, how he would twist under the pain of double jealousy. Poor little Georges, who had sent her on this mission with masochistic joy, flagellating himself with the thought of her in another's, a dirty imperialist's arms, hoping she would fail so that he could have her, finally, as an outcast in disgrace. No wonder she felt this excitement, realizing that she was already launched on her first single-handed assignment of top priority, the importance of which might even change the course of history.

"I don't suppose Mme. Nicole would approve of this," Walter said, taking the pipe out of his mouth with his right hand and putting it on the table.

"Why not?"

"She was pretty sore at the guy who took Jeannette off to Algiers."

"But there is a difference between taking a girl to Algiers and inviting her to listen to Fauré."

"Shouldn't you be up there?"

"At Mme. Nicole's?"

"Yes."

"Not until ten o'clock."

"It's half past nine."

"I'm not going."

"Not tonight?"

"Not any night. You saw how it was; I cannot face it. I would prefer anything—the Seine—but not that."

"Then it wasn't me that put you off."

She shuddered. "It was everything—the house, those poor little stupid girls in their chiffon, the idea of taking off one's clothes in cold blood in a cheap room with a strange man. It made me sick. I was *dégoûtée*." She gave his hand an extra squeeze. "All day I have thanked God that it was you who had to be the first. You were so kind, so understanding."

"You know, at first I thought you were putting on some kind of an act. Then I began to realize that there was something about you—your clothes, your look, your voice, maybe—something that didn't fit the picture. Funny, isn't it, meeting you in a place like that?" He laughed softly. "It's one of those things no one would believe if you told him. Why, they wouldn't even put it in a movie script, they'd say it was too improbable." He stopped and looked at her questioningly. "But what are you going to do now? You said it was the only kind of work you could get."

"I shall try and find something in the *quartier* where I live —sewing, embroidery, translating—something I can do *chez moi*."

"Where do you live?"

"In the *troisième arrondissement*, near the Place de la République."

"You have an apartment?"

She laughed. "I have a room—one room on the second floor, above the shop of an ironmonger."

"With your education and knowledge of English you ought to be able to get some translating work."

She shrugged her shoulders. "One must know the editors."

"Maybe . . ." He stopped, obviously deciding against the suggestion he had in mind.

They listened in silence until the sonata was finished, fingers entwined, hers soft and yielding, his hard, enfolding. When he got up to change the record, she got up, too, following him to the bookshelves, not to look at the records on the bottom shelf but to examine the titles of the books above them. The upper rows were mostly French novels in paper covers, not the sort of thing that would interest him. It was the shelf above the records which he seemed to have requisitioned for himself, filled, as it was, with books in English—

weighty textbooks on economics, money, foreign exchange, and even *Das Kapital*, which made her wonder.

Walter squatted at her feet, putting the Fauré away. "What will it be now?" he asked, but before she could answer he said, "How about Tchaikovsky's 'Francesca da Rimini' as long as we're in the romantic mood?"

"Perfect," she said, unbuttoning her jacket and taking a deep breath, like a sigh of satisfaction.

Walter put the record on the phonograph and came back to her, putting an arm around her waist, not aggressively, but gently, discreetly. "These are only a few of my books," he said. "The others I keep in my bedroom."

"A weighty collection. Is that all you read—economics?"

"The books in my room are mostly history. I like history. Right now I'm struggling with Villefosse."

"René Héron de Villefosse? Which one of his are you reading?"

"*L'Histoire de Paris*, but it's slow going with my feeble French."

She could feel his hand and arm grow tense as the passionate phrases of Tchaikovsky filled the room. She turned her head and looked up at him. "I could give you lessons."

"Yes, you could," he said, then, seeing her upturned face, kissed her quickly on the lips, shyly, a little frightened by his own audacity.

She did not say a word, letting her head fall on his shoulder as if it were a grateful refuge, while he led her slowly back to the couch.

CHAPTER FOURTEEN

"THE identical symptoms," Brigadier Derek Dunglass said, wiping his mouth with an upward stroke to keep his mustache in place. "The same tickle on the roof of the mouth, the same tingle in the spinal column, the same butterfly buzz in the pit of the stomach."

"What's the matter? Are you ill?" Eleanor asked him.

"Desperately."

"Why didn't you tell me?" she said anxiously. "We could have put it off. And this food at the Métropole—it's too rich for an ill man." She realized that he had devoured a dozen Marennes without turning a hair.

"Good God, don't worry about the food! It's the best possible medicine. The richer the better."

"Don't talk nonsense, Derek," she said crossly.

"I'm quite serious. For my ailment the remedy is good food and good wine. It distracts the other senses, and, at this moment, my other senses are in urgent need of distraction."

Eleanor laughed. She realized now what he was getting at in his oblique British way. It was the sort of thing he used to say to her, and it made her feel warm and contented. When he had called on the telephone to ask her to lunch with him she had hesitated, knowing, the way women know those things, that the old enchantment, the earlier precious abandon which she had cherished, could not be revived; that they were two different people, older, calmer, more cautious than the pair who had met and loved thirteen years before. Yet she had agreed to meet him at the Métropole because she wanted to feel again the glow which his ridiculous hyperbolic flattery invoked. The years were dropping away, and she was glad that she had accepted the invitation.

"*Rien ne change*," he went on, his agate-blue eyes fixed on her, affectionately, gaily. "It's like a fairy story—in the nursery sense, of course—this finding you again in the dark forest of bureaucracy, still beautiful, still soft and gay and lovely. I pull away the dead branches of your prison, and what happens? At the sight of you I am once more the young, dashing guardsman. No, don't start counting my gray hairs. They mean nothing whatever. It's the spirit that has been touched with youth and vigor. You laugh. You don't believe me. You think I'm just talking myself into a state of—"

"Don't say it."

"Oh, I wasn't going to be clinical. I'm keeping this on a high poetic plane for the moment. The rest, the blinding surge of passion, that comes later, after the coffee and brandy."

"Go on. Don't stop, I love it. Just like old times. Is it your memory or do you practice these speeches with your wife?"

"With Daphne? Good God no! Why, if I talked that way to Daphne, she'd put me to bed with a cup of Ovaltine and send for the doctor."

"Wise woman."

He raised his sandy eyebrows and looked at her with the expression of an eager child. "I say, how jolly! Then you are going to put me to bed!"

"Send you," Eleanor said.

"Cruel," he said in mock tragedy. "Alone in a cold, cold bed!"

"You're hopeless, Derek. I believe you never think of anything else."

"When I'm with you, I don't. What do you take me for?"

"A middle-aged, married soldier."

"Alone in Paris," he added.

"Why is it that every Anglo-Saxon male thinks of Paris as free territory for making passes?"

He looked surprised. "Really, Eleanor, you disappoint me. Don't tell me you've reached that prosy age where you reduce everyone to categories. I refuse to be pigeonholed as a typical Anglo-Saxon male. When I make passes—wonderful American phrase!—it is deliberate, calculated, and nongeographic. My passes result from the peculiar effect on me of an individual and have nothing whatever to do with seeing girls with naked breasts in night clubs. I make very few, I'm choosy that way—only two real ones in many years. The first of those was in New York . . ."

"And the second?"

"You should not have asked that, but as long as you have, I'll tell you. It was also thirteen years ago, right after the first one, at a hunt ball in Dorset, and the girl's name was Daphne Truitt."

"That's all, the whole story?"

"To all intents and purposes, barring a pinch here and there of some provocative behind, there is nothing else worth mentioning. So you see, my dear, I'm not just the gay blade, sniffing about for a bit of fluff in Paris. I'm a simple, plodding bigamist who takes his responsibilities seriously."

Eleanor was laughing, having the time of her life. "So, you feel it your duty—"

"Sacred," he said solemnly, raising his right hand. "Sacred duty, and good God, what fun!"

"Oh, Derek, you're wonderful," Eleanor said, wiping the tears of laughter from her eyes with her napkin, "and I love you so dearly—but let us be serious for a moment. I want to know how you happened to be at that party of Percy Warren's the other evening."

"Very simple indeed. René Peyraud called me to say that he was arranging a party for one of his tycoon American clients, and unless Christian and Lettice and the de Tonvilles and I came to his rescue, his boredom might well bring on acute dyspepsia. So, being a loyal little band, we accepted. Besides, of course, as we all agreed, it was an ideal chance to have a really bang-up meal at the expense of a dull chap who wouldn't know a woodcock from a snipe."

"So that's what you think of us," Eleanor said defensively.

"Quite. We're a smug little lot. Fancy ourselves no end. Our creed is that everyone else is a crashing bore."

"And who belongs to this disgusting coterie, just those you mentioned?"

"Exactly, with the possible exception of old de Tonville. I think he finds us a bit too flippant."

"I should think he might." She looked at Derek searchingly, not quite sure that he was not pulling her leg. "So you came just to make fun of us," she said critically.

"Not at all. We came to eat and enjoy each other's company. The Warrens and the Lockes were nothing more than supernumeraries—like the waiters. Then, of course, we found you, and that upset our plans a bit."

"In what way?"

"No need to explain my reaction. I was, quite naturally, prejudiced in your favor."

"Kind of you, I'm sure," Eleanor said stuffily.

"Don't mention it. I'm that way—inherent Scottish gallantry. But I had really nothing to do with it."

"With what? You are annoying, Derek. Don't talk in circles."

"But you always interrupt me. I was about to say that it was René and Christian who made the proposal to invite you to join our charmed circle. Lettice was all against it at first, having some silly belief, inherited from her preposterous father, that Americans are savages because they shift their forks from the left to the right hand before eating. She was brought around in the end by Christian's impassioned oration in your defense."

"Why should he defend me?" Eleanor asked.

"You should know better than I. You must have said something that amused him, something very naughty in impeccable, idiomatic French."

"I don't make lewd cracks to strange gentlemen."

"Well, whatever it was, you won him."

Eleanor was pleased. She had been favorably inclined toward St. Avit, but now she fancied him as most attractive. It was Lady Lettice who nettled her. "Look," she said, holding up her fish fork, on which was speared a piece of Sole Maison. "I don't shift. I haven't shifted since I was ten years old."

"Lettice didn't really accuse you of shifting. She merely remarked that, as a race, Americans are shifters, and shifters must be shiftless or they wouldn't shift so much."

"A narrow-minded snob," Eleanor said tartly. "What was the attitude of the de Tonvilles?"

"Only Jacqueline was involved. Old Hubert has no interest in these matters. He's a nonvoting member. To be quite frank with you, my dear, her attitude disturbed me."

"Against?"

"Quite the contrary, too eagerly pro. It aroused a suspicion which I've had for some time that the dear girl has Lesbian tendencies. Her enthusiasm for your physical attributes had an alarming ring."

"What an awful thing to say. I'm afraid, Derek, you have an evil mind."

"If jealousy is evil, yes. You see, if Christian or René should fall for you, as they undoubtedly will, I would know how to defend myself, but if you and Jacqueline started hitting it off, I should be quite helpless."

Eleanor laughed. "Don't worry, Derek, I'm not the type. Besides, I don't believe a word of it. It's just your imagination. Why shouldn't she say something nice about my figure?"

"That's the point, she never mentioned your figure."

"But you just said that she said . . ."

"That you had a mouth that was made for kissing. 'Une bouche de cerise, faite pour l'embrasser,' is the way she put it."

"How charming."

"Good God! There you go. I should never have told you."

"Don't be an idiot, Derek. You're just trying to annoy me."

He laughed heartily and took a long drink of the cold Pouilly Fuisée. "Oh, my dear Eleanor," he said finally, looking at her with affection, "it's such fun, this. Remember how I used to say things, all sorts of naughty things, just to shock you, to make you blush. How beautifully you blushed. Dear God, I can see it now, starting at your neck and working down like a veil of rose chiffon, tinting your breasts, flowing on until it finally made a lovely little rosebud of your navel."

"Derek, please," she pleaded. She could feel the flush on her cheeks. "You mustn't."

"There it is," he said, delighted with the effect of his words.

"You're doing it now. We ought to rush up to my hotel so that I can kiss the rosebud before it fades."

"Derek!" She was cross now. "Unless you stop, I'm going to leave."

"Let's both leave." He waved to the waiter. "*L'addition, s'il vous plaît.* We can have coffee *chez moi.*"

Her composure returned. She had not been angry with him, not really. With herself, yes, because she had felt the old dissolving sensation in the pit of her stomach. She knew that unless she held herself rigidly in check she would succumb to the fever of desire. She was determined to resist it, not for any moral scruples or sense of duty, but because she was afraid that it could never be the same—as beautiful, as complete. The memory was too precious to be tampered with.

Eleanor said nothing when Derek told the driver of the taxi to go to the Hotel Napoléon in the Avenue Friedland. There was time enough to tell him when they got there that she was not going up to his room. No argument was to spoil the pleasure of this short ride. As the taxi started, he put his arm around her and kissed her temple.

"Eleanor, darling, kiss me," he whispered, his bristly mustache tickling her cheek, evoking memories that made her shiver with pleasure. She could feel her resistance ebbing, but she struggled to hold firm, not moving her head, keeping her eyes on the back of the driver. His right hand was on her cheek, pressing gently, firmly. She tried to stiffen the muscles of her neck, but they had gone flabby. Before she knew it she was kissing him, as she had once kissed him, as she had never kissed another man.

"Derek," she said when they broke for breath, "please, not here in the rue François Ier." She took his arm from her shoulder and placed it in his lap with a pat of finality. "Anyone might see us."

"And take heart," he said with complacency.

"Suppose someone saw you and told your wife."

He smiled. "Daphne would be rather cute about it in her funny way. She'd wait until after dinner when I was reading the *Times* over a glass of brandy, then she'd say quite casually, 'Poor dear, so you had to kiss that girl in a taxi. What was the matter? Wouldn't she go up to your room?' "

"Now I know she's a wise woman."

He looked surprised. "Does a remark like that imply wisdom?"

"Infinite."

"Really! You women are quite beyond me."

The taxi stopped at the curb in front of the Hotel Napoléon. Derek jumped out, offering her one hand while fishing in his pocket for his wallet with the other.

"*Numéro deux Boulevard Jean-Mermoz, Neuilly*," Eleanor said to the driver, then turned to Derek. "No, my dear, I'm going home."

"But you haven't had your coffee," he said, looking crestfallen.

"I never touch it."

He stood there, his body holding the door open, his left hand inside his coat, like a picture of Napoleon. "But Eleanor, my dear, see here, we haven't yet discussed the initiation."

"That was ten years ago," she said, smiling at him from the far corner of the cab.

"I mean our little group. We're taking you in. I promised them I'd arrange it."

"When?"

"That's just it, when?"

"Is it to be lunch, tea, or dinner?"

"Dinner, nothing less. Do come in where we can discuss it quietly."

"Sorry, Derek, but I must go home. I promised the children."

"You promised me."

"No, I didn't."

A light of comprehension came over his face and he frowned. "So, that's what you meant by Daphne being a wise woman."

"Yes, Derek dear, I'm the girl who wouldn't go up to your room."

"Dash! What an idiot I am."

"But I love you just the same. Now close the door, I must be running."

"What about the dinner? Have you an evening next week?"

"Is Sam included?"

"Good God, no!"

Eleanor smiled. "I'll have to look at my book and give you a ring." As he started to close the door she pointed to her lips. "Lipstick," she whispered. "Wipe it off." And she blew him a kiss.

CHAPTER FIFTEEN

"BY the way," Sam said, "I'm flying to the States on Tuesday. The cable came this afternoon. They want me for the appropriation hearings."

Eleanor's heart stopped a beat and she was rather ashamed of it. A decent, wifely heart should not exult thus at the prospect of a husband's departure. Yet it did, without any prompting, showing that she must take measures to keep it in its place. "You were expecting this, weren't you?" she said calmly.

"Yes, Sherrill told me it was apt to happen."

They were returning from a cocktail party, one of those steadily recurrent affairs which consume the daily hours of seven to eight-thirty of every American civil servant in Paris. They were all the same, those cocktail parties: the same people, the same martinis, Scotches and sodas, and indifferent champagne; the same soggy sandwiches of sweet American bread from the commissary; the same bowl of cream cheese surrounded by potato chips which cracked in two when one tried to scoop; the same noise; the same inane conversation with men who were only intelligent while at work, and with women who liked cocktail parties. Eleanor hated them, yet she went dutifully each day, arriving at seven-thirty, patiently chatting in an agony of boredom, a frozen smile on her face, until Sam arrived, gulped one drink, and took her home.

They were circling the Place Victor Hugo, and Eleanor wondered what had happened to the statue of the author, which she remembered from her youth. The place where it had stood was an unsightly mass of rubble, mud now in the evening rain. "How long will you be gone?" she asked, trying to put a note of anxiety into her voice.

"Two weeks, three at the most, I should say. It's one of those things which depend on the whim of the Appropriations Committee."

"It's flattering that they should need you."

Sam did not reply to this, but she gathered from the smile of satisfaction which hovered about his face that he was pleased. At any rate, he was so deeply absorbed in his own thoughts that she could safely retreat into the warm cocoon of her private, inner mind without fear of arousing his suspicion. The plan came to her instantly, in a flash, fully conceived and detailed. The initiation, as Derek had called it, the dinner, would be hers, at her house, now that Sam was leaving; an exquisite, calculated meal, perfectly balanced, with the right wines, and she in her new dress, the slightly theatrical one that Balmain had made her, with its yards and yards of beige-pink surah flaring out from a tight-corseted waist and a bodice—if you could call it that, for it did no more than cover her breasts—embroidered with soutache and brilliants. The flowers on the table and in the drawing room would match her dress—roses and gladioli of that particular strange, decadent, indeterminate color which the florist on the Place de l'Alma would surely be able to find for her. It would take place next Wednesday or Thursday—better Thursday, more time to prepare, to polish every detail.

The Marquise de Tonville took off her cape of black Persian lamb and tossed it on a chair. "It is so warm, so delicious," she said to Eleanor, happy in the fact that the central heating was effective enough for her to display her neck and shoulders, which were alabaster white, with a smooth skin of satin, contrasting with Eleanor's, which were shell pink, *matte*, reflecting no light.

"I'm afraid we Americans have a weakness for overheating," Eleanor said.

"But it allows one to show one's lovely dresses," the marquise said. "Like yours, my dear, which is a dream."

"Thank you," Eleanor said, trying hard not to blush, realizing that Mme. de Tonville was looking, not at the dress at all, but at her mouth, her neck, and remembering what Derek had said, but not minding the scrutiny as much as she knew she should. She turned to Christian de St. Avit. "Do you find it too hot?"

"Any temperature which allows you ladies to display yourselves is acceptable," St. Avit said.

At that moment Walter Haines entered the room and Eleanor thought she could hear the eyebrows of the coterie rising. She had asked him on the previous day, after she had learned from Mme. de Tonville that the marquis was indisposed. The dinner had been planned for seven—two men and a lady on each side of the table, with herself at the head, reigning—and she did not wish to spoil the design. Had she asked Derek to propose the seventh, it would have been a stranger to her, and not wishing this she had hit on Walter, not because he fitted, but because she fancied that it would be good for him, give him a sight into a world which he knew nothing of, yet must know if he were ever to move up in his service. Besides, he had that air of dedication, of intellectual poise which raised him above the level of blatant mediocrity. He might not amuse them, but he would not offend them, of that she was sure.

She introduced Walter to Mme. de Tonville, to Christian de St. Avit, to Derek, while the butler passed champagne in lieu of cocktails. She explained that she had chosen him carefully to replace the missing marquis, adding that his role would be to leaven their levity with a properly serious note. She spoke in French, the only admissible language of the group, hoping that Walter would understand that he was not to revert to English, even to her. Then Lady Lettice entered the room, followed by Maître Peyraud, and the party was on. At once they were all talking, drinking, eyeing each other appraisingly, the women sizing up the dresses, the men taking in with pleasure the contours of exposed feminine flesh, ample and varied enough among the three women to satisfy any taste.

Lettice Burnham, like a plump partridge, her freckled neck fairly bursting out of a gown of copper taffeta, came stalking to Walter, pinning him down with her china-blue eyes. "An American, I suppose," she said in English, breaking all rules.

"Yes, indeed," Walter said pleasantly, and with unmistakable pride.

"I might have expected," she said, noting that his face was better than the cut of his hair or his dinner jacket. "And why were you asked? Do you act in the cinema?"

Walter laughed, thinking this was a sample of the wit his hostess had told him to expect. "I'm afraid not, nothing as glamorous as that."

"I suppose you write books about the perverse sex habits of the natives of Georgia."

"Not even that."

"You must do something."

"Naturally . . ."

"I mean something notable, that people talk about."

"Why do you say that?" Walter asked. He was still taking it all in fun, as if he were the end man feeding the interlocutor.

"Mrs. Locke told you, of course . . ."

"Oh, yes, and I told her that she was taking a chance," Walter said. "But I shall do my best not to disgrace her."

"Well, if you insist on being so bloody modest, I shall have to get the story from René," she said.

"Who is René?" Walter asked.

"That chap over there," she said, "the one talking to your hostess; the one with the Oriental eyes who looks more lecherous than he is. He knows everything about everybody." She stalked away toward Peyraud to satisfy her curiosity as dinner was announced.

In its small, intimate way the dinner was quite regal, with Eleanor sitting like a queen at the head of the table, the roses spilling out of a great bowl in the center, matching, as she had wished, the muted, indefinite pink of her gown, the candles throwing a discreet light on the faces of Derek, Mme. de Tonville, and the Count of St. Avit on her right, and on Peyraud, Lady Lettice, and Walter on her left. With no questioning critical eyes to watch her from Sam's seat, she ruled firmly, benevolently, like the Speaker of the House, letting only one guest talk at a time, giving the floor with a nod or a smile. Under the exhilaration of the food, which surprised them all by its excellence, and the wines, which Derek had helped her choose, and the atmosphere, which was pleasantly reminiscent of prewar elegance, they became expansive and articulate, that is, all but Walter and Eleanor, who were satisfied to listen.

"There are two ways of looking at it," Maître Peyraud said

judicially, having been tossed the ball after a speech by Jacqueline de Tonville in which she had deplored the vulgarizing effect of mass production and mass entertainment. "One is your way, my dear Jacqueline, that what we see and hear is lacking in taste and, in consequence, is changing the aspect of Paris, hiding the façades of Gabriel and Mansart behind enormous billboards which advertise second-rate articles of commerce or third-rate film plays in a manner which is hardly that of Toulouse or Chéret, or even of Picasso. Granted it is bad, offensive. But let us look at the cause and the motive."

"Money," Lady Lettice muttered, causing Eleanor to look at her with a frown and a finger to her lips.

"You are quite right, dear Lettice," René Peyraud went on. "Money is at the root of it. But money, alas, has been at the root of almost every tragedy that has attended our race since Fouquet decided to spend public funds on a grandiose scale. There is nothing new about our adoration of money. What is new, and perhaps encouraging, is the growing propensity to spend. Now, money is only evil when it is hoarded and idle. The moment it starts circulating it becomes a force for good, dispensing pleasure as it passes, lifting up the downhearted, curing the ill, lending a gaiety and light to lives that have been mean and dark. This phase, the phase of bad taste, may be only a primary manifestation, due to the fact that this new tendency is so widespread, so universal that it concerns the great mass of the little people who have yet to learn about form and color and harmony. Give them time, and the things upon which they rush to spend their *sous* will no longer satisfy them. By having seen and heard and experienced, they will acquire the critical faculty and will accomplish their own metamorphosis from worms to butterflies. What we see going on around us is due to a heretical change in the attitude toward money. Observe the word '*sou*' which I just used. It is unknown to the postwar generation, whereas it once was the symbol of that French proclivity, of which we boasted, to gain but never to spend. So, give us time, dear Jacqueline, for vulgarization is only the priming coat to any good picture."

Eleanor noticed that Walter had been nervously fiddling with a wineglass throughout René's discourse. She looked at him inquiringly, wondering if, after all, he wished to have a word. He caught her eye, blushed, and cleared his throat.

"It has always been believed," he announced in an unnaturally loud voice, still twirling the stem of the glass, his eyes on his plate, not daring to look at his adversaries, "that the subject of money was of interest solely to the economists . . ." He shook his head sadly. "I'm afraid my French is not up to it."

"In English, then," they all cried.

"By all means," Lady Lettice added. "It will be refreshing to hear an American on the subect of money."

"As I started to say," Walter went on in English, with more confidence, "it has always been assumed that money, the theory of money, was solely of interest to economists and bankers. They are the ones who have written the tomes on the subject. Yet the more I read these works, the more I am drawn to the conclusion that money is, in reality, a philosophic abstraction which creates a state of mind, a mass state of mind, a state of mind deriving from the special set of circumstances surrounding the artificial basis on which the concept is built. Take, for example, the American idea of money, which seems to interest so many people these days." He glanced up at Lady Lettice, who smiled at him provocatively. "In America, money is credit, debt. The more you borrow, the richer you are, and the lender is eager to aid you to the limit. The more extravagant your proposal, the better he is pleased. As a result of this approach, we have pyramided the greatest, the most fantastic development of resources since the fall of the Roman Empire." He stopped, suddenly fearful that he was sounding pompous. "I'm sorry," he said, "I didn't mean to bore you."

"But you are not at all," St. Avit protested. "On the contrary, I find your theory fascinating. I am eager—we all are, I am sure—to know what you believe to be the French idea of money."

Walter looked pleadingly at his hostess, but she gave him no pity, nodding for him to answer Christian's point if he could. "Well, as I see it," he went on, "you French think of money as gold. I may be wrong, but I believe that the mental image which forms in the mind of every French peasant and bourgeois shopkeeper when the word 'money' is used is one of bars or coins of golden metal. It is probably this very finite concept of money as being tangible and portable which promotes the desire to save and hoard."

"Splendid! Perfect!" Christian exclaimed. "You have touched us on the heart. Ever since the last French king left the throne we have worshiped the louis d'or as sovereign."

"Why, then," Lettice asked, "do you use the word *'argent'* and not *'or'*?"

"To fool one another," Jacqueline de Tonville answered. "We do not wish people to know that when we say silver we are dreaming hungrily of gold."

"And what about our English neighbors?" René Peyraud asked, leaning forward to address Walter across Lady Lettice's freckled bosom. "I think it only fair to us that their secret be exposed."

"I don't think it's any secret," Walter said, smiling at Lady Lettice. "Like the French, the British have an empiric idea of money; only, instead of being a single metal, it is all the raw materials of an empire. I would hazard the guess that you think of the pound sterling as representing the rubber and tin of Malaya, the tea of Ceylon, the diamonds of South Africa—everything, in fact, all the products of your colonies and dominions."

"What do you say to that, Derek?" Eleanor asked.

"Well—er—I'm afraid I really never gave it much thought," Derek answered. "I dare say Haines is quite right—the pound is the Commonwealth, and the Commonwealth is the pound. Sound, I expect, from a philosophic point of view. As for me, I think of the pound as a bang-up meal in Paris."

"You're just a glutton, Derek dear," Lady Lettice said, "without the true-blue British Empire spirit."

"You're no one to talk, you live here," Derek countered.

"Dull as they are, I rather like your views," Lettice said to Walter with an unusually charming smile. "Why don't you write an article about it?"

"I doubt if I could," Walter replied modestly.

"Don't worry," René Peyraud said, "Jacqueline will write it. I watched her taking mental notes. It will probably appear next week in *Le Figaro*."

"I had not thought of it," Jacqueline de Tonville said, "but it is not a bad idea." She turned to Walter with a smile. "Perhaps Monsieur Haines will take a cup of tea with me tomorrow afternoon."

"You had better take care," Lettice warned Jacqueline. "Mrs. Locke may not fancy you running off with her prize."

"Oh, he's not mine," Eleanor protested. "He's my husband's."

Lady Lettice turned and looked at Walter in amazement. "Fancy! I would never have suspected."

"I mean his economic assistant," Eleanor added, blushing.

Christian de St. Avit raised a glass of pink champagne that the butler had just filled. Its color was not forthright like *vin rosé*, but a delicate, yellowish pink which thoughtfully matched the roses and Eleanor's dress. "I propose that we drink a toast of welcome to our new friend," he said, "our new sister, our new companion in the secret order of intolerance, who, from now on, shall be known among us as Eleanor. May it please her to find our little band the only remaining haven of wisdom and wit, and to be bored to death in the company of the dull, scheming, petty, envious, and ignorant who comprise the rest of the world."

They all raised their glasses and looked at her, saying, "Eleanor," before they drank—all, that is, save Walter, who was mystified by the whole performance and merely drank without saying anything.

"You are very kind—" Eleanor started to say.

"There you are quite wrong," Lettice interrupted. "Kindness is a form of self-indulgence we do not practice."

"How shall I put it then?" Eleanor said, a little perplexed.

"I shouldn't try," René answered.

"But I insist," Eleanor said. "After all, the initiate is supposed to say something, and I haven't had a word all evening."

"Dear God," Jacqueline said, raising her eyes to the ceiling. "If it's maudlin I shall become ill."

"Pay no attention to her," Derek said to Eleanor. "Jacqueline adores being ill. She thinks the pallor becomes her."

"Well, it does," Jacqueline said indignantly.

"Please," Eleanor persisted, "let me say that I join you, my dear companions, with a sense of nostalgic relief. At first you frightened me with your airs of superiority, but now that I know that you are merely cosy, wicked people whose sole desires are to snub the ignorant and deflate the pretentious, I feel as I do when I visit the felines in the Jardin d'Acclimatation—at home among you."

"Amen," René said, sighing with relief.

"Will someone tell me what this is all about?" Walter asked, still bewildered.

"No, dear boy," Lettice replied, patting his arm, "they will not. You are much too young."

"But Christian will tell you about his kingdom," René said.

"Ah, do tell it, Christian," Jacqueline pleaded. "I adore your kingdom. It is so romantic."

Christian gave them an angry look and was silent.

"Won't you tell me?" Eleanor asked. "I don't know the story."

"It's not a story, and it's not for you, Eleanor," Christian said crossly. "It may be for Mr. Haines, but not now."

CHAPTER SIXTEEN

"WHAT does Lady Burnham do?" Walter asked. He was giving Christian a lift home in his car. It was a clear, cool night, too late for heavy traffic on the Avenue de la Grande Armée. The only other cars were exceeding all speed limits, blinking their lights at each cross street, but never slowing. Walter kept to the right, letting them rush past him, driving with his usual caution in spite of the exhilaration of Eleanor's dinner.

"She is Lady Lettice, not Lady Burnham," Christian corrected. Mindful of his own lineage, he was a stickler for correct address.

"I thought her name was Burnham."

"It is," Christian explained, "but being the daughter of an earl she is a lady in her own right."

Walter still did not understand why she was not called Lady Burnham, but he found the subject too dull to pursue. "Does she do anything?" he asked.

"She writes when the mood is on her, rather amusingly, too. Surely you have read *Love is the Joker?*"

"No, I haven't."

"Hardly your dish, but great fun."

"Well, I must say I enjoyed the evening," Walter said with real feeling. "It was certainly nice of Mrs. Locke to ask me."

"I fancy she thinks you are worth educating," Christian said.

"What do you mean by that?"

"Just what I said."

"But I am educated," Walter protested.

"In a university, yes, but that is nothing. That is what Strindberg referred to when he said that education is everything that is left after one has forgotten all that one has learned. Where do you live?"

Walter was bewildered again. These people, these friends of Livy's wife, had such a cryptic way of talking. "On the Ile St. Louis," he replied automatically, still worrying about Strindberg's views on education.

"Really!" Christian exclaimed. "Somehow I thought of you as living in the most modern part of Passy."

"I like old Paris," Walter stated simply.

"Then Eleanor was right—you are worth educating. I must come and see you sometime. I have a particular weakness for the Ile St. Louis."

"Would you like to come now?" Walter asked. "I have some good Scotch." He said it to be gracious and hospitable, not thinking for an instant that St. Avit would accept at this late hour.

"It is very kind of you. I should be delighted," Christian said with enthusiasm. "I am not in the least sleepy."

My God, Walter thought, if Germaine should wake up! But even if she did, he consoled himself, she would probably not come into the living room. She was tactful that way. In any event, he was caught now. If St. Avit should discover her, he would have to rely on him as a French gentleman to be discreet and keep his mouth shut.

When they reached the apartment Walter turned the key in the lock as gently as possible, opened the door carefully, turned on the light in the foyer, tiptoed into the living room, switched on the lights, then returned, took Christian's overcoat, and laid it on the console without saying a word. Christian smiled inwardly, realizing at once that someone else was in the flat, someone whom Walter did not wish to awaken.

Walter turned on the lamps, saying in a low voice, "Make yourself at home while I fetch the drinks." Then he disappeared into the dining room while Christian speculated on the sex of the roommate.

Walter was squeezing soda from the syphon into the whiskey glasses on a tray, concentrated on his task, when the door to the foyer, which he had carefully closed, opened and Germaine looked at them sleepily. She was wearing Walter's dressing gown of Stuart tartan over her nightdress, and on her feet were the rabbit-fur *pantoufles* Walter had bought her the day before. Leaning over the coffee table, Walter did not see her, but Christian did, and smiled. Even thus, without make-up, her eyes dulled with sleep, her hair a churning mass of copper, she was different from what he had expected: not the little bleached-hair tart that most Americans fell for; more refined, more simple in a well-bred way, more out of his own drawer, even in a way familiar. . . .

Christian stood up. "I ask your pardon for disturbing you," he said courteously in French.

Walter straightened up with a jerk, almost dropping the syphon, and blushed. "Did we wake you?" he asked stupidly.

"Sorry," Germaine said in English, without embarrassment. "I heard a noise, so I came to investigate." She stepped back into the foyer. "I shall leave you to your drinks."

"Why not join us?" Christian said gallantly.

"Yes, do," Walter echoed.

"But I am not dressed," Germaine protested, starting to

close the door. She had a sensation of fright. Christian's face was vaguely, disturbingly familiar.

"You are as totally covered as we in your lovely Scottish robe," Christian said. "Enter, Lady Macbeth, and fear not this poor Macduff."

Now that the fat was in the fire, Walter saw no reason to continue the farce of false modesty. "Don't be silly, Germaine. Come on in and join us in a nightcap."

"*Bon, si tu veux,*" she said, thinking that the harm, if it were harm, had been done, as this man with the voice and the manner which kept strumming on an unresponsive chord had already seen her. "*Fais-moi un whiskey-soda, pas trop fort. Je reviens dans un instant.*"

Walter felt that some explanation was justified, but he had no idea of how to express it. He decided that whatever he said might only make matters worse, so he said nothing and handed Christian a highball.

Christian settled back on the sofa and sipped his drink. "You are a very lucky man," he said.

"I don't deny that," Walter answered, proud that his taste was approved by a Frenchman patently as eclectic as St. Avit.

"A most beautiful flat on the Ile St. Louis and a charming girl to look after you. Really, dear fellow, I envy you." He lowered his voice. "Tell me, what is her name?"

"Brisson—Germaine Brisson," Walter replied. "An exceptional girl, *agrégée* in history from the Sorbonne, and speaks perfect English."

"So I noted. But you should not allow it. You should make her speak French with you. That is the way to learn a language."

"Oh, we do," Walter said emphatically. "We speak only French. In the beginning, of course, it was mostly English—

that's how we happened to meet—but now it's only French. We read together, out loud to each other, every evening."

"What a charming picture!" Christian said, smiling with delight at the mental image. "And what are you reading?"

"*L'Histoire de Paris* by Héron de Villefosse."

"Lucky fellow! They all want to educate you—Eleanor, Lettice, Jacqueline, and Mlle. Brisson. Watch out or you will suffer from overeducation." He jumped to his feet as Germaine entered the room.

"This is the Comte de St. Avit, Mademoiselle Brisson," Walter introduced them.

Germaine came over to the couch and shook hands formally with Christian. She had put on lipstick and brushed her hair. They both looked at each other as people do who believe they have met before but cannot remember when or where. Christian was the more annoyed of the two, believing himself incredibly stupid for forgetting such a beautiful face. His mind kept bouncing back into the past, trying to locate the place, the environment, the circumstance. Normally, he would have asked her frankly where they had met, but some vague suspicion that the circumstances were unpleasant prevented him. He had no wish to end the evening on a wrong note.

"Your friend Mr. Haines gave us a brilliant talk on the theory of money," he said in French, watching her as she sat down on the fauteuil that faced Walter's, his mind still searching for identification.

"That is his particular field of knowledge, is it not?" she said, looking at Walter.

"Of study, I should say," Walter answered modestly, then turned to Christian. "There was a story they wanted you to tell me, a fairy story about a kingdom. You said it was for me. Well, somehow, sitting here cosily at midnight, drinking our nightcaps, I think we are in the mood for a fairy story. Won't you tell it to us?"

"I'm afraid it would bore Mlle. Brisson," Christian said warily, still looking at her, still waiting for the clue, hoping that her voice, if she could be drawn out in talk, would help to unlock the door of his memory.

"On the contrary, it would amuse me," Germaine said flatly, without conviction, knowing that, like herself, St. Avit had not yet recalled the time, the place, and hoping desperately that they would continue to elude him.

"It is not an amusing story," Christian said, "unless one is so bound by cynicism, like René Peyraud, that it appears ridiculous. That is why I would not speak of it at dinner, because René believes that it is a momentous joke which I have devised, a wicked commentary on the misguided people who strive to federalize Europe."

"You don't believe in European Union?" Walter asked.

"Indeed I do, with all my heart," Christian said emphatically.

"Then, why do you speak of the Federalists as misguided?" Walter said.

"To answer that is to tell my story." Christian took a drink of whiskey, lit a cigarette, sat back on the couch, his blond head resting on the brocade cushion, his blue eyes fixed on the chandelier, and launched forth on his doctrine of empire. He began with a brief review of history, starting with Clovis and the kingdoms of Austrasia and Neustria, proceeding through the House of Pepin to Charlemagne, the pivot of his thesis; then the Hohenstaufens, the Capetian kings, the houses of Valois, Burgundy, Hapsburg, and Bourbon, down to the Napoleonic conquests. All this, he explained, was to demonstrate that Europeans had, since the beginning of their history as rooted people, been conditioned to the need of a symbolic ruler, that under the democratic form, introduced by Rousseau from atypical Switzerland, they had become unstable, fickle, agnostic, and defenseless, unable to rule themselves because they lacked that spiritually unifying force which, by history and tradition, had always been a Christian ruler.

It was soon after he had started that Germaine, with a shock which stopped her heartbeat, remembered. It came to her suddenly, that indelible picture of the young leader of the F.F.I. band operating in the Vendée, standing there against the shadowy outline of the ruined Château de Talmont, the moon shining on his blond hair which waved in the wind while he urged her, with considerable eloquence, to bring her forces under his command for the sake of France. In those days he went by the name of Capet, taken, she knew now, because of his devotion to the monarchs, but there was no mistaking the voice, the hair, the thin, wiry body. Even though he was now in a dinner jacket, whereas on that night in 1941 he wore a torn tweed jacket over a black turtle-neck sweater, she knew that it was the same man, the same man who had stood there with a young priest at his side, speaking, as he was speaking now, with conviction, with passion.

His words did not interest her. They were, to her conditioned mind, nothing more than the hollow deceptions, the opium for the people, that had been foisted on the ignorant, as Marx had taught, since the Catholic Church had first fostered the feudal system. She shut her mind to them, trying to recall how she had been dressed that night, if she had worn anything on her head which had shielded her face from the moonlight. It was difficult to remember, but she hoped, suspected, that she had had a kerchief over her head, tied peasant fashion. That had been their only meeting, and it had been at night, she wearing a man's uniform, with that kerchief.

Her voice, her accent, would be his only clue. She decided to speak, if she had to, only in English.

Walter listened, fascinated by Christian's argument, so alien, so remote from his own fundamental beliefs. It was a new side, a new facet of the European mind, one he had never met and which had never occurred to him. His first instinct was to reject it summarily as arrant romantic nonsense, having no place in the modern world. But as Christian elaborated with logical clarity the spiritual need for a king-emperor above and beyond the democratic process of the people's voice in the rule of city, commune, and state, showing that it was the only means of breaching the barriers of language and mores which divided the countries of Western European christendom, he began to wonder. Charles the Great was the prime example, Christian argued. He had brought the Germans, the French, the Lombards, and the Italians into a single, unified empire under the banner of the Church, while allowing self-rule to the cities and communes. Thus unified, Europe had been able successfully to defend itself against the encroachment of the Moslems in the west and of the Avars and Czechs in the east.

"It is a concept which is difficult for an American to digest," Walter said when Christian paused.

"In fact, impossible for you to understand," Christian added, "because your roots are grounded in the proposition that all men are created equal, and that, therefore, kings and princes are vain and immoral objects before God."

"Yes, I think that's true," Walter said thoughtfully. "My country is populated by people who fled from kings and dictators."

"There is a vast difference between a benevolent Christian monarch and a dictator," Christian said. "The true European distrusts all dictators. We are essentially democratic. We believe in, and will defend, our right to a voice in government. That is why Hitler was cremated in Berlin and Mussolini hung by the heels in Milan. Stalin and his hordes will suffer the same fate if we have the sense to pursue our historic course."

"Which is, as you see it, the revival of the Holy Roman Empire," Walter said.

"If you wish."

"What would you do about the Protestant elements in France, Germany, and Holland?" Walter asked.

"Exactly what the English do about the Catholics—allow them complete freedom to practice their own religion. Do this and they will be as loyal subjects of the emperor as the English Catholics are of their Protestant monarch."

Walter smiled. "Well, it's a beautiful thought," he said skeptically.

"But one which does not suit our American saviors," Christian added. "You want us to be in your own image."

"Experience has shown us that the federal state is about as good as any method yet devised for protecting the rights of the individual in an industrial civilization," Walter argued.

"Therefore it should be good for Europe."

"I don't see why not."

"Ah, my dear Haines, that is the true Puritan speaking. What is good for me must, of necessity, be good for you. You are incorrigible missionaries, you Americans, and that is our greatest danger."

Germaine affected a deep yawn and got up from her chair. She had listened to more than she could stand without bursting forth with her own dialectics to deflate St. Avit. Everything he had said had marked him in her eyes as the epitome, the essence, of imperialistic reaction. This puling death rattle was, in its way, more disgusting, more degraded than the blatant capitalistic appetite of Wall Street. She would retire now, before that silly young man, whom she had once rather admired in the moonlight as a brave leader of the Résistance, recognized her as a disciple of the one great power on earth, the power of the masses, which he could not comprehend.

"If you don't mind," she said in English, "I shall go to bed."

Christian jumped to his feet. "I have bored you, then," he said in French.

"On the contrary," she persisted in English, "I found your fairy story very interesting. Good night, gentlemen." She went out of the room quickly, without turning.

"I must be going, too," Christian said. "It is late."

Walter got to his feet. "I'll drive you home."

"I can find a taxi."

"Not at this hour. Besides, I want to hear why you consider us a danger."

They walked out of the apartment and descended the stairs.

"Because you would be doing what the Bolshevics seek to do—impose a pattern on us which is neither natural nor traditional," Christian said.

"But you cannot compare a federal Europe with a Communist Europe," Walter insisted.

"True, but if you, with your might and your dollars, led us, cajoled us, into a form of union for which we are not spiritually or historically prepared, the resulting discord might well bring us into the lap of the Soviets."

"Where do you live?" Walter asked when they were in the car.

"At the corner of the rue Spontini and the rue de Longchamps."

"Let's see now, that's—"

"Your quickest route is *les quais* to the Place de l'Alma, then the Avenue Président Wilson to the Place d'Iéna . . ."

"Of course, and there we get the rue de Longchamps."

Walter started the car and drove straight on, around over the Pont Louis-Philippe, turning left on the Quai de l'Hôtel de Ville.

"But you do believe in federal union, provided there is a king to head it up," Walter went on, intrigued by the idea.

"Precisely," Christian said. "The federal form for democratic government and the king-emperor for spiritual unity. The federal form without a monarch would mean the same chaotic situation which now entangles Europe, engendered by fear, distrust, and jealousy."

"And a king without the federal form would be tyranny," Walter mused. "Very interesting. It's a new idea. I have to get used to it."

"I doubt if you ever will," Christian said amiably. Nothing was said for a while as they sped down the deserted quays and crossed the end of the Place de la Concorde. Finally Christian spoke again. "You know, I believe I've met Mlle. Brisson before."

"Really!" Walter exclaimed, pleased that his judgment of her caste was being confirmed. "When was that? While she was a student?"

"No. During the war in the Résistance."

"That's right. She was in it. That's where she learned her English."

"She had another name in those days, but then, we all did."

"You were in it, too?"

"Yes, in the same district."

"What was your name?" Walter asked.

"I called myself Capet."

"I must ask her if she remembers you."

"I would not do that if I were you," Christian said solemnly.

"Why not? Is there something . . . ?"

"She will not like to be reminded."

"Then there is something," Walter said. "I suspected it. She doesn't want to talk about those days."

"She was brave, but misguided. I admired her, but we could not agree."

That's it, then, Walter thought, she was a collaborator. He could see how the stigma would have made her an outcast, a pariah, but he saw no reason for him to resurrect her sins when she had so patently repented. If she wished to bury the past, he would help her. She wanted a new life and he was willing, eager, to give her the chance for it. "Poor girl," he said, "I feel sorry for her. I have a feeling she hates herself for what she did."

"You think she no longer believes?" Christian asked, surprised and not a little shocked by Walter's sympathy, not realizing that no thought of Communism was in his mind.

"She believes in nothing, least of all in herself. When I met her she was on the point of throwing herself in the Seine."

"That's what happens when one loses faith," Christian said sadly. "That's the trouble with France, with Germany, with Europe. It is searching for a new faith. Without one, it will commit suicide."

"She's worth saving."

"Everyone is worth saving."

CHAPTER SEVENTEEN

LIVY had barely unpacked his bags and hung his suits in the closet when the desk called to announce the arrival of Mr. Alfred Wellman. Livy told the clerk to send him up at once. He had never met this junior partner of Pomeroy, Greenough and Sedwitz, but he had every intention of giving him a piece of his mind for changing the instructions he had so explicitly given to Lew Pomeroy in New York. Lew had been high in his praise of this man Wellman, saying that he knew his way around and could be trusted to handle the matter discreetly and efficiently, but all the time he had spoken there had been that sardonic smile on his face, as if he thought Livy was behaving like a publicity-hungry debutante. "If that's what you want, Livy, you can probably get it," he had said, "but I warn you that with your Republican background it's going to come high." There had been no point in trying to make him understand that an ambassador was a man of rank and position far beyond that of a partner in a banking house. Lew was too much of a cynic to fancy rank of any sort which did not earn at least one hundred thousand dollars a year. To spend money to get a twenty-thousand-dollar job was to him the rankest folly. He had not said it in so many words, but Livy knew well enough what had gone on in the back of Lew's mind. He also knew that Lew would turn heaven and earth to aid him, and that no one, not even his New York partners, would ever know that Livy had sought the post.

There was a knock at the door. "Come in," he called, but he purposely did not move from where he stood by the window, looking out at Lafayette Park. He heard the door open and a voice ask, "Is this Mr. Locke?"

"Yes, Mr. Wellman," Livy answered, turning slowly, "I'm Livingston Locke. Come in and sit down, and kindly tell me why I'm here instead of at the Mayflower."

"You got the message on the train, I hope," Wellman said. He was a scholarly-looking young man who appeared to be in his early thirties. The crew-cut of his sandy hair, the slightly mussed gray suit with the jacket unbuttoned, showing a Phi Beta Kappa key hanging from the watch chain that stretched across his waistcoat, were the readily recognizable trademarks of Harvard Law School.

"Yes, I got it," Livy said coldly. "But why the Hay-Adams? Is the Mayflower full up?"

"I take full responsibility for the change," Wellman said with easy assurance. "I told Lew on the telephone that I was going to do it, but it was too late to reach you. You had already left for Penn Station. This is a better locus of operation than the Mayflower for your tactical campaign."

"But I always stay at the Mayflower. They know me there," Livy said huffily.

"Lew explained that to me. But the point is that the man who is coming to see you"—he looked at his watch—"in fifteen minutes would prefer to come here."

"What the hell difference—"

"There are too many people around the Mayflower who would know him," Wellman went on, ignoring Livy's annoyance, "and might start speculating and asking questions.

Whereas here it is only a short step from his office and he can drop in without exciting comment."

"Who is this fellow?" Livy demanded.

"A man named Leon David from the White House staff."

"Oh," was all Livy could say as his anger suddenly vanished.

"He's an assistant to the Appointments Secretary and he will ask you a few pertinent questions—biographical questions —so that your qualifications can be weighed against those of other candidates for the same post."

Livy pulled a chair over next to the couch. "Here, sit down," he said. "Let me get this straight. What post are you talking about? I never mentioned anything specific to Lew."

Wellman sat down in the manner of Harvard men, leaning far back, his spine on the edge of the seat, his legs crossed, showing rumpled, garterless socks. "The ambassadorship to Holland," he said. "It's the only opening at the moment. I hope it suits you. I gathered from Lew that—"

"Yes, yes, that's fine," Livy interrupted, impatient now in his growing eagerness. He got up from the couch. "I had better order some drinks."

"Don't worry, that's all attended to," Wellman said. "I took the liberty of ordering a couple of bottles of old sour mash bourbon and a bottle of Scotch. They were told to bring it up as soon as Leon arrives."

Livy was impressed. This young man was all that Lew Pomeroy had said he was. "Why so much?" he asked lightly, smiling to let Wellman know that he was not being critical.

"Well, at five-thirty a few friends of yours will be dropping in to greet you. Leon will probably duck out before they come. And, by the way, have you been around to E.C.A. yet?"

"No," Livy said, "I just got here. They are not expecting me until tomorrow morning."

"That's fine," Wellman said cryptically. "I don't want any

of them dropping in on our little party. That was another reason for not putting you up at the Mayflower."

"Who is coming?"

"Just a few—George Alexander, the congressman from your district, Guy Kirby and Huntington Ferris from State, Emerson Mallet of the Federal Reserve, and Senator Donegan."

The telephone rang and Livy walked over to the desk to answer it. "Yes, that's right," he said into the receiver. "Tell him to come up to 407." He hung up and turned to Wellman. "It's your friend David."

"Don't be put off by him," Wellman advised. "Leon's a smart boy, but sometimes he's a little abrupt."

Livy opened the door for him and he walked in casually, ignoring Livy, going straight to Wellman; a thin, bald young man with thick lenses in his horn-rimmed spectacles, wearing a ready-made suit of the wrong shade of brown and a red foulard bow tie with white polka dots. "Hi, Chuck," he said. "What's your trouble now?"

"Don't kid me," Wellman said, still sitting on the back of his neck. "You know why you're here. This time I'm paying you back for past favors. I've brought you the man you're looking for, Leon. Meet Mr. Livingston Locke."

David turned and nodded to Livy, then sat down on the couch next to Wellman. "Nice suite you've got here, Mr. Locke," he said, surveying the sitting room with its heavy imitation William and Mary furniture and its walls covered with blue silk brocade. "I like this hotel, it's quiet and handy."

"For you," Wellman said.

"Yes, and for Mr. Locke, too," David said. He turned to Livy. "You work for E.C.A., don't you?"

"In Paris," Livy replied, going to the door in answer to the knock of the waiter. "Just put everything on that table over there. We'll serve ourselves." He walked back to the couch and sat down in the chair that faced David. "I'm chief of the Fiscal and Payments Branch."

"And before that?" David asked, with a deadpan, like a prosecuting attorney.

"Senior partner of Gwenn, Thackeray & Co.," Livy said, in a way which made it sound as imposing as the chairman of the Finance Committee of U. S. Steel.

"The bankers, eh," David commented. "How long were you with them?"

"Ever since I left college in 1927."

Wellman unwound himself and got to his feet. "What can I mix for you, gentlemen?" he asked.

"Just a light one, Chuck," David said. "I've got work to do. A little bourbon and a lot of water."

"Make mine a Scotch and soda," Livy said. The feeling had been growing within him ever since this man Leon David had arrived that he had seen him before. "Didn't you use to be with S.E.C.?" he asked.

"That's right," David said with a sardonic smile. "You remember me, eh? On the Ulysses Power and Light reorganization. That's where I first ran into Chuck. His job was to pull the wool over my eyes."

"But you were too fast for me, Leon," Wellman called from the table where he was mixing the drinks.

"You fellows made yourselves a bundle out of that deal," David said to Livy, dropping the smile and putting back the deadpan. "What college did you go to?"

"Harvard."

"And Groton before that?" There was a note of sarcasm in David's voice.

"Precisely," Livy said, with pride, thinking of the Rector.

"Maybe it's not as good as you think," David said. "A lot of senators are afraid of that background."

"It was F.D.R.'s," Livy argued.
"Yes, and maybe that's the reason. You're a Democrat?"
"I've always been an enrolled Republican," Livy answered frankly.
"This is going to be a tough one, Chuck," David said, taking the drink that Wellman handed him.
"Nothing is tough—not for you," Wellman said. "I'm telling you, Leon, Mr. Locke is your man—broad international experience, knows all the financial and political leaders of Europe, speaks fluent French . . ."
"Are you married?" David asked, ignoring Wellman's sales talk.
"Yes."
"Living with your wife?"
"Yes, and we have two children, a boy and a girl. You know, Mr. David, that you can find all this in *Who's Who*."
"We don't pick ambassadors from *Who's Who*," David said rudely. "How long are you going to be in Washington?"
"That will depend on the House Appropriations Committee. I came over to testify."
"Have you your statement prepared?"
"Yes indeed. I brought it with me."
"Let me have a look at it."
Livy went over to the desk and took a mimeographed copy of his report out of his brief case, bringing it back to the couch and handing it to David, who gave it a quick glance, then folded it and put it in his side pocket.
"I'm afraid I can't let you have that," Livy said. "It hasn't been cleared with the Administrator yet."
"Don't worry about that," David said blandly. "The Administrator is not going to know that the President has seen it."
There was a loud knock at the door. Wellman looked at his

watch. "That must be one of your guests," he said to Livy. "I told the front desk to send them right up."

"Well, I'll be seeing you, Chuck," David said, rising. "I wish you luck, Mr. Locke."

"Thank you, Mr. David," Livy said, walking to the door with him. "The luck is in your hands."

"Not mine, the Boss's."

Livy opened the door and faced the red, beaming countenance of Senator Donegan. The Senator's quick eye took in the presence of Leon David and Wellman. "Glad to see you, Livy," he said heartily. "I take it things are progressing. What is it, Leon? Ambassador to Costa Rica?" He stalked into the room, saw the bottles and glasses on the table, and headed in that direction.

"You'll have to ask the Boss," David answered.

"Don't double-talk me, Leon," Donegan said, pouring a good hooker of bourbon. "I'm seeing the Boss personally on this one. Come clean, now, what is it?"

"Holland," David replied. "But there are others, Senator, others with a lot of backing."

"To hell with the others," the Senator said confidently. "I'm backing Livy Locke, and you can tell that to all the boys in the East Wing."

Leon David ducked out, closing the door quickly behind him. The Senator watched the exit out of the corner of his eye and chuckled. "Don't worry about him, Livy," he said, "he's only a messenger boy."

"Thanks for the help, Mike," Livy said. "How is your campaign outlook?"

"No better than when I saw you in Paris."

"Do you know Mr. Wellman, Senator?" Livy asked.

"Sure, I know Chuck."

"He'll be in touch with you when you need help. He's my personal representative in Washington."

"You're a smart picker, Livy," Donegan said.

"With your weight behind it, Senator, I think we can push this ambassadorship over," Wellman said.

"Look, Chuck," Donegan said, bringing his drink over to the couch and sitting down, "you heard me tell Leon, didn't you? I'm going to speak to the Boss about this, and not on the telephone, either."

"That will cinch it," Wellman said.

The Senator smiled and slapped Livy on the knee. "When you see your wife, tell her the little woman was tickled pink with those scarfs and the perfume."

"I'll write her today," Livy said, pleased that Eleanor had done her part so effectively.

"Chuck, you should have been in Paris with us," Donegan said to Wellman. "What a town! And this Livy has an assistant . . . How's Walter, anyway?"

"He was fine when I left him the day before yesterday," Livy answered, full of mellowness and the milk of human kindness.

"Keep an eye on him, Livy, he's going places, that boy," the Senator said.

There was another knock on the door and the sound of voices in the hall. Livy nodded to Wellman. "Open the door for them," he said, not wishing to leave the Senator, knowing that, of all the guests whom Wellman had asked, Donegan was the most important for his purpose.

CHAPTER EIGHTEEN

"I FORGOT to ask you where you were going," Eleanor said. She had thought, when Christian had suggested a lunch outside Paris, that he had in mind Marly, or Bougival, or St. Germain-en-Laye, but here they were, swinging from the new parkway into Route Nationale No. 10, already a good thirty kilometers from Paris.

"To Pontchartrain," Christian said. "It's not far now. We turn off at Trappes on Route 12, and we'll be there in ten minutes. Are you hungry?"

"Hunger is my greatest weakness," Eleanor replied, adding, "particularly in France."

"We shall eat well at this place, better even than in Paris, where the good cooks are ruined by tourists who have no discrimination."

"I have to take care. I've already put on weight in the few months I've been here."

Christian let his eyes wander from the road for an instant while he looked at her. She was in a gray suit which fitted her well, with a little gray felt beret on her blond head. He knew what she meant. Her figure was good as it was, rounded and firm and feminine, yet she could not afford another kilo. Ripe, he thought, ripe to be picked and eaten. When she had accepted his invitation to lunch in the country, he assumed that she knew what she was doing. She had excited him from that very first moment when he had sat next to her at Peyraud's dinner, even before it had become evident to him that she and Derek had been lovers. That night the observant Jacqueline had warned him to have a care. "Locke does not seem like a husband one need fear," he had replied. To which Jacqueline had answered, "I was thinking of dear Derek." So he had had to plot his campaign with care, for to cuckold two men, with a woman who gave every evidence of punctilious respectability, was not a simple undertaking. The departure of Locke for the United States had been an unexpected bit of good fortune, defining his time limits to Saturdays and Sundays when Derek was in Kent with his Daphne. He had taken the immediate advantage, asking her lightly, in a good Samaritan voice, if she would be amused by a little drive in the country and a lunch at a nice inn. She had accepted with the proviso that he get her back to town in time to dress for an Embassy cocktail party that she reluctantly felt it her duty to attend.

The front of the inn was already crowded with parked cars, but Christian managed to squeeze in his little Peugeot. The proprietor greeted him at the door effusively, as a favored customer, bowing deeply to Eleanor, then leading them to a table by an open window which looked out on a garden massed with tulips, jonquils, and lilac.

"I like your friend Haines," Christian said as they drank their *apéritifs*, his a sherry and hers a dry martini.

"Sam tells me he's an able young man," Eleanor said. "I wish he were not quite so solemn, so serious. He needs to develop a lighter touch if he is to rise in his profession."

"You did well to ask him to your dinner. I think he was amazed to learn that one can talk of serious matters without being ponderous."

"I'm sure you're right," Eleanor said. "He called me the next day to thank me and apologize for having held forth on the subject of money."

"He did it well, as a matter of fact," Christian said. "Only he should not have scowled so, like a frightened pedagogue."

"He'll learn."

"If you and his girl take the trouble to teach him."

"His girl? What do you mean?" Eleanor asked.

Christian sipped his sherry, looking at her quizzically. "Perhaps I should not have spoken," he said. "I forgot that you are an American, your French is so without accent."

"But I must know," Eleanor said eagerly. "Is he in love with some girl? Is she French? Do tell me about her."

"If I do, it must be between us. Above all, your husband must not know."

"He'd be the last."

"Ah, well," Christian said, encouraged by her dismissal of Locke, "you may remember that he took me home after your dinner."

"Yes, he offered you a lift. I heard him."

"We went first to his apartment on the Ile St. Louis for a whiskey and soda. It is quite charming. Not at all what I expected."

"And he told you about this girl?" Eleanor asked impatiently.

"There was no need. She appeared while we were talking, emerged from his bedroom like Lady Macbeth, clad in a tartan robe."

"I don't believe it. I don't believe a word of it. You're making this up."

Christian ignored her disbelief as the waiter served them with *queues d'écrevisses au gratin* and the sommelier poured a *champagne nature*, all of which he had ordered by telephone.

"She goes by the name of Germaine Brisson and is pretty enough to look well even in a man's dressing gown."

"You mean that she lives there as his mistress?" Eleanor asked, incredulous.

"They are certainly not married."

"Oh dear, how mistaken one can be!" Eleanor exclaimed, with a sad shake of her head. "Here I was, convinced that he was a shy, rather puritanical scholar from the Middle West, and he turns out to be living with a . . . What sort of a girl is she?"

Christian was smiling, not at Eleanor's wrong judgment but at the insight into her character which her words had revealed. "Precisely the sort of girl you would expect him to fall in love with—extremely intelligent, educated, probably from a good bourgeois background."

"But if she is a lady, how could she . . . ?"

"What an extraordinary statement, my dear Eleanor. Do you assume that all ladies are vestal virgins?"

"Don't be dense, Christian, I meant nothing of the kind. I meant that young girls who are well brought up and well educated don't, as a rule, become men's mistresses. I'm afraid you're as gullible as Walter Haines. Just because this girl is pretty and attractive and listens to you talk in wide-eyed wonder you refuse to admit that she's nothing but a little . . ."

"Little what?" Christian asked when she hesitated.

"*Grue*, tart, if you insist on having the word."

"No," Christian said thoughtfully, "I do not misjudge people, least of all women. I would have placed her accurately even had I met her at Haines's for the first time."

"You knew her before?"

"I had met her once in the Vendée under rather strange circumstances." He ate his *queues d'écrevisses* and drank some wine with a faraway look that made Eleanor wonder if he, too, had had an affair with the girl. "No, Eleanor," he went on, "she is not a tart in any sense of the word. She is a strange person, suffering, I should say, from some grave inner conflict."

"So she finds protection in Walter's arms," Eleanor added, with a trace of the feline.

"Probably."

"He loves her, you say."

"I think so, though I doubt he would admit it even to himself."

They ate in silence for a while, Christian thinking that perhaps he had erred in telling her about Germaine, not because it might harm Walter—he was convinced that Eleanor would be loyal on that score—but because of the effect of this news on his own plans. She had gone on record with him as believing that ladies do not have affairs. Furthermore, any attempt on his part to seduce her today would immediately be linked in her mind to this affair of Walter and Germaine, and she would feel constrained to uphold the role of the adjusted, happy wife who needed no protecting arms.

"You know," Eleanor said, breaking the silence, "I think it is probably the best thing that could have happened to him."

"I'm not sure. That will depend on Mlle. Brisson."

"But if she's what you say she is . . ."

"If she is willing, if she is ready, to devote herself entirely and completely to Haines."

"Isn't the fact that she is willing to live with him evidence that she is?" Eleanor asked.

"Partial proof only," Christian argued. "You must remember that the intellectual—and make no mistake, she is an intellectual—is able to make a clean break between reason and heart. She may give him her heart without reserve, but if she does so in the belief that her heart is of small importance compared with her powers of thought, then she may, in the end, destroy him."

"How?"

"By trying to mold him into something which he is not."

"Really, Christian, you make her sound fascinating. I must meet this creature."

"That, I fancy, might be dangerous for Haines."

"Of course," Eleanor said, "it would have to be done with the utmost tact. You'll have to help me devise a way."

"I want no part of it."

"Don't be mean, Christian, you must help me; you're the only one who knows them both."

"See here," Christian said emphatically, "I did not bring you out to Pontchartrain on a lovely Saturday in April to discuss Mlle. Brisson."

"Don't blame me. You brought the subject up."

"And I regret it exceedingly. You seem more interested in her than you are in me."

"My interest is in Walter Haines."

"Which is even more disheartening."

Eleanor laughed. "You make such pretty speeches," she said in a motherly way. "Now, what is that story which Maître Peyraud asked you to tell the other night?"

"He was pulling my leg."

"But there is a story. Jacqueline de Tonville told me there was."

"It's not a story, it's a political theory, and it is even less appropriate to this luncheon than Mlle. Brisson."

"Then you're not going to tell me?"

"Some day, but not now," Christian said firmly. "Right now I want to talk about you. You give me that comfortable feeling of having known you for a long while, and yet I know so absurdly little about you, only the fact that you are married, have two children, and give the impression of being contented with your lot."

"What more is there to know?" she said, trying to disarm him with that very impression of contentment which he had noted. "That is the whole, simple, humdrum story."

"If it were, we should not be lunching tête à tête in Pontchartrain," he said, smiling at her.

"That's absurd," she said crossly. "You can't make me out to be a thwarted, unhappy woman just because I allow you to take me to lunch in the country. I thought our little coterie were supposed to be friends who enjoyed each other's company."

"Oh, that is quite true," Christian said, still smiling. "We enjoy each other immensely, for the very reason that we are aware of each other's weaknesses. That knowledge gives us a camaraderie which would otherwise be quite impossible. Take René Peyraud, for example. We accept the fact that he enjoys flattering beautiful women, while preserving a Proustian attitude toward his fellow man. As for dear Lettice, there is no secret among us of her rather Victorian nymphomania—"

"I think I would rather not hear any more lurid details," Eleanor interrupted. "Unless, of course, you wish to confess your own perversions."

"You think I am indulging in malicious gossip," Christian said. "If I had said these things about others not in our group, you would be right. We, however, believe that we are civilized and enlightened to the point where we can accept our friends as they are, not as they would have others believe them to be." He studied her face as she picked at her *poularde à la crème*, knowing that she had been horrified by his revelation, that everything in her upbringing rebelled against facing the real facts about people's natures. "Perhaps," he went on, "we have been too hasty in inviting you to join us. That was largely my fault. I thought you exquisite and intelligent, and assumed, why, I do not know—it was stupid of me—that you were emancipated."

"Emancipation is a matter of ideas, not of words as in Henry Miller," she said hotly.

"Then you can accept my friends as they are?" he asked.

"Of course I can," she maintained stoutly. "I have, haven't I? Only I do not wish to discuss their private lives, which are none of my business, nor yours."

They finished their lunch in virtual silence, remarking once in a while about the food or the flowers or the warmth of the sun for April, apathetically, as if they feared that any subject not limited to the obvious and immediate might be as controversial as the last. Christian could have pursued his argument and convinced her that to be shocked by words and not by facts was a form of mental dishonesty inherent in the Puritan mind, but he preferred to let her annoyance cool off, turning its direction, as it did so, from him to herself. He was satisfied that he had judged her correctly, that she was brimming with a desire which had been frustrated by years of living with a man who was both pompous and frigid, that she would not—could not—release herself except with the simulated trappings of what she would call "love." Some other men, most other men, in his place would have used that opening, feigning an until-death-us-do-part devotion that was electric, at first sight; and she would have melted under it, wanting to believe every word, shutting her mind to all small voices of doubt or caution. But this he would not do, because to do so would be to soil his own honor, to be untrue to himself as well as to her.

When lunch was over and they got into the car, it was

Eleanor who tried to dispel the gloom. "So our little group are all supposed to be abnormal," she said lightly. "I find that thought most amusing."

Christian, who had started to back the car into the main road, put on the brakes and looked at her in amazement. "But who, my dear Eleanor, would care to be normal?" he asked. "Would you have us like a row of *poulets de Bresse,* all fat, all stupid, all the same flavor?"

"What gave you the idea that I am not one of those fat, complacent *poulets?*" she said, laughing.

He went on backing the car and turning it into the road. "I thought you were a special, sensitized specimen, but of course I could have been wrong."

"What vices did you tag me with?" she asked, still laughing. "Was I a siren or a Lesbian?"

"I fancied you as a sort of passionate nun, thwarted by her vows," he said, heading the car down a side road.

Eleanor gasped, settling back in the seat as if the wind had been knocked out of her. "Well, of all things!" she exclaimed when she got her breath. "Is that the impression I give? Is that what they said about me?"

"That is the conclusion we came to. Very flattering, don't you think?"

"I'm not quite sure. Was this view unanimous?"

He smiled broadly as he drove through the little village of Jouars les Mousseaux. "Yes, even Derek had to agree," he said pointedly.

She made no comment, although she was grateful to Derek for having voted with the majority. "Where are you taking me, anyway?" she asked, relieved, now, to find a new topic.

"I thought we would go around by the valley of the Chevreuse. The road is prettier and I would like to show you an ancestral house."

"The feudal keep of the St. Avits?" she asked.

"No," he said, "that is near Mont de Marsan, whence the family stems. We are Gascon in origin and temperament. This château which I will show you is merely a shooting lodge built by a rather ambitious ancestor who had an idea that proximity to the court of Louis XIV might aid him financially."

"Did it?"

"Family history is silent on the point, but I have always suspected that his friendship with Fouquet paid off."

The aspect of the countryside had suddenly changed. Fields had been replaced by scrubby woods of oak and alder as the road descended into a narrow valley that ran between two clifflike plateaux. Soon the valley widened, the woods on the left becoming taller and finer, and those on the right gradually yielding to a vista of heather and bog. At a turn in the road they came upon an entrance drive which led into the dark wood. It was guarded by two massive stone piers and elaborate wrought-iron gates.

Christian stopped the car and sounded his horn. There was a small lodge well inside the gates, and from it emerged a very old woman with a black shawl drawn tightly over her shoulders. As soon as he saw her coming toward them, Christian jumped out of the car and ran toward the gate, waving.

"*Bonjour, Juliette,*" he called. "*Comment ça va?*"

The old woman stopped and peered at him from myopic eyes. "But no, it is not possible!" she exclaimed in a high, cracked voice. "Monsieur le Comte, what a pleasure for my old eyes! What brings you here in April when the birds are nesting?"

"I have a friend with me who would like to see the Château de St. Hubert," Christian said. "Open the gates, my dear Juliette, and lend me the great key."

"Oh, but it is a pity to see it as it is," the old woman

scolded. "All the furniture in dust covers and all the lovely carpets rolled up."

Old Juliette unlatched the gates and Christian swung them open, then together they walked to the car. "Juliette," Christian said, "this is my friend Mme. Locke, an American who likes to see those places where the history of France was made."

"Good day, Madame," Juliette said, shaking the hand which Eleanor extended from the car window. "Monsieur le Comte does not deceive me. I know him, oh, since he was no bigger than a rabbit. He has a great sentiment for this place. You probably have no wish to see an empty old château, but he will insist on showing it to you and telling you all the stories, the true ones and the ones he makes up in that naughty mind of his."

"Has he a naughty mind?" Eleanor asked with a twinkle in her eye.

The old woman winked at her, lifting both hands in a gesture of despair. "He likes to tease, madame, and make one believe all kinds of fanciful things."

"I'm glad you warned me," Eleanor said in a stage whisper.

The old woman fetched Christian the key, and he drove slowly up the long, winding road, which was rutted and weed-grown. Suddenly the car emerged from the wood into a broad circular field, fringed at its edges with massive rhododendrons, except on the segment which faced them, where there rose, like the proscenium of an amphitheater, a classic building of gray, weathered stone. The road half-circled the field at the border of the rhododendrons until it arrived at a broad expanse of gravel in front of the horseshoe steps which led to the entrance of the château. Christian parked the car, helped Eleanor out, and led the way up the stone steps to the balcony. Here they stood for a while by the balustrade, looking

HÔTEL TALLEYRAND

out over the commanding view of the valley and the distant rolling hills of the forest of Rambouillet.

Christian, gazing, his eyes misty with memories, seemed unaware of Eleanor's presence. "All that you see there," he said finally, with a sweeping gesture of his arm, "is where the kings of France hunted, riding with their hounds and hawks, and where, nowadays, the presidents of the Republic waddle out with their ministers of state to murder pheasants driven into the muzzles of their guns." He laughed bitterly. "The pot hunters have replaced the sportsmen."

"Do you like to shoot?" Eleanor asked. She had not pictured him as a sporting man.

"I adore it," he said passionately. "I live for the days of autumn and winter when I can come here. Oh, we haven't the quantity of game they have." He nodded toward the distant forest of Rambouillet. "But the birds we have are high and difficult, really sporting shots that look no bigger than sparrows when they come rocketing over." He turned abruptly and put the great key in the oak door, as if the talk of shooting was a subject too precious to be pursued.

They entered into a large octagonal foyer, originally a *salle de garde*, very high, with an elaborate domed ceiling and with the eight walls paneled in oak, each emblazoned with a relief carving portraying objects and instruments of the hunt. The atmosphere was dark and musty, the only light coming from the open door. As her eyes became adjusted, Eleanor could discern the details of the boiserie and of the marble-topped consoles, on each of which was a portrait bust of a bewigged gentleman. Christian told her the history of the château, how it had been built by Guy Bazac, the fifth count of St. Avit, in 1650, as a shooting lodge where he could entertain his friends at court. Most of the rooms on the ground floor, including the foyer, he explained, had been entirely done over in the eighteenth century by an earlier Christian, who had fled to England during the revolution.

As they moved from room to room, Christian told Eleanor the story associated with every picture, every bibelot, every tapestry. They might be, as the old woman had warned, figments of his imagination, but she did not care. There was a sincerity, a sentiment, a passion in his voice that could only stem from deep affection. It was the story of his family and it was flavored with intense devotion and loyalty, as if the clan represented the continuity of all that was firm and noble in French civilization. This was a side of his character which she had not divined. So far she had thought of him only as a cynical young man of rather impertinent assertiveness who seemed to be quite sure that every woman was longing to go to bed with him. The conversation at lunch had served to confirm this impression and she had almost reached the point of disliking him. Now, however, as she listened to him, as she saw him look at each object with reverence, as she sensed the love and pride, her feelings toward him changed; she admired him as a man of sentiment and honor.

The only bedroom on the first floor was at the southern end, with two tall windows looking out over the valley. "This is original," Christian said as they entered it. He smiled. "My namesake, the eighteenth-century Christian, had the good grace to leave us this historic room untouched." The walls were hung with tapestries depicting Diana in various hunting episodes, and a huge bed dominated the room with its four posts of carved, gilded oak and its tester of embroidered velour.

"The master's bed, I take it," Eleanor said.

"No, not the master's," Christian corrected. "That is upstairs. This was the room reserved for royal and noble visitors. According to legend it was on that bed, in 1651, that the great Nicolas Fouquet, Marquis de Belle-Isle, Inspector of Finance, proposed to Marie de Castille. It was there, on that mattress, that she realized her ambition of capturing the richest man in France."

Eleanor smiled. "It is what we would call a very French story."

Christian walked slowly over to the bed, stepped up on the dais, then turned to Eleanor, a hand resting on one of the massive pillars. "I wonder," he said quietly, seriously, "if it is not typical of all ambition. My dear Eleanor, it is the one story connected with this house which I dislike. It is a mean, sordid story. When love-making is used for gain or advancement it is nasty and dirty. It has always been my hope that some day I will be able to exorcise the ignoble act of Marie by making love to some woman on that bed who has no further ambition than the fulfillment of her desire.

"What has prevented you?" Eleanor asked, unable to suppress a smile.

"I have yet to find the woman." He stepped down from the dais and walked toward the door. "I had you in mind, you know, but it didn't work out. A pity, isn't it?"

"I wouldn't say it was a pity," Eleanor answered, following him across the salon and into the foyer. "I think it's all much better as it is."

"For the moment, yes," Christian said, and waited for her to pass into the sunlight before he closed the door and locked it carefully.

CHAPTER NINETEEN

GERMAINE took out the worsted suit that she had worn the night she met Walter. Ever since he had staked her to a new wardrobe, nothing really expensive, but new, at least, and more in the mode, made for her by a little copyiste she knew in the rue Washington, this old garment, this uniform of Party-hack days, had been carefully packed away in a suitcase which she kept in the closet in the dining room. As the chatelaine of Mr. Walter Haines's apartment at 26 Quai d'Orléans she had felt it was too worn and too dowdy to be in keeping with her role. Even on Thursday mornings when she made her weekly stroll to the Pont Neuf and instructed an old woman how to get to the Hôpital de la Charité, giving her a folded copy of *Le Figaro* which concealed her brief report on O.S.R. and O.E.E.C. activities, she wore her new clothes.

But on this morning, this Thursday, the woman, one whom she had not seen before, younger than the others, more the student type as she herself used to be, had whispered as Germaine wrote on the margin of the newspaper, "Go to the room of Le Boiteux at three this afternoon. It is important." Quickly she had written on Le Figaro in large letters, "Directly, or by taxi from the White Dove?" When the girl had read the question which Germaine had pushed toward her, she had said, "Directly, on foot. Keep away from the White Dove."

Germaine suspected that it had to do with the mimeographed copy of Walter's report which Locke had taken to Washington and which she had passed on at the Pont Neuf a week ago. That she had procured it she had considered a minor triumph. Yet it had been so easy, nothing could have been simpler. Walter had brought home a copy for her to read, proud of his brain child, wanting her to know that he had composed it, every word of it. It had been stamped "Confidential" at the top and bottom of each page, which meant, she knew, that he should not have shown it to her, or even taken it from the Hôtel Talleyrand to his flat. What she did not know was that the classification was merely temporary, to prevent release before it had been approved by the Administrator and recited by Locke before an open hearing of a congressional committee. She had read it carefully, finding that she could flatter Walter with complete honesty, for it was an excellent report, clear, precise, and well reasoned. What it lacked for her purpose, for the purpose of the Cominform, were the figures, the detailed listing of each country's balance-of-payments position, its holdings of gold and valuta. She had remarked to him, after she had finished reading it, that it would be more comprehensible to her were she to know these details. He had been so flattered by her interest, so delighted that she wanted to know, to learn about his work, so happy to find himself, for the first time in their relationship, the teacher and not the pupil, that he had promised eagerly to bring home a copy of the composite O.E.E.C. statistics on the following day, warning her, however, that they were highly confidential and had been supplied by each government only on the condition that they were not for public consumption. This he had done, leaving the document in the flat for only twenty-four hours, so that she had had to copy the figures furiously from the moment of his departure in order to have them complete before his return.

Without a hat, dressed in the old suit and wearing the old, soiled rubber-soled moccasins, she walked out of the house and crossed quickly over the high bridge which connects the Ile St. Louis with the Ile de la Cité. Le Boiteux lived in a shabby pension in the rue Henri Barbusse which catered to stanch Party members. She knew the place. It had a bar and a restaurant on the ground floor, where she had often eaten with Le Boiteux and Georges Persan, and even, on occasion, with Le Crépuscule himself, the great, the formidable, the feared Crépuscule who was the link with the Cominform and, for all she and the other comrades knew, with the Bolshevics and the Politburo. She walked slowly, merely strolling, until she reached the Boulevard St. Michel; then, being on safer ground in the student quarter, where girls dressed as she was were usually going somewhere with a purpose, she changed to a brisk pace. At the Place Edmond Rostand she took the rue Gay-Lussac, preferring to approach the rue Henri Barbusse from a small back street than directly from the boulevard. It took her longer than she expected, as the streets back of the Institution Sourds Muets and the Ecole Lavoisier kept turning at abrupt angles. She finally found herself back on the Boulevard St. Michel and had to retrace her steps on the little rue Val de Grace to the point where she had crossed the rue Henri Barbusse without knowing it.

Georges Persan, who was sitting at a table on the terrace of the bar-restaurant, saw her coming and ostentatiously got up and walked to the door which led to the pension rooms above. Germaine realized that this was her signal and went in at the same entrance, where she found him waiting at the foot of the narrow stairway. As soon as she had closed the outer door he turned and went up without greeting her.

Le Boiteux was seated in a frayed upholstered armchair by the window, which looked out over the vegetable garden of the deaf-mutes across the street. He did not get up when she came in. He never got to his feet when it was not necessary, for the ankle which the Gestapo had twisted and broken in their fruitless attempt to make him disclose the names of the Communist leaders of the F.T.P. had never healed properly and pained him when his weight was on it. He was a heavy, taciturn man whose bitterness was as pervading as his blind faith in the power and the glory of the Party. Like all who were selected by Le Crépuscule for the work of this special cell, he was unmarried and without ties of family. A typical man of the north, dour and physically brave, he had been born in Douai but had lived his adult life as a foreman of a factory in Puteaux. Since the war he worked only for the Party, living here in the pension in a single bare room and acting as agent and legman for the boss, Le Crépuscule.

"Take another look in the hall, then lock the door," he commanded in a low, grating voice.

Persan stuck his head out of the door, glanced up and down the corridor, and closed it again, sliding the bolt. "No one there," he said.

"Comrade Brisson," Le Boiteux announced, pulling Walter's report, folded in half, out of his inside coat pocket, "Le Crépuscule wishes me to tell you that he finds this interesting but that it must be translated."

"He's read it, then," Germaine said, unable to hide her pride.

"How could he find it interesting if he had not read it?" Le Boiteux growled. He held the report out toward her. "Here, take it. You are to do the translation."

Germaine stepped forward and took it from him. She saw at once that her copy of the statistical tables was missing. "Where is the part I copied out?" she asked.

"Those figures are clear enough as they are," Le Boiteux said.

"Why did you copy them?" Persan asked. "Why didn't you bring the original as you did the text?" He was sitting on the bed, eyeing her with a mixture of adoration and hate.

The only other chair was a small cane-bottom one which was pushed under the deal table by the wall. Germaine pulled it out and sat down. When she spoke, it was to Le Boiteux and not to Georges. "The figures supplied by O.E.E.C. are highly secret. They were in the apartment only for one day. I had to work fast to copy them all."

"You're sure they are correct?" Le Boiteux asked.

"Absolutely. I checked them back twice," Germaine said, tossing her head in confident assurance.

"Can you get hold of the original again?" Le Boiteux said.

"Impossible. Even to try might arouse suspicion," Germaine stated emphatically.

"Le Crépuscule is not satisfied with them," Georges Persan remarked.

"Let me handle this," Le Boiteux snapped at Georges.

"What do you mean, he isn't satisfied with them?" Germaine shot back at Georges, her eyes blazing. "He'll never get a more authentic or more important document out of the Marshall Plan than that. What did you want me to bring, phony figures dreamed up by some dumb American? My God, Le Crépuscule doesn't realize what he has."

"Wait a minute, wait a minute," Le Boiteux growled. "Calm yourself, comrade. He knows what's important better than you do. These figures you brought don't agree with those he has from another source."

"What other source?" Germaine asked.

"That's none of your business," Le Boiteux said severely. "Your job is to get authentic information, not press handouts."

"That's just what I got you," Germaine snapped. She was angry now, seeing her triumph deflated by ignorance.

Le Boiteux reached in his pocket and drew out another sheaf of folded papers. "Look at this," he said, holding it out to her.

It was a printed pamphlet which, in form and content, seemed identical with that which she had copied, only it lacked any designation of classification. The title, too, was the same as the one Walter had brought home to her. It read, "Balance-of-Payments Positions of the Fourteen Nations of the Organization for European Economic Cooperation as Presented to the Finance Committee on March 27, 1950." She turned to the tables. The first one she came to was on Italy. She tried to recall if the figures were the same, but she could not; there had been too many tables, too many sums for her to remember them all.

"Well, what do you say now?" Le Boiteux asked.

"It looks like the same report," Germaine said, perplexed. "It has the same heading, the same date of the meeting. The only difference that I can see offhand is that the other was marked 'Secret' on the top and bottom of each page."

"Was the word 'Secret' printed or stamped?" Georges asked.

"It was printed in the same type as the report," Germaine replied. "Tell me, in what way do the figures differ?"

"In one report the gold and dollar holdings of at least four countries were larger than in the other," Le Boiteux said. All the time his eyes were on her, studying her carefully, as if he suspected that she might be double-crossing them.

"In which were they larger?" she asked.

"He didn't tell me," Le Boiteux said stonily. "He just said that there was this discrepancy."

"Let me take this," Germaine said, waving the pamphlet. "I'll see if I can get Haines to explain the difference."

"No, you don't!" Le Boiteux almost shouted. "That's not to leave this room. Give it to me."

"Here it is," she said, tossing it to him. "I don't suppose any of you dimwits ever thought of checking with the press reports. These figures were in every paper the day after that meeting on March twenty-seventh. I remember seeing them."

"Didn't he tell you to check them, Georges?" Le Boiteux asked.

"Like hell he did," Persan grunted. "I haven't been in on this until this moment and you know that damn well."

Le Boiteux picked up his cane and pointed the rubber ferrule at Georges' legs. "Look under the bed there. You'll find the whole file of *L'Humanité* for this year." Persan got down on his knees and pulled out a pile of newspapers. "They're in chronological order, so just look at the date on the top copy of each pile."

"This one says April fifth," Persan said on pulling out the third pile.

"Bring that lot to me," Le Boiteux ordered, "and push the others back carefully so as not to get them mixed up." The pile in his lap, Le Boiteux went through it quickly with his big fingers and pulled out the issue of March twenty-eighth. He glanced through it. "Not in here," he said.

"Try the twenty-ninth," Georges suggested.

Le Boiteux replaced the issues of the twenty-eighth and pulled out the next one. "Here it is," he said, reading the article hastily, then turning to the third page, where the tables were. He held the paper out to Germaine. "You read the figures while I check it with this report. Just read the gold and dollar holdings of each country."

Germaine made no effort to take the newspaper. "Let Georges read it," she said. "You fellows don't trust my eyesight."

"Don't be an idiot," Le Boiteux grumbled.

"We'll soon see who the idiot is," she said caustically. "Go on, Georges, read it to him."

Persan got up and took the paper, switched on the single bulb that lit the room, and put on a pair of heavy horn-rimmed spectacles. He studied the figures first before starting to read. His voice showed that he was quite indifferent as to the result of this inquiry. It did not concern him. He had no responsibility in the matter and would be equally pleased whoever was in the wrong. When he had finished, he raised his head and asked, "Well, are they the same?"

Le Boiteux did not answer, but only sat there, scowling at the report in his hands.

"Of course they're the same," Germaine said sarcastically; then she laughed, a hard, brittle laugh. "Imagine what clever sources Le Crépuscule has to check on me! Brings you a press release that was printed in every paper in the world! That's a hot one! I hope he was paid handsomely."

"Comrade," Le Boiteux said, looking at her sternly, "it is our duty to check and double-check, to believe no one, not even you."

"Okay," Germaine said calmly, satisfied now that she would receive the credit she deserved from higher up. "But next time do your checking before you start accusing me." She got up. "Is that all? I must be back before Haines returns."

"Just a minute," Le Boiteux said, more pleasantly than she had ever heard him. "How is it going? Has he no suspicions?"

"If he had, you would never have had those figures," Germaine said.

Le Boiteux smiled. "He still thinks you just the little whore from Mme. Nicole's?"

"No, I had to change that," she replied. "I am now an ex-collaborationist who was forced to go there because I could get no other work."

"Hasn't he questioned the fact that there's nothing about that on your identity card?" Georges asked.

"He hasn't seen my identity card," Germaine said. "I've seen to that."

"Just the same, you had better have one that shows you've been to court," Le Boiteux said. "The woman who meets you next Thursday will drop it on the sidewalk."

"Is it fun sleeping with this character?" Persan asked with a leer.

Germaine flushed with anger. The barb had hit where she thought herself invulnerable. "Shut up, you dirty-minded—" she started to say.

"Easy, comrade," Le Boiteux interrupted. "Don't pay any attention to his talk. Tell me, have you met any of Haines's friends?"

"Only one," she answered, frowning. "That put me in a tough spot." She turned to Persan. "Georges, do you remember that night at the Château de Talmont when a young chap from the F.F.I. who called himself Capet came to see us about joining up with him?"

"He had a bloody priest with him," Georges added.

"Well, a few nights ago," Germaine went on, "Haines brings a man up to the apartment for a drink. He introduces him as the Comte de St. Avit and my blood starts to run cold. Not that I recognized him at first—I didn't—but I felt sure that I'd seen him somewhere, I could not remember where—Toulouse, Oxford, Maquis—and then it came to me suddenly that it was that Capet."

Georges Persan had risen from the bed and come forward to Le Boiteux's chair. "Look, comrade," he said, "I don't like this. It isn't good. That guy knew all about Comrade Brisson, knew she was the F.T.P. leader for the Vendée, knew she was a Party member—"

"But he knew me as Solange Ramé," Germaine interrupted, "and he only saw me that one time, and it was night and I had on a uniform with a kerchief over my head."

"If you recognized him under another name, why shouldn't he recognize you?" Georges asked irritably.

"Because he didn't. I could tell," she answered defensively. "Besides, we were speaking English and how would he know that Solange Ramé could speak English?"

"What makes you so sure he didn't recognize you?" Le Boiteux asked.

"Because he's a stupid aristocrat who would have said so at once if he had," she replied. "I know the type—nothing to do but chase after women and regret the passing of the Bourbons. He thought I was attractive, but the look in his eye was lust, not recognition."

"I'll bet it was both," Georges said.

"Where did your economist friend meet a man like that?" Le Boiteux asked.

"At a dinner at his boss's house," she replied.

Le Boiteux pushed himself up with his strong arms and, with the aid of his cane, limped over to Germaine. "Just take care, comrade. Keep out of that fellow's way. We can't afford to have this go wrong after such a good start."

"Don't worry, I'll handle it," she said confidently.

"What did you say his name was?" Le Boiteux asked.

"Le Comte de St. Avit," she answered. "Haines called him Christian."

"Make a note of that, Georges," Le Boiteux said to Persan. "Monsieur le Comte de St. Avit. We'll get a line on him." He held out his hand to Germaine. "Good luck, comrade."

She shook his hand, then turned to the door, saying, "Au revoir, Georges."

"I'll go with you," Persan said.

"No," she said. "I'd better go alone."

"She's right," Le Boiteux said. "She must not be seen with you, not even in the corridor. You stay here with me, I want to talk to you."

Germaine ran down the stairs and into the street. Her victory was forgotten. Only the words of Persan stabbed her mind like hot needles. Did she really enjoy living with Walter? What if she did? What difference did it make as long as she could bring Le Crépuscule the right documents? And there was always the consoling thought that if anything should slip up, Walter could prove his innocence and would not suffer. Oh, God! why did that jealous, slimy Georges have to bring that up?

"Listen," Persan said when the door was closed and bolted, "do you realize what a bad angle this is, her meeting up with that de St. Avit who used to call himself Capet?"

"You're right, comrade, it's not good," Le Boiteux said. "That is, if he recognized her. She says he didn't and she's a smart girl. She hasn't made a mistake yet."

"Look at it this way," Georges Persan argued. "If the American is a pal of St. Avit, then he's sure to come there again. If he didn't recognize Solange the first time—"

"Germaine, you idiot!" Le Boiteux shouted. "Never mention that other name. It doesn't exist."

"All right, Germaine. If he keeps on seeing her, sooner or later he's going to remember, and when he does, he'll put two and two together and tip the American."

"She said she'd keep out of his way."

"No, she didn't. That's what you said. She told you not to worry, she'd handle it."

Frowning, Le Boiteux poked the torn carpet with the rubber ferrule of his cane. "We can't afford to take any chances, Georges," he said finally. "She's clever, yes, but sometimes the cleverest have to be watched for their own good." He looked up at Persan with an ironic smile. "You've bought yourself the job you've been looking for. I want you to tail her and find out if she sees the count again. Keep a close eye on the two of them—who comes to the apartment, and where they go together. Have the motorbike handy in case they use his car. And don't forget to report to me every morning."

Georges put on his battered felt hat and picked his raincoat off the bed. "Now you're talking, comrade. I don't like the looks of this."

CHAPTER TWENTY

"SORRY, Christian," Walter said into the telephone. "It's kind of you to ask me, but I have to make it a practice to refuse all luncheon dates on weekdays. My time is too uncertain."

"I quite understand," Christian's voice said. "It would not have occurred to me to bother you had the matter not been important."

"Could we make it later, say at six-thirty?"

"*Malheureusement*, no," Christian said. His voice sounded fretful and serious. "I have something to tell you that cannot wait. It is urgent, very urgent. It concerns your work, your mission."

"Could we make it downtown? Somewhere near the office, say Weber's or the Crillon Bar?"

"For reasons I cannot explain now it will have to be *chez moi*," Christian answered impatiently. "Don't worry, I shall not keep you long. In an hour and a quarter you will be back at your office. *Entendu?*"

"It's against my rules, Christian, but as you say it concerns E.C.A. I'll do it." Walter looked at his watch. "It's twenty-five to one. I'll be there at one sharp."

"*Merci infiniment, mon vieux.*"

Walter hung up the receiver, picked the car keys from his

desk and fiddled with them. He wondered what information Christian might have which he so urgently wished to disclose. It concerned E.C.A., he had made that clear. Had he heard something from a friend in the Quai d'Orsay which involved NATO or EPU? Or was it that fanciful scheme of his for the reconstitution of the Holy Roman Empire?

Smiling to himself, he got up and took his hat from the tree in the corner. The picture of Livy's face if he tried to promote the theme of European monarchy was enough to make the prospect of the lunch agreeable.

Old Etiennette, dressed correctly in black, with a frilly starched apron and a minute lace cap on top of her gray hair, greeted him at the door with the friendly smile she reserved for Christian's men friends and told him that *Monsieur le Comte* was waiting in the salon.

"I apologize for asking a busy diplomat to come way out here for lunch," Christian said as Walter entered the room. "I wish to present my dear friend the Abbé d'Albret."

A slender man with the rugged face of a soldier, but with soft, compassionate eyes, dressed in the long white robes of a Dominican, came forward and shook Walter's hand. "It pleases my friend here to give me the title of Abbé," he said pleasantly, "but it is not correct. I am not a Superior but merely a humble priest of the order."

"I prefer it. It suits you much better," Christian said. "In any romance of the eighteenth century you would appear as the Abbé, not just plain Father d'Albret."

"Alas, I am not a character in a novel by Diderot," the priest said.

"Indeed you are not," Christian exclaimed. "You are more important than those social butterflies." He turned to Walter. "It might interest you to know that he is the leading character in the most vital story of the twentieth century."

The Dominican lifted his arms. "How you exaggerate, my dear Christian," he said. "My role is infinitesimal."

"What is this important story?" Walter asked, convinced that he had been right in his guess that he was to be indoctrinated with the theory of European empire.

"The struggle between those who believe in the sanctity of the individual and those who seek to enslave the mind of man," Christian answered in a voice that was far less pompous than the statement. He poured three glasses of sherry from a decanter and handed one to Walter and one to the Abbé. "The story started with Mussolini's march on Rome, continued with Hitler and the Nazis, and is now reaching its diabolical zenith with Stalin and his Bolshevics." He raised his glass to the priest. "The Abbé d'Albret has been in the forefront of the battle from the beginning."

"You look hardly old enough, Father," Walter said politely.

"In 1922 I was a novice at Montauban," the Abbé said modestly.

"It seems hardly possible," Walter remarked, seeing, however, the little telltale lines about the priest's eyes. "That was twenty-eight years ago."

Etiennette announced that lunch was served, and Christian ushered his guests to the table at the far end of the long yellow room.

"May I suggest, for reasons which will be obvious, that we do not speak French while we are lunching," Christian said in English. "I would have preferred to speak of this matter after we had finished eating, over a glass of brandy, but knowing, Haines, that you have to be back at the Hôtel Talleyrand by half past two, I thought it wiser to launch into the subject at once."

"You men of the Marshall Plan seem to work very hard," the priest said in excellent English.

"There is much to be done and time is short," Walter said.

"I must confess, Haines," Christian said in a voice that was unnaturally serious, "that I asked the Abbé d'Albret to join us today because I did not have the guts to tell you what I have to tell you without his moral support. I was afraid that if we were alone you might think I was butting in on matters that were none of my affair, that you would believe neither my words nor my motives, and that your resentment, your anger, would cause you to dismiss all that I said from your mind."

Walter looked astonished. "For God's sake, man, what are you trying to say?" he asked.

Christian put down his knife and fork and looked Walter squarely in the eye. "That your mistress, who now calls herself Germaine Brisson, is a highly placed agent of the Cominform," he said, pronouncing the words slowly and deliberately.

Walter's heart stopped a beat, but he let no sign of shock or surprise appear on his face. For an instant his mind was frozen by the appalling revelation; then, as it began slowly to function, he had a sensation of complete unreality. He had the illusion of not being there at all, of watching a victim facing his accusers. "You are making a very direct and explicit accusation," he said coldly.

"Because I know what I'm talking about," Christian said.

"If you have proofs, you have naturally taken them to the police," Walter said.

"Not yet, because that would wreck your career. I owe it to you, as a gentleman and a friend, to give you the opportunity of getting out of this before the police are notified."

"Thanks, that's mighty magnanimous of you," Walter said sarcastically. "Now I'd like to hear what your proofs are."

"You tell him, Abbé," Christian said.

"This is a most unpleasant task," the priest said slowly, "for

I have observed your reaction to the news, which leads me to believe that you love this unfortunate and misguided girl."

"We'll leave that out of this," Walter said angrily.

"Very well, we shall pass that by," the Abbé said patiently, taking a little black notebook from the folds of his white robe. He fingered the pages until he found the one he sought before speaking again. "If you will be patient with me, I will tell you briefly the history of this woman. She was born in Toulouse on August 14, 1926, the daughter of Professor and Madame Gabriel Santerre and christened Ninon after her maternal grandmother. Her mother died when she was three years old and she was brought up by her father and a Mlle. Boudreau who acted as housekeeper for her father after the death of his wife. She had one brother, Jacques Santerre, who was her senior by six years and whom she adored. He was killed fighting with the Maquis in 1941. In 1940, during the period of the so-called phony war, her father sent her to the home of Professor Hinch-Bidley at Oxford for safekeeping and in order that she might become proficient in English. She resented deeply having to leave her father and brother. The bitterness of this forced separation from her family in time of danger seems greatly to have colored her life in England, for it was there, when she was only fourteen, that she first began to consort with undergraduates of Communist leanings. In 1941 she persuaded Professor Hinch-Bidley to allow her to work in London for the French underground movement. She next appears in Brittany in January, 1943, as an active member of an F.T.P. brigade under the name of Solange Ramé. Soon after, she was given command of the F.T.P. forces in the Vendée, and it was there that the Comte de St. Avit and I met her for the first time."

"The second time was at your apartment," Christian added.

"In 1945 and 1946," the Abbé went on, "she was active in Communist Party affairs, first in La Rochelle and Bordeaux and later in Paris. During that period, always under the name of Solange Ramé, she achieved the recognition of Thorez and other leaders for her tireless and ardent efforts. It was only in 1948 that she again disappeared. The story was carefully circulated that she had gone to Russia to take an important post with the Bureau of Propaganda. As a matter of fact she never left Paris. She was attending school, a very secret school, the school for Cominform spies. When she graduated, it was under the name of Germaine Brisson, and she was assigned to duty in the cell of a man named Pierre Fantin, who is known as Le Crépuscule." He closed the little book and looked up at Walter with a wistful, sad expression.

"How do you know all this?" Walter asked. He had hardly touched the poached egg in a pastry patty that Etiennette had served him, letting it grow cold while he listened, his thoughts in a turmoil, remembering the secret balance-of-payments figures he had brought home for Germaine to read.

"I make it my business to know what the enemies of Christ are doing," the Abbé said. "In this case I have taken special pains because of her father, who for years has helped me with my English studies."

"When, according to your informant, was it that she appeared as Germaine Brisson?" Walter asked.

"The first we knew of the new personality," the priest answered, "was when she called on Fantin in December of last year."

"That was four months ago. What was she doing before I met her?" Walter asked, still doubting that she was using him.

"We do not know," the Abbé confessed. "She was kept very much in hiding, probably waiting for an assignment."

"Has it occurred to you that she might have changed her mind during that period and run out on the Party?" Walter said.

"Had she done that, she would have changed her name again," Christian said. "She would have communicated with her father and become once more Ninon Santerre."

"Not necessarily," Walter argued. "She may have been too ashamed to do that. Just let me tell you how I met her and you will see what I mean." He went on to describe in detail his visit to Mme. Nicole's establishment, referring to the Senator merely as a friend, but repeating her conversation and describing her behavior, both there and subsequently at the Bar Condé, at la Méditerranée, and at his flat.

"She could have been planted at the brothel," Christian said. "If the proprietress is a Communist and you were a periodic client, that would have been a neat method of introducing her."

"No," Walter protested, "that doesn't hold water. In the first place, if that was planned, she would have tried to behave like the other girls in order to allay suspicion. Secondly, who ever heard of a whorehouse madam being a Communist? The two things are mutually exclusive."

The Abbé smiled. "Not according to the Bolshevics," he said. "It is their custom to use the impulses of sex for their own ends."

"Well, I just refuse to believe that Germaine is not on the level," Walter said stubbornly.

"You wish to believe her an apostate," the Abbé said thoughtfully. "You may be right, but until we are sure, it is for you, for us, for the free world, a dangerous assumption."

"Look, Father," Walter said earnestly, "it doesn't make sense. Why should the Communists spy on me or my work? There are no secrets in E.R.P. or in the European Payments

Union. It's all an open book. You can read it in the papers." As he spoke, he knew it was not the truth, but he had to say it now, as much to defend himself as to protect her. "If they were going to all this trouble to plant a spy, they would do it in NATO or in M.D.A.P. or in the Embassy, and certainly not in the apartment of a lowly economic assistant at E.C.A."

"Can you afford to take the chance, Haines?" Christian asked.

"What do you want me to do?" Walter said hotly. "Throw her out? Kick the poor girl into the Seine without giving her a chance to defend herself?"

"We're not suggesting that you kick her out," Christian said. "That would help no one. It would be better that you give her an opportunity to prove what she really is."

"What do you mean?" Walter asked.

"Let her continue to live with you," Christian explained, "giving her no reason to believe that you have any suspicions. Then bring home a document, one of a confidential nature, not so confidential, mind you, that it would give help to the enemy, but one which would not, at least, be given to the press. Then we shall see."

"Who will see?" Walter asked.

"The Deuxième Bureau," Christian answered.

"You mean to notify them?"

"It is our duty," the Abbé said.

"That means that our security officer will know," Walter said, turning pale. "I thought you said you were doing this out of friendship for me."

"That is true, Haines," Christian said. "I was convinced that you were an innocent victim, and I still believe so, I want to believe it, but . . ."

"Oh, God!" Walter moaned, putting his head in his hands. "What a mess! What a sickening mess! If I don't report this myself to the security officer, I'll be suspected of being an accomplice." He dropped his hands on the table and looked from Christian to the Abbé with an imploring, tragic expression. "Look, gentlemen, listen to me, please. I wanted to leave this out of the discussion, but I can't, not now. I love Germaine. Do you get that? I love her and I refuse to believe that she is a Communist spy."

"There was no need to tell us," the Abbé said gently. "We understand. We know what a bitter, cruel blow this is."

"If you mean that, Father," Walter implored, "then give me a little time. I don't ask for much, twenty-four hours will be enough. Just give me one chance to talk to her before you notify the police."

"I'm afraid we cannot afford—"

"Give it to him, my dear Abbé," Christian interrupted. "I'll vouch for him."

"What will you tell her?" the priest asked.

"That the Comte de St. Avit recognized her as a Communist he met in the Résistance," Walter said, "under the name of—what was it?"

"Solange Ramé," Christian answered.

"And that you know she came over from England," Walter continued, "and that the story she told me about having learned English as the mistress of a British officer was a lie."

"There was a Britisher with her band," the Abbé said.

"But you said she learned her English at Oxford," Walter said.

"Quite true," the Abbé assented, "but it may be useful for you to say that she did not learn it from Sergeant Onslow, who was dropped with her from the same R.A.F. airplane. It will prove to her that you know what you are talking about."

Walter got up from the table. He had eaten nothing. "I

shall call you tomorrow," he said to Christian. "What is your number?" He took out a notebook and pencil.

"Kléber 65-09," Christian replied. "I shall be here until one-thirty."

The Abbé d'Albret got up from his chair. "Let me say to you, as one who has had much experience, that conversion is not an easy task. I shall pray for your success."

"I believe that Germaine Brisson is already a convert," Walter said stanchly.

"Love moves in a mysterious way," the Abbé said, with a compassionate smile.

Walter bowed stiffly and walked out of the room, followed by Christian. In the foyer, old Etiennette handed him his hat and raincoat. She shook her head disapprovingly. "But monsieur has not eaten his lunch," she said.

CHAPTER TWENTY-ONE

WHEN Walter got back to his office he tried to work, but found that it was impossible. His mind was incapable of focusing on the document before him. It insisted on retracing every moment since he had first met Germaine in the foyer of Mme. Nicole's, every word she had said, every gesture she had made. In the process of chronological recall there came to him, parenthetically, the history of the development of his sentiment toward her, how it had begun with interest and pity, how it had changed to suspicion and wariness, how it had grown to respect and admiration, and how it had flowered into adoration and—yes, love. That was the word he had used to Christian and the Dominican, and it was true. Was it reciprocated? Did she love him?

He glanced at his engagement pad, then got up, took his hat from the tree in the corner, and walked into the outer office. "I'm going out," he said as he passed Janice Callery's desk. "Leave word at the visitor's bureau for Vince Barrett that I'll see him tomorrow morning."

"Will you be back for your five o'clock appointment?" Janice asked.

"I don't know, I don't think so," he said vaguely, moving toward the door. "What was it, anyway?"

"With Dr. Malfatti of the Italian Delegation."

"Put him off until tomorrow. I want to talk to Vince before I see him."

"Where can I reach you?" Janice asked, her pencil poised above her notebook.

"I don't know," he said, and walked out of the door in a daze.

"What's eating him?" Miss Kleinholz asked when the door had closed.

"God knows," Janice said. "Did you see how he looked? As if he'd lost his last friend."

"Maybe he has. Maybe she ran out on him," said Miss Kleinholz, to whom all troubles were romantic in origin.

"I'll stake my next paycheck that it's not a girl. Not with him. Our dear Walter's mind may run to figures, but they're not feminine figures. Now, with Mr. Locke it's different."

"Don't kid me," Kleinholz said crossly, "Mr. Locke's as cold as yesterday's *pomme de terre*."

"Says you. You should have seen him give me the once-over when I wore that Beresford blouse."

"That's cute, that blouse," Kleinholz said reflectively. "Say, maybe it was that cable about Mr. Locke's testimony."

"Why should that upset him?" Janice asked. "It went over big, didn't it?"

"Well, you know he's funny that way. It's his report, every word of it, and he's not getting any of the credit."

Walter crossed the rue de Rivoli and entered the gardens of the Tuileries. It was a day for children: warm, with a diluted sun which opened the tulips and lent a clean whiteness to the sails of the toy boats bobbing about on the basin. Everywhere mothers, aunts, grandmothers, nurses sat by their perambulators, knitting, sewing, gossiping while the older children scampered about, tossing their balls, chasing each other, calling in their high, chirping voices, never still for an instant. It was a spot which Walter loved, with its symmetrical flower beds, its trees in precise, orderly lines, its obelisk-pointed vistas, one to the great square of the Louvre, the other past the horses of Marly to the Arc de Triomphe. This garden had always seemed to him the apotheosis of Paris, of the grandeur of its history. Yet today he saw none of it; not even the ubiquitous children could divert his mind from the horror, the dismay, the terrible, haunting doubt.

He sat down on an iron chair, unaware of the life that ebbed and flowed about him. The woman who sold the tickets had to speak to him three times before he realized that she was addressing him. He gave her the twelve francs which was the rental for the chair, and withdrew into the dark recesses of his agonized mind. Now that he had relived every moment of the past weeks, his thoughts had lost all semblance of order. He had found nothing, except, of course, her desire to see the true balance-of-payments figures, which gave the slightest indication of her disloyalty, nothing to bear out this cruel and detailed accusation. Why had they done it as they had? Why had de St. Avit asked him to lunch and faced him with the story? Was it to find out if he, too, were a Communist agent? Or was it, as Christian had stated, in order to warn him as a friend, so that he could be the first to alert the police?

The suspicions of jealousy on Christian's part which had flashed through his mind, at first, had vanished as he had listened to the story the monk had told. No, it could not be that. They had both been too earnest, too worried, too obviously sure of their ground. But why were they mixed up in it at all? What business was it of theirs what Germaine Brisson was? They had spoken of their duty to France, to the free world, but all that sounded farfetched for a priest and an idle nobleman. Yet it was not easy to judge; sometimes people like them, with no regular work to occupy their minds, got crazy, elevated notions, like St. Avit's scheme for the return of the Holy Roman Empire. How that had made Germaine laugh. How scornful and sarcastic she had been that following morning when he had recalled the count's theory while they were drinking their café au lait. There had been a bitterness in her voice that was quite unlike her, and the bitterness had been more against de St. Avit than against the theory. She had called him a stupid idiot, a ridiculous playboy who was no fit companion for serious people, making it plain that she did not wish him to associate with that sort of parasite.

He got up from his chair and started walking toward the Louvre; not that he had any idea of going to a particular place, but only to move, to walk, to do anything that would help to prepare his mind for the meeting with Germaine. He went on slowly, at his usual measured pace, until he reached the Avenue Paul Déroulède, which bisects the gardens where the palace of the Louvre begins; there he turned right to the river. Crossing the roadway, he followed the river's edge, where there were fewer pedestrians.

His mind returned to that morning after the visit of de St. Avit. Yes, it was as if she had been warning him to see no more of the count. At the time he had been flattered, thinking that she was jealous of his ability and did not wish him to accept lower mental standards in his friends. Could it have been that she recognized the count? She had never said that she had, or even intimated that there was anything familiar about him other than as a typical specimen of a class she had once known. Suppose she had? Suppose she knew who he was? Would she not have kept quiet about it for the very reason that she did not wish him to know that she had once been a Communist? That, in all probability, was why she was so silent, so secretive, so sad about her past—because she was ashamed of it; ashamed, not of having been a collaborationist as he had suspected, but of having been an active, dedicated Communist. It was fear, then, fear of the consequences of her apostasy which had caused her to disappear into the dark haven of Mme. Nicole's establishment. It was just as logical a story as that of the Abbé d'Albret. Had he not admitted that he knew nothing of her work or whereabouts from the time when she had gone to see some man they called Le Crépuscule (he must remember that name) up to the moment Christian had found her at his, Walter's, flat?

His feet were carrying him methodically in the direction of the Ile St. Louis. He was not conscious of their purpose, any more than he was aware of the fact that he had left his car parked on the Place de la Concorde in front of the Guaranty Trust Company. His mind went on revolving, revolving with its endless hypothetical questions. There was the argument of the name. Why, if she had given up the Party, had she not given up her Party monicker? Shame, he had said to Christian. But there could be other reasons. Her identity card, for example. If that said Germaine Brisson, she could not get a job, even at Mme. Nicole's, who was scared to death of the police, under any other name. Solange Ramé. No, that was the one she had used in the Résistance. The real name, the one she was born with was Ninon— Oh, God, he must try to remember what it was! That was the most important fact of all, for it established her as an entity, as a person of flesh and blood, with roots, with a background, not just a red wraith floating about in Communist cells. Santé . . . Santelle . . . Sentire . . . Santerre. That was it—Santerre. Daughter of the Toulouse professor. It fitted in, too: the daughter of a pedagogue, cultivated, reserved, intelligent, thoughtful, affectionate, and . . . Oh, my love, my love, my sweet, tragic Germaine!

How long he had been sitting there, smoking one cigarette after another, stamping the butts out viciously in the ashtray, before she came in, he did not know.

"You?" she said, with a startled expression. "What are you doing here?"

"I came home," he said dully, seized with a panic inside now that she was here.

"Yes, that I can see. But why? Are you ill?"

"I'm upset. I couldn't work, so I came home."

She walked into the room and sat down on the arm of the chair which faced him. She was quite in control of herself. The momentary shock of finding him in the flat at half past four had vanished. It had been a sudden, automatic guilt feeling, because she had come directly from her meeting with Le Boiteux in the rue Henri Barbusse.

"What has gone wrong?" she asked sympathetically.

Walter put out a cigarette and looked at her. "Why have you got on that old suit and those shoes?" he asked. "You told me you'd thrown them out."

"I wear them for marketing," she said.

"Have you been marketing?"

"Yes," she lied, not liking the questioning.

"But you have no bag, no parcels."

"I was looking for *rognons de veau*. I couldn't find any. What's the matter with you, anyway? Why all these silly questions?" She saw the pile of butts in the ashtray in front of him and began to wonder, to tighten up inside, with the bands of fear beginning to bite.

Walter put his elbows on his knees and clasped his head in

his hands, taking a deep breath, which he exhaled like a sigh. "I'm in a jam, Germaine," he said, switching to English.

"What kind of a jam?" she asked in English, following his lead, and worried.

He got up from the chair and came over to her. Taking her chin in his hand, he lifted her face until their eyes met. "Tell me honestly, Germaine, what are your feelings toward me?" he asked gravely.

"My feelings? What do you mean, my feelings? I'm here, am I not? I'm yours."

"Is that all—just gratitude for three meals a day and a home?"

"Don't be silly, my dear," she said quite calmly, though the worry was deep. "You know me well enough to realize that I would never have stayed with you, given myself to you, unless I was . . . unless I was fond of you."

Walter looked into her eyes which seemed so honest, so trusting. "Today I told someone something that I had never even admitted to myself. I told him that I loved you." He could feel the muscles of her chin react involuntarily, but her eyes never wavered.

"So they have found out at your office that I am living with you," she said. "That is why you are upset."

He took his hand from her chin gently, letting it slide along her smooth cheek and through the waves of her hair, and walked back to his chair. "No, they don't know at the office," he said as he sat down. "It was the Comte de St. Avit to whom I said it."

She laughed to cover the excitement, the release of adrenalin which she could feel seeping through her. "So you have been discussing me with that silly young man."

"He asked me to lunch with him today." Walter lit another cigarette and noticed that his hands were trembling. "Tell me, have you ever seen him before—before the night I brought him here?"

"Not that I remember," she lied.

"He says he met you in the Résistance, when you were called Solange Ramé."

She shrugged her shoulders. "That may be. There were so many of us in so many places."

"That was your name in those days?"

"Yes, that was my Maquis alias. We all took fake names." It seemed wiser to admit this, as it did not involve her in anything beyond that night at the Château de Talmont.

Walter took a deep inhale and crushed the cigarette out. "Now listen, Germaine, listen carefully, and remember what I say, and, God knows I mean it with all my heart. I love you. Everything between us hinges on that."

"Of course, my darling Walter," she said softly. The words, which had come unthinking to her lips, were better, she thought, than any she could have devised.

"There was another man at this luncheon in de St. Avit's apartment, a Dominican father whom the count calls the Abbé d'Albret. He seems to know a lot about you, says he's a friend of your father, Professor Santerre of Toulouse. He said that your real name is Ninon Santerre and that—"

"Did you believe this nonsense?" Germaine cried, her knuckles white as she clenched her hands together. Her response was automatic. More than her mind had been conditioned to the strict, unswerving maintenance of her cover. Her whole being knew its lesson, knew how to react instantaneously to any situation, no matter how surprising or dangerous. Not even what she felt about Walter, whatever it was, for she had never allowed herself to dwell on it, could alter or diminish the role which she had assumed. The clenching of her hands was fear. She knew that. But she also knew that it would seem to him like anger if her words were the right ones.

"I don't know what to believe, Germaine. That's why I came home to talk to you."

"It's a pack of lies," she said in a strained, excited voice. "It doesn't even make sense." She fished in her purse. "Here's my *identité*—read it, see for yourself." She held it out to him, but he made no move to take it.

"Look, I don't give a hoot what your name is—Solange, Ninon, Germaine—that's all beside the point as far as I'm concerned. There's only one thing that matters and that is their statement that you are a member of the Communist Party. Are you, or are you not?"

"I was, when I was in the Résistance," she admitted, her eyes flashing with what Walter thought was angry pride but in reality was fear.

"Are you now?" he insisted.

"No," she said emphatically. "I hate politics. I'm through with it."

"Do you know a man who is called Le Crépuscule?"

"Don't be silly," she said scornfully. "That is not a name. It means 'twilight.'"

"You haven't answered my question," Walter said relentlessly. "Do you know a man who goes by that alias?"

"Of course not."

"And you were not born Ninon Santerre?"

"I told you already, it's a pack of lies."

"Did you ever live at Oxford with a Professor Hinch-Bidley?"

"Never."

"Were you parachuted into France by a Royal Air Force plane in 1943?"

"No."

"Did you ever know a Sergeant Onslow?"

"No—wait a minute, yes, I did know Sergeant Onslow."

"Where?"

"In the Résistance. He was the Englishman I told you about, the one who taught me English."

"Your lover?"

"Yes."

"But you told me he was an officer."

"*Officier, sous-officier*—what's the difference?"

He put his head in his hands again and sighed. "Oh, God, Germaine, what's going to happen to us?"

"What do you mean?" she asked anxiously. "Don't you believe me?"

"I want to believe you, God knows I want to, but that's not going to stop them," he moaned.

"Stop whom?"

"St. Avit and the priest. They're going to notify the Deuxième Bureau, and that will mean the finish of my career."

Now she was really alarmed. "How can they, with just a pack of lies? Just because that jackass thinks he met me when I was in the F.T.P., does that prove that I'm a Communist agent?" That was the wrong thing to say. She knew it the moment it had left her lips.

Walter caught it, and his heart sank. He had not accused her of being an agent. He had only asked her if she was a member of the Party. She had convicted herself by the use of the word. He got up from his chair and walked over to a window, standing there, looking out at the ivy-draped prow of the Ile de la Cité. It was a long time before he spoke, and when he did, it was without turning to look at her. "Either this is a criminally unfair accusation against an innocent person, or it is true, or partially true."

"Then you don't believe me," she muttered.

"Whatever the answer is," he went on slowly, ignoring her comment, "it will now be brought to light. The police will make their inquiry, and the case will be closed, one way or the other. Nothing, no verdict, no suspicion, no accusation can take away from me the happiest moments of my life. God, they were wonderful! If you've been acting, Germaine, then you're the finest living actress and should give up politics for the Théâtre Français. You won me, captured me heart and soul." He sighed. "I had plans for us, too. Such glorious plans."

"You wish me to leave?" she asked quietly.

"On the contrary," he said, still looking out of the window, "I hope you will stay right here. For you to leave would be construcd as an admission of guilt. No, my dear, if we are innocent we must carry on as we have, with our heads high." He wheeled about and faced her. "We have nothing to fear, have we?"

Her head was in the hollow of her arm on the coffee table. Her whole body was shaking with sobs.

CHAPTER TWENTY-TWO

"BUT you cannot be so innocent, my dear Walter, as to think that all this money is being poured into Europe for purely philanthropic reasons," Germaine said. It was four o'clock in the morning and they were still in the living room, still dressed as they had been when she had returned from her meeting with Georges Persan and Le Crépuscule to find Walter waiting for her. A nearly empty bottle of whiskey and two syphons of soda stood on the coffee table between them. Both held half-filled glasses in their hands.

"I neither think it nor said it," Walter protested. "The purpose is thoroughly selfish. We believe that if Western Europe falls into the orbit of the Bolshevics, we alone, without allies, cannot survive."

"So, even if the masses hunger for socialism, you will buy them off with your Wall Street dollars," she argued.

"We have nothing against socialism," Walter said. "The British have it. It is one of the leading political forces in France, Belgium, Germany, and Austria. That's the trouble with you Communists, you're always playing fast and loose with words. When I say 'socialist,' I mean Mollet's party and the Labor Party in England. When you say it, you mean Stalinist Communism."

"Which is the only true socialism," she maintained. "The

only socialism which holds to the teachings of Marx and Engels."

Walter laughed. "Have you read your Lenin and your Stalin? Do you know to what degree they have twisted and changed the teachings of Marx?"

This had been going on more or less steadily for eight solid hours. Ever since that moment in the night when she had told him of her love, she had striven to gain her only avenue of escape—his conversion to Communism. He knew the truth. There had been no longer any purpose in denying it. Now the struggle had reached its apex. The moment had come. She was up against it: the crisis, the terrible, paralyzing decision whether to continue the cold, lonely battle or retire into a haven that was sheltered and warm. It was a sudden turn in the road that was unexpected, beautiful, and frightening. At the start of this mission her faith in her invulnerability had been serene. She had been as sure of herself, of her destiny, of her hard will to follow the flame of the people's revolution, as her leaders were. They had tested her and found the steel flawless, and so they had trusted her to carry on alone. How could she know that there remained in her a vestige of the past, an inert bacillus which, under the gentle, trusting, honest warmth of Walter's care, would spring to life, investing her mind, her heart, her body with a sentiment so uncontrollable that it drowned all sense of principle, of duty? In her frantic efforts to find a solution, a compromise, anything which would allow her to keep her faith and Walter, she had tried to convert him to Stalinism. But she realized now that that was hopeless, that he was too firmly planted in the rank soil of economic self-determinism to be shaken from his belief.

"Let me tell you something, my dear Germaine," he was saying, sitting on the corner of the couch now, next to her chair, putting his glass down on the table and his hand gently on her arm. He was telling her about the standard of living of the factory workers in the United States, giving her figures, comparative figures of work hours in terms of purchasing power between them and workers within the Soviet Union. She listened, not intently; she had heard the arguments before, read them in capitalist journals, believing them to be trumped-up statistical lies; but what she did hear was his conviction, his earnestness, the solid foundation of his belief. She could feel it in the touch of his hand, see it in the fire of his dark eyes as he looked at her. This was no fanaticism, no blind faith. It was his final answer, his $x =$, his q.e.d. to a carefully reasoned problem. He had worked it out for himself, step by step, gathering all the factors, not just from his side, but from hers, too, from Engels, Marx, Lenin, Stalin, and Eugen Varga, scrutinizing, weighing the validity of each posed solution until he had distilled all into a rational hypothesis.

It was this sensation of observing the human mind at work which first touched her. A long-forgotten chord had been struck. Out of the dim, uncertain past she seemed to hear the voice of her father bringing light and reason to a passage from Milton's *Comus*. She had loved him then, in those days before the Hitlerites struck, and he had sent her cruelly away to England. Yes, she had loved him, worshiped him as a symbol, as the man of reason. Then, in her exile, her resentment, she had tried to perform her own reasoning on matters more vital to the fate of the working masses than Milton's poetry. She had come to a conclusion—or had she? Had she come to it the way her father had come to his, or Walter now in his long and thoughtful analysis was coming to his? Had she not, rather, read and listened and believed because she wanted to believe, because she wanted to turn the world inside out and scrub it clean of the grime of centuries of tyranny which had torn her from her home and killed her brother?

"You see, darling," Walter went on, "the solution which Marx proposed was violent because in England in 1867 he could not conceive of a situation wherein the limited company, in its greed, could ever visualize profits as stemming from any other source than the lowest wage for workers. If I had lived in London in those days, I would have probably been his devoted disciple. Factory conditions were such that any man of good will and compassion would have preached rebellion against the capitalists. What he didn't see, couldn't see, was that time and reason and the very urge for profit would bring a solution that did not involve violence. Violence is never a solution for anything. All it breeds is tyranny and oppression, because you cannot impose a solution in an evolving society without secret police and concentration camps. Do you see my point? Do you see what it means to live in a world where you and I can discuss these things quietly and rationally without fear of arrest?"

Germaine did not answer. She lifted her glass and drained the dregs of stale whiskey and soda. She knew he was right, that in her world, the Bolshevic world, no argument, no discussion, no reasoning, except in self-abasement, was admissible. To listen, even, was treason—deviation was their word for it—and was punishable by anything from dismissal to death, depending on the nature of one's position and duties.

"Maybe you don't want to answer now," he said gently. "Maybe it's better that you think it over quietly by yourself." He picked up her hand and kissed it. "I know what a terrible decision it is, my sweet, but you have to make it, there's no dodging it—that is, if you love me."

She looked at him with a smile that was an attempt at courage, but tears were in the corners of her eyes as she nodded assent.

"The awful part of it," he went on, "the tragic part, is that there is no compromise solution for us. Most people can live and love with divided political allegiances. In the States, if you were a Republican and I were a Democrat, or here in France, if you were a Socialist and I were a Radical, we could argue like cats and dogs, then kiss and play Ravel. But the differences between free democratic people (my definition of the word) and Soviet Communists are so fundamental, so inimical, that they would destroy us both. I would be fired at once for endangering the security of the state, and you—well, you know better than I do what your fate would be."

"Pour me just a drop," she said, handing him her empty glass. He poured out the last of the whiskey and filled the glass with soda. "I understand perfectly. It's quite clear. I must either renounce communism or leave this apartment tonight."

Walter looked at his watch. "This morning," he said, smiling. "Any time before noon."

"Would you believe me if I said I had given up the Party?" she asked.

"Yes, because you said you loved me. If lovers cannot believe each other, then there is no hope for the world."

"Is there a hope?" she asked bitterly.

"God, yes! Sure there is. How could I go on doing what I'm doing unless there was hope?"

"That's what I said to myself."

"But our hopes were different."

"I wonder."

"Yours was for a classless society where all, in blind faith, took orders from a Politburo. Mine is for freedom and reason and sanity."

"That is an oversimplification."

"Granted, my dear, but don't forget that it is a quarter past four and I've been going through hell . . ."

"Oh, my dear Walter," she said, leaning over and stroking his forehead and running her fingers through his hair. "I know what hell is. We have been walking through it together, my love, like Dante and Virgil."

"You do love me, don't you, Germaine?" he asked, with a look of pleading.

She slid from her chair and, kneeling before him, buried her face in his knees, crying like a tired child. "I should not. I have no right to," she said, her voice muffled by sobs. "But I do, I do." She lifted her tear-stained face. "They will kill me. Yes, my love, they will murder me."

"You mustn't say that, darling," he reassured her. "You're tired now, as I am. We'll both be calmer when we've had some sleep."

She got to her feet. "No, Walter, I must go. It's no use. It would only kill both of us."

He got up and took her arms. "Listen, Germaine—"

She pulled herself free and started for the door. "Please, darling, don't argue. I must go. There is no other solution."

"If that's your decision," he said sadly.

She stopped in the doorway and faced him. "It's common sense. Can't you see that?"

"That you should choose the Party rather than me?"

"Oh, my darling," she pleaded, "don't say that. It's because of you, because I love you, that I must go. If I stay here you'll be ruined, finished, disgraced. *You* may believe that I have renounced the Party, but your people won't. They'll say I have pulled the wool over your eyes. They'll say that I lied to you so that I could continue my spying. It took them years to believe in the apostasy of Malraux and Koestler, and they were never secret agents, not real ones, just amateurs. So what makes you think they'll believe me, a member of Le Crépuscule's apparatus?"

Walter's face brightened. Suddenly all the fatigue, the discouragement left him. He could feel his heart pounding new blood, new energy, new hope into his body and his brain. He rushed forward and grabbed her in his arms. "Oh, God!" he cried. "Oh, dear, merciful God! We're saved, my love! We're saved. That's all that counts. There isn't any fear, there isn't any trouble as long as you've chosen me."

"Do you realize what you're saying?" she pleaded.

He put his hands on her small waist and held her at arm's length. "I know this," he said slowly, with confidence, "that you and I will have a long, hard struggle, that there will be moments of danger and discouragement, but that together, loving and trusting each other, we can be happy."

"What about the Deuxième Bureau?"

"They will not be warned."

"Can you trust de St. Avit and his friend the priest?"

"They'll believe me."

Germaine shook her head in doubt. "I'm afraid, Walter."

"Of what the Party will do?"

She shrugged her shoulders. "Yes, a little, but more of what your government will do."

"If I have the courage to face that, have you as my—"

"But Walter, my love, think of your position, your work. It would be madness for us to go on living together."

"As man and wife?"

She tore herself from his arms and ran down the foyer into the bedroom. When he found her, she was lying on the bed, her face in the pillow, sobbing. But there was a different sound to her weeping. There was a note in it of choking, overwhelming joy.

CHAPTER TWENTY-THREE

WALTER stopped at the little bar in the rue Cambon where, in the old days, he used to have his second cup of morning coffee, and telephoned to Christian de St. Avit. He told him in guarded language, the kind of language that Foreign Service officers are taught to use when discussing classified matters on the telephone, that there was no need for him or for the Abbé d'Albret to notify the authorities, that everything had been satisfactorily settled, and that he would arrange within the next few days to see him and explain what had transpired. After hanging up he ordered an *exprés*, which he felt he must need after the emotion of his sleepless night. Actually he felt fine, better than he had felt in months, full of energy and lightness, as if he had achieved some singular and important triumph, which he had, when he came to analyze it. He was very pleased with himself.

Christian's reaction to the telephone call, on the other hand, had been one of extreme doubt and misgiving. He was more than ever convinced that Walter was a gullible adolescent who was being outwitted and traduced by the cleverest, most ruthless agent of the Cominform in France. He felt sorry for Walter, whom he admired for his simple integrity, but he was determined that this American civil servant must either be shown the light or sacrificed for the good of the

Atlantic community. He sat on the edge of the bed, his hand still on the telephone, and planned his course of action.

He lifted the receiver and called the Abbé, to whom he repeated what Walter had said. The priest was less skeptical. He had been impressed by Walter's forthrightness and thought that there might be a good chance that he had succeeded in converting the professor's daughter.

"I had in mind calling Mme. Locke, who is the wife of Haines's *patron*," Christian said. "She may be able to exert some influence on him."

"Not yet, my dear Christian," the Abbé said. "Let us give him the benefit of the doubt for a little time. In the meanwhile I shall endeavor to find out if she is still seeing Fantin."

"Mme. Locke is a woman who can be trusted," Christian persisted.

"A woman will always protect her husband," the priest argued. "She will warn him at once if she suspects that he may suffer from the indiscretions of his assistant."

"But her husband is in the United States."

"All the more reason for you to leave her alone."

"You have a way of reading my mind, my dear Abbé," Christian said, laughing.

He had hardly replaced the receiver when the telephone rang. It was Eleanor's voice which greeted him cheerily.

"Derek just called to say that he has to stay in Paris for a meeting on Sunday," she said.

"Poor fellow," Christian said, "he loves his dear Daphne so much. I was just about to call you to ask if you would care for another drive in the country tomorrow."

"Derek asked me the same thing. He said he just had to get out of Paris on a Saturday."

"Of course, I understand," Christian said, with a touch of bitterness. "He has first call on your heart."

"My heart belongs to Daddy, young man. That's why I'm taking no chances with either of you two seducers. I'm giving a picnic. Derek is bringing the wine, I'm bringing the chicken, cheese, and salad, and you are to bring the strawberries."

"For three?" Christian asked.

"Oh, no, there'll be the children, that's five, and Walter and his fiancée, that's—"

"His what?"

"His fiancée. Haven't you heard? He's engaged to be married. He sounded quite flighty with joy on the telephone. I can't wait to meet her."

"Did he tell you her name?" Christian asked, more worried than ever.

"Not her family name," Eleanor answered. "He merely referred to her as Germaine."

"That's the girl."

"You mean the girl he was—his mistress?"

"Yes, Germaine Brisson."

"How perfectly fascinating!"

It was arranged that they were to meet in the square in front of the Château de St. Germain at noon. From there they would proceed in file, following Derek's car until he found a suitable spot in the forest for their picnic.

Christian put on his slippers and went into the bathroom. At least, he thought, this would give him an opportunity to observe the happy couple at close hand.

"I must say Haines has found himself a mighty pretty bit," Derek whispered to Eleanor, wiping his mustache with a paper napkin.

"Isn't she a love, and so intelligent," Eleanor whispered in reply, looking at Germaine where she sat at the other end of the steamer rug, leaning against the trunk of a tree, with

Walter close to her, touching her, smiling at her with love and pride.

"You've lost a suitor," Derek mumbled as he bit into a second joint of chicken.

"I'd be careful if I were you," Eleanor cautioned. "He looks like the jealous type."

"Oh, I wasn't talking about myself," Derek said. "You couldn't lose me if you tried—and you did try."

"Why, Derek, how absurd," Eleanor said.

Little Charlotte, who was sitting at her mother's side, eating cut-up chicken with a spoon from her own special dish, looked up. "What's absurd, Mummy?" she asked.

"Brigadier Dunglass said that I have not been kind to him," Eleanor explain to her daughter. "Now that is absurd, isn't it?"

"Yes. But Mummy, what does 'absurd' mean?" the child asked.

"It means foolish, silly, untrue," Derek answered. "It's a word you must learn, young lady, because you will find it most useful as a defense. All grownup ladies use it when they don't want to admit that they are wrong."

Little Charlotte looked at him quizzically across her mother's lap, not quite certain that he was being serious, but wanting to believe him, and repeating to herself out loud, "Absurd, absurd."

"I pride myself on having recognized you," Christian said to Germaine. He was prone on his stomach, across the end of the rug, propped up by his elbows, eating a hard-boiled egg.

"Was it my face or my voice?" she asked pleasantly, all feeling of rancor against Christian having vanished, remembering him now only as the earnest pleader for unity.

"A combination of both, I suppose," he replied.

"But I had a kerchief over my head and my back was to the moon," Germaine said.

"There was enough light for me to distinguish your features."

"It's a face one doesn't forget, my dear Germaine," Walter added proudly.

"Which was hardly an asset in your recent occupation," Christian commented. He was still far from convinced that she was no longer working for the Communist Party. The mere fact that she had agreed to become Walter's wife was suspicious, for by so doing she could gain more, with less danger of being discovered.

"But the war is over and we no longer have to hide our identity, Captain Capet," she said pointedly.

"Are you a captain?" young Colin asked. He was lying next to Christian, listening to them talk.

"I was, during the war," Christian answered.

"In the Maquis?"

"Yes, in the Maquis."

"And were you in the Maquis, too?" Colin asked Germaine.

"We both were. That's where we first met," Germaine said.

"Did you live in the woods?"

"Sometimes," Germaine answered, "and sometimes in abandoned houses."

"We slept by day and fought by night, like Red Indians," Christian added.

"Golly, that must have been fun!" Colin exclaimed.

A motorcycle came chugging along the road, which was twenty yards away. Germaine, who was facing in that direction, saw it pass the opening in the bushes through which they had entered their woodland glade. In the brief instant that it took to pass that narrow space, she saw that it was ridden by Georges Persan and that Le Boiteux was riding pillion, holding on to Georges's belt. She dropped her head quickly, leaning forward to pick a sandwich from the plate in the center of the rug, hoping desperately that Le Boiteux, whose face had been turned toward them, scanning the glade, had not seen her. She knew at once that they were tailing her—the usual check when there was the slightest suspicion. Out of the corner of her eye she saw Christian's hand extend across the rug. That was it, she thought, the count was the reason. She had promised Le Boiteux to avoid him.

Christian picked up the plate and offered it to her. He saw that the blood had left her face as she took a sandwich and straightened up. He heard the motorcycle stop and saw her hand tremble as she lifted the sandwich to her lips. He knew fear when he saw it—he was an old acquaintance of fear, for only the brave know it intimately—but he could not decide why it had come to her so suddenly. Had she seen someone pass on the road? Or was it himself, his doubt, his suspicion which she had sensed?

Derek stood up and pulled the cork from a bottle of claret. "Colin, my lad, pass the cups," he commanded. "What's a picnic without wine, women, and song? Charlotte, my dainty miss, you will have to supply us with the song."

Charlotte blushed and hid her face in her mother's skirts.

"She won't sing, she's afraid," Colin said with disgust as he passed out the paper cups.

Charlotte lifted her head angrily. "That's absurd!" she shouted.

"Good girl! Well played!" Derek cried. "You're as quick to learn as your mother."

Charlotte got up on her knees and, with one hand on her mother's knee to steady herself, sang "Au Clair de la Lune" defiantly, in a high piping voice.

They all applauded enthusiastically.

"Now Colin, you do 'Sur le Pont d'Avignon,'" Eleanor said.

Colin looked sheepish. "Please, Mummy, you know I can't sing," he pleaded.

"That's absurd!" Charlotte shouted.

"Oh, shut up!" Colin said angrily, his face getting redder.

"Colin, dear, no temper, please," his mother warned.

Colin was standing by Germaine. Suddenly he felt an arm around his waist. "Come, we'll sing it together," she whispered to him softly. She took the lead, starting off in a rich, throaty contralto, Colin joining, at first hesitatingly, then louder and with confidence.

As she sang, Germaine thought she saw a face some distance off in the wood, peering through the undergrowth, and a sharp fear stabbed her heart, but she did not waver in her singing.

"Walter, you've been hiding things," Eleanor said when the song was over. "You never told us that Mlle. Brisson had a lovely voice."

"I didn't know it myself," Walter confessed, looking at Germaine with admiration.

"We've jolly well got to have another one after that sample," Derek said as he walked around filling the cups with wine. "But first we must drink to the happy couple." When the last cup was filled, he raised his own, holding it out toward Germaine and Walter. "As I look at you two, I am drawn to the uneasy conclusion that Franco-American relations have not been so solidly cemented since the Marquis de Lafayette effectively aided General Washington in trouncing the forces of the late and unlamented King George III. I am all in favor of this international getting-together in holy wedlock. There's nothing like a double bed to promote confidence and understanding. But, mind you, don't gang up again against us British. If there's to be another tea party, let's have it in London, with the red carpet down and the Life Guards out with their swords at the salute. Or, if that sounds too much fuss and feathers for your dear republican hearts, there's a little cottage near Ashford in Kent where an old crock of a soldier and his long-suffering wife will not only give you tea but a bed and all that's left of the wine cellar. God bless you both, and may your lives together be long and happy in a world that is free from tyranny and discord."

"Hear, hear!" Eleanor and Christian cried, and they all drank.

"Thank you, Brigadier," Walter said. "We won't forget that invitation, will we, dear?" And he gave Germaine a sly kiss on the temple.

Germaine felt for Walter's hand and squeezed it with the force of fear. "Oh, God, darling, I think I'm going to cry," she whispered in his ear.

"Now I think we should kiss the bride," Derek said.

"Don't be silly, Derek," Eleanor said. "One does that at the wedding."

"Have I to wait that long?" Derek said, crestfallen.

"When is the wedding?" Colin asked.

Germaine and Walter looked at each other questioningly. "We haven't even discussed that yet," she admitted.

"As soon as I get clearance from the State Department," Walter said, and his blood ran cold. This was the first time he had thought of it—Germaine would have to be investigated and given a clean bill of health.

"Do you have to have their permission to get married?" Christian asked.

"Yes, if one marries a foreigner," Walter replied, trying to hide his cold fear.

"You mean an F.B.I. check and all that?" Eleanor asked.

"I'm really not sure. I'll have to find out," Walter said. He felt suddenly hemmed in, as if they were trying to threaten him, to injure him, to rob him of his happiness. He glanced at Christian, but Christian was leaning over, dishing out the strawberries, and he could not see his face.

"Can I came to the wedding?" Colin asked Walter.

"Of course," Walter answered, smiling wanly.

"And me, too?" Charlotte asked, jumping up and clapping her hands.

"You shall be the flower girl," Germaine said gently.

On the ride back from the Forêt de St. Germain to Eleanor's house in Neuilly, where they were to reassemble for tea and cocktails, Christian contrived to take Eleanor alone in his car, letting Derek take the children, while Germaine went, as she had come, with Walter. After the events of the picnic he was convinced that he must talk to her, in spite of the advice of the Abbé d'Albret.

"I hope that Derek's feelings were not hurt," Christian said, as they started down the long *allée* toward the château.

"Because you insisted on taking me alone in your car?" she asked, then answered her own question: "No, he's not the kind to be upset by that sort of thing. Besides, he loves the children."

"I had to talk to you."

"I thought you were not yourself today," Eleanor said. "What's the matter?"

"It's your friend Walter Haines. I'm worried about him."

"Because he's marrying that girl?"

"Yes."

"Why should you worry? I think she's charming, and so cultivated. Just because she was his mistress—"

"It's not that, my dear Eleanor. That is in her favor. I know all about her. She's a Communist agent, planted in his apartment to spy on your government. Her name is not Brisson at all, it is Ninon Santerre."

"Wait a minute. Drive slowly. Let the others get on ahead." Eleanor put her hand to her throat. The news had so stunned her that her heart was throbbing. She turned and looked at Christian. "How do you know this?" she asked.

He told her the whole story, beginning with his meeting with Solange Ramé in the Vendée, and then how the Abbé d'Albret, through the scouts of Catholic Action and his friends in the Sûreté, had pieced together the entire history from Toulouse to the apparatus of Le Crépuscule.

"Why didn't you tell Walter, warn him in time, instead of telling me?" she asked coldly.

"Eleanor!" he exclaimed indignantly. "What do you take me for? Of course I told him, told him everything, even more in detail than I have told you. He came to lunch at my flat with the Abbé. We laid the cards on the table."

"My God, Christian, what did he say?"

"I think he believed us finally, but not in the beginning. He asked for twenty-four hours in which to have it out with her, face her with the facts and get an answer."

"When was that?"

"The day before yesterday."

"Has he talked to you since?"

"Yes, he telephoned the next morning to tell me that everything has been arranged satisfactorily. He said there was no further need to alert the police."

"What did he mean?" Eleanor asked.

"He whispered to me today that she had confessed everything and had renounced her allegiance to the Communist Party. That is when he asked her to marry him."

Eleanor sighed a deep sigh of relief. "Thank God it's all right, then. Mercy, how you frightened me, Christian."

"See here, Eleanor," Christian said soberly, "if I thought it was all right I would not have told you. I would have helped him to bury the disagreeable past."

"Oh, no," Eleanor said, frightened again. "Don't tell me, please don't tell me you think she's lying."

"Communist agents of her position and training do not just walk out because they fall in love. To begin with, they don't fall in love, not in your sense of the phrase. And if they did, they would never live to enjoy it."

"But did you see her today? Did you watch her face? She is in love, Christian. I know it. I can tell," Eleanor said desperately.

"Yes, I watched her," Christian said, "and I saw what looked like the symptoms, for, believe it or not, I can spot them as well as you can. But I don't trust her. They're too devious, too clever. Think what an opportunity it would be for her to be married to one of your career men."

"The State Department will never let him marry," Eleanor said sadly. "They are sure to learn about her past."

"Then he will resign, you mark my words."

"How tragic! How terrible!"

"The fatality of love."

"It shouldn't be fatal, Christian, not in that way," Eleanor said. "It should be beautiful and gay and full of hope and wonder. Oh, Christian, if you'd ever been in love, you'd know."

He reached for her hand and pressed it to his lips as they drove by the machines of Marly. "I could be in love, my dear, quite easily."

CHAPTER TWENTY-FOUR

WITH his diplomatic passport and Lambert Charlton there to meet the plane and whisk him through the formalities, Sam Locke was able to stride past the guard at the glass door that separates the arriving passengers from the Republic of France at Orly Airport a good quarter of an hour ahead of those who had traveled with him from New York. He looked buoyant and confident, unruffled and unmussed by a night of brief dozing in the Constellation. He kissed Eleanor on both cheeks, French fashion, with an enthusiasm that was anything but normal. Eleanor assumed that this self-satisfaction was attributable to the warm reception his report had received from Congress, about which she had already received inklings from Carroway.

When they got into the car he told the chauffeur to drive to the Hôtel Talleyrand and settled back in the corner, sidewise, so that he could face Eleanor as he talked to her.

"Jim Carroway tells me that your testimony went down well with Congress," Eleanor said.

"They were easy on me," Sam said, with false modesty. "They're like most people: they want the facts, and if you know what you're talking about, they'll listen. I told them what they wanted to know."

"You have every right to be pleased," she said pleasantly.

"Paul was very happy about it."

"I don't doubt it."

"By the way, how are the children?" he asked.

"Flourishing," Eleanor replied. "We had a lovely picnic in the Forêt de St. Germain on Saturday."

"This little trip was very successful," Sam said, not interested in the picnic, nor in his children now that he knew they were in good health.

"So it would seem."

"Oh, I don't mean the testimony necessarily." He smiled as if he had some delicious secret on his mind. "I've got a piece of news for you, Eleanor."

"Well, what is it?" His cat-and-mouse attitude and the smug smile annoyed her. She had a premonition that whatever the news was, she was not going to like it.

"It's not official yet."

"So you can't tell me."

"Listen, Eleanor, this is strictly confidential and not to be discussed with anyone, not until I give you the word." He leaned over and whispered in her ear so that the chauffeur could not hear. "Ambassador to Holland."

"Who?"

He tapped his chest with his index finger.

Eleanor took a deep breath to cushion the shock. This was the second jolt in two days, and it was telling on her. She let out her breath in a sigh which she hoped her voice would cover up. "Oh, Lord, Sam, when does this happen?"

"Probably within a month. The appointment is on the President's desk. He's sending it over to the Senate before they recess."

"But Sam, how did it happen? Who recommended you?" she asked, suspecting that he had engineered it himself.

"I haven't the faintest idea," he lied. "It came as a bolt from the blue. I was thunderstruck."

"Did anyone ask you if you wanted it?"

"The President himself. He asked me to call on him at the White House. Of course I thought it was to discuss E.C.A. matters. You can imagine my surprise when he offered me this."

"What did you say?"

"What could I say? I accepted it. You can't tell the President of the United States that you don't want to represent him as an ambassador. It's a tremendous honor, Eleanor. It's terrific."

"But *do* you want it?" she asked, still incredulous.

"Want it? My dear Eleanor, no man *wants* responsibilities of this kind. It isn't a question of what I *want*. It's a question of duty. If I could order my own life, I suppose I'd have a farm in Virginia, hunt in the fall, fish the Restigouche in the spring, and shoot quail in South Carolina in the winter. But a man in my position can't just do what he likes with his life, any more than Sherrill or Paul. The country needs men like us in times like these to represent us abroad. You can see why they picked on me instead of some politician with money and no background. They weighed this post carefully and came up with my name because I'm a gentleman, I've experience, I know Europe, and I have the proper background and education."

"I wasn't questioning the choice, Sam," Eleanor said in a defeated voice. "You'll be a better ambassador than most of the ones they pick from civilian life. There's no argument about that. Only it's so contrary to what one hears—you know, about people putting up huge sums to get posts like that."

"They're the ones who go to Honduras and El Salvador. When it comes to a place like The Hague . . ."

"I suppose they have to use a different yardstick."

"What's the matter, Eleanor? You don't seem pleased."

"Pleased?" she said, sitting up straight and looking at him. "Of course I'm not pleased. I'm horrified. The last thing I want to be is an ambassadress."

"Damn it, Eleanor," he said, annoyed, remembering the dream, "you have no right to take that attitude. You have a duty to perform as much as I have. You're my wife. You should be giving me a leg up instead of trying to pull me down."

"Don't worry, Sam," she said sadly, "I'll do my duty. I'll put on the old frozen smile and shake hands and say pretty things and tell the dear Queen what lovely bouncing children she has."

"Really, Eleanor," Sam said bitterly, "you are the most uncooperative wife that any man in public life ever had. Sometime I'd like to know what you'd really like."

"Sometime I'll tell you," she said calmly.

The car stopped. They were in the courtyard of the Hôtel Talleyrand. Sam jumped out with his briefcase in his hand. "Tell Lucien to unpack my bags. I'll be home at seven and I want an early dinner," he barked at her, then slammed the door of the car and stalked off.

Eleanor motored home to Neuilly in a state of listless depression. Her mind could not find any future beyond one of infinite, aching boredom, of meaningless words spoken to endless rows of nameless people who meant less to her than the trees which lined the Champs Elysées. The word "duty" kept up a steady repetition, hitting her consciousness like the cold drops from an icicle. There was no escape that she could see, or that, if she could have found it, she would have the courage to face.

By dinnertime Sam had forgotten his annoyance. The

thought of the new title, the new glory, the new position, with all its trappings and fanfare, was too absorbing to allow Eleanor's disapproval to weigh on him for long. He had, as a matter of fact, forgotten it almost the moment he had entered the Hôtel Talleyrand and had run into Sherrill, who had heard the news through his own pipeline to Washington, and who had congratulated him warmly, with a hearty, prolonged shaking of his hand. Now, after two good martinis, he was inclined to be patient and generous with Eleanor, knowing that she would, in the final analysis, live up to the role and do her duty with uncomplaining proficiency.

There was a long silence before Eleanor spoke. She wanted to be sure that her words, by their arrangement and essence, conveyed the correct proportions of her fear and confidence.

"I'm sorry about this afternoon," she said. "It was beastly of me to be so mean about your appointment."

Sam chuckled. "I guess I sprung it too abruptly. I could see that the news bowled you over."

"I do congratulate you, Sam. I think it's wonderful. I should have said that in the car, but—"

The telephone rang and Eleanor, who was sitting nearest to the desk, reached over and picked up the receiver. "*Allo.* Yes, he's here. Just a minute, please." She offered the receiver to Sam. "Someone for you."

Sam got up from his chair, took the receiver, and answered, standing by the desk. "Oh yes, McEwen. What is it? Oh! Can't it wait until the morning? I see. Well, if it's that urgent, why don't you come right over. I can give you a half-hour before dinner. Do you know the way? Yes, that's it, and turn right on the rue d'Orléans. One block over the Boulevard Jean Mermoz begins." He hung up.

"Tell Julien to put dinner off for three-quarters of an hour," he said to Eleanor.

"I really think it's outrageous, Sam, disturbing us as we are about it sit down to dinner," Eleanor said, walking to the door. "After all, we are not at war. Is there anything so important that it can't wait for two hours?"

Sam shrugged his shoulders. He, too, was annoyed at being bothered at this hour. "Apparently it is a most urgent matter," he said.

When Eleanor returned from giving her instructions to Julien and the cook, she found her husband mixing a third martini. "I suppose it's Sherrill's doing," she complained. "That man is so intense about his work that he forgets that other people lead ordered lives."

"No, it isn't Sherrill this time," Sam said. "It's a man named Frank McEwen, the security officer. He's probably found someone's safe unlocked."

"Well, why doesn't he lock it and report to you in the morning?"

"We'll have the answer soon enough. He wouldn't tell me what it was on the telephone. Come, have another cocktail, I want to drink to the new ambassadress."

"No, thanks. You can drink to that poor creature if you want to. One drink is all my dizzy head can stand at this point."

Sam held up his martini and chuckled. "Who would have imagined it? Who would have thought that little Eleanor Cumming, the bluestocking debutante of Southampton, would end up as Her Excellency the American Ambassadress?"

"Please, Sam, don't rub it in," she pleaded.

When Julien announced that a gentleman had arrived who wished to speak to Mr. Locke, Sam turned to Eleanor and asked her to wait for him in the salon; he preferred to talk to

McEwen in the library, where there was less chance of being overheard by the servants.

Julien held the door open for Eleanor to pass, then Sam said, "Show the gentleman up here."

Frank McEwen looked a little frightened and apologetic as he entered the library and shook hands with Locke. He had a pink baby face, surmounted by a crew-cut of red hair. The effect was too youthful to be impressive.

"Will you have a cocktail?" Livy asked.

"No, thanks," McEwen said, "I don't drink. Besides, I want to get this over with as quickly as possible. You said you hadn't had your dinner yet."

"Sit down," Livy said pleasantly, motioning to the armchair by the desk where Eleanor had been sitting. He took out his cigarette case and offered it to McEwen. "Have one?"

"No thanks, I don't smoke."

Livy lit his own cigarette and said, "Well, what's the urgent story?"

McEwen cleared his throat, then patted his mouth with his hand. "Mr. Locke," he asked, "did you know that Walter Haines is engaged to be married?"

Livy raised his eyebrows and smiled. "Well, that is news! No, I didn't. When did it happen?"

"According to him it was about two days ago."

"Did he tell you about it?"

"Yes, sir, only a half-hour ago."

"Funny, he never mentioned it to me," Livy Locke said. "I had quite a long talk with him this afternoon, when I got in from Orly, and he never said a word about it."

"He said he wanted me to be the first to know."

"Well, that was thoughtful of him," Livy said complacently. "Is he an old friend of yours?"

"No, sir, I hardly know him. He came to me because I'm the security officer."

Livy knitted his brow. The statement puzzled him. "I don't quite see the point. Is she foreign?"

"Yes, sir, she's French," McEwen answered. "He came to me because he knew that he would have to get clearance before he could marry her."

"Of course," Livy said. The tone of his voice was less cordial. He was beginning to get annoyed that his dinner was being delayed by so trivial a matter. "What's so urgent about that? Is she pregnant?"

"It's worse than that, Mr. Locke," McEwen said earnestly. "If you don't mind, I'd like to tell you the story he told me."

Livy glanced at his watch. "Go ahead, but remember, you've got only twenty minutes more. My wife does not enjoy being kept waiting for dinner."

Frank McEwen was not embarrassed by the curt injunction. He knew that what he was going to say would make Locke forget all about his dinner. Sure of himself, feeling the confidence which comes with having the ball in one's own territory, he pulled a small notebook from his pocket, opened it, and holding it where he could refresh his memory with the names and places, recited the story as Walter had told it to him. He made no attempt to color the facts. On the contrary, priding himself on his objectivity as an investigator, he followed accurately, with his trained memory, the words of Walter, interspersing throughout "he said" and "according to Haines." There was no editorializing, nor did he draw any conclusions when he had finished the story with an account of the picnic in the Forêt de St. Germain.

As Livy listened the color had gradually left his face, his jaw had become set, and his eyes, which had never swerved for an instant from McEwen's face, had taken on a bright, piercing light.

"Let me get this straight," Livy said in a low, cold voice. "You say he took this girl on a picnic with my wife and children on Saturday?"

McEwen nodded. "That's what he told me. They went to the Forest of Saint Germain and then came back here to your house for a cocktail."

Livy got up. "I'm going to ask my wife to come here. I think she ought to corroborate that part of the story."

"Sure. That's right. I will have to talk to her anyway to make my check."

Livy went out into the hall and called loudly, "Oh, Eleanor! Come to the library."

The voice of Julien came from the floor below. *"Je crois que Madame est dans sa chambre, Monsieur."*

"Bien, dites-lui de venir ici," Livy commanded, and returned to the library.

"If you don't mind, Mr. Locke," McEwen said, "I would like to do the questioning."

"Ask her anything you like," Livy snapped. He walked over to the desk and stood there, looking down at his empty cocktail glass. "This is the damnedest thing that has ever happened to me . . ."

"Nothing has happened to you, Mr. Locke," McEwen said quietly.

Livy turned on him. "He's my assistant, isn't he?"

"But you knew nothing about it."

Eleanor entered the room, smiling graciously. "Have you two finished your business?" she asked.

"No, we haven't," Sam said abruptly. "Sit down, Eleanor. Mr. McEwen has a few questions he'd like to ask you."

Frank McEwen had stood up when she came into the room. "Good evening, Mrs. Locke," he said.

"How do you do, Mr. McEwen," Eleanor said. She turned to Sam. "My husband apparently thinks that we've met before."

"This is no time for formalities," Locke said. "Sit down, Eleanor."

She sat in the chair that her husband had vacated and looked at McEwen with an amused, quizzical expression. She liked the looks of him. He was as American as peanut butter with his blue-green ready-made suit and his necktie of bright abstract design.

"Eleanor," Sam said, standing between them, his back to the desk, like a referee, "I want you to listen to McEwen and answer his questions as honestly as you know how. This is a very serious matter."

Eleanor looked up at him and then at the security officer. She had a sudden premonition that they wanted to talk to her about Walter and Germaine. If that was it, she would— McEwen's voice took her attention.

"Mrs. Locke, I understand that Mr. Haines brought a young lady to a picnic you gave on Saturday. Is that correct?"

"It is quite correct," Eleanor answered.

"Can you recall her name?"

"I believe it's Mlle. Brisson—Germaine Brisson." She wondered how this man had learned. Had Christian's friend told the police?

"Did he say she was his fiancée?"

"Indeed he did. He told me he was engaged when I called him about the picnic. That's why I asked him to bring her."

"Did you know anything about her? Did you know who she was?" McEwen asked in the same polite, reassuring voice.

"Not then, not when I asked him to bring her," Eleanor replied.

"So he told you about her at the picnic. Is that it?"

"No. He told me nothing about her," she said defensively.

"Then who did?" Locke asked angrily.

"Do you wish me to answer my husband's question?" Eleanor said, looking at McEwen.

"If you please, Mrs. Locke," McEwen replied.

"Before I do it, I would like to know where you got your information about Mr. Haines's engagement," Eleanor said.

"See here, Eleanor," Sam interrupted, "Frank McEwen is doing the questioning, not you."

"It was Mr. Haines told me, Mrs. Locke," McEwen said politely. "He told me the whole story. You see, he has to get cleared by State before he can marry her."

Eleanor heaved a deep sigh of relief. "Oh, I'm so glad he did," she said. "Then there's no more problem, is there? He's told you everything. Now you know what she was and how she has been saved because of her love for him."

"Don't be a fool, Eleanor," Sam snapped. "It isn't as simple as that. Why, I wouldn't believe that woman—"

"Would you mind giving me the name of the person who told you, Mrs. Locke?" McEwen asked, hoping to keep Locke's anger out of it.

"It was a friend of Mr. Haines. His name is Count Christian de St. Avit."

Frank McEwen took out his notebook again and consulted it. "Yeah, that's right, Saint A-v-i-t," he said, as if to himself, then closed the book and looked at Eleanor. "Why did he tell you this?"

"Because he wanted to warn me that it might get into the

hands of the French police. Being a friend of Mr. Haines, he was anxious that it be kept in the family—our family, the American family."

McEwen smiled at her. "That checks exactly with what Haines told me," he said, putting the notebook back in his pocket. "Is there anything else you could tell me about this girl, Mrs. Locke? Any details which Haines might have overlooked?"

"Only my impression of her, my judgment after having seen her and talked to her on Saturday."

"I think that is beside the point," Sam interjected. "Frank is interested in facts, nothing else."

"As a security officer, Mr. McEwen will know that impressions people give by their behavior are often more revealing than so-called facts," Eleanor said firmly.

"What were your impressions?" McEwen asked, as if to placate her.

"That both Haines and Mlle. Brisson are genuinely, sincerely in love with each other," she said emphatically.

Frank McEwen got up from his chair. "I must apologize for keeping you people from your dinner. Thank you, Mrs. Locke. You've been very helpful." He rubbed his hand through the thick brush of his hair as he walked slowly toward the door. "There's just one more point, Mrs. Locke," he said, stopping and turning to face her. "Do you think it possible that this girl is faking her renunciation of the Communist Party just so she can marry Haines and continue to get inside information?"

Eleanor rose from her chair. "I don't believe it for a minute. When a woman really loves a man, she doesn't lie to him. That's what I meant when I said that she truly loves him."

McEwen smiled. "Well, let's hope you're right, Mrs. Locke.

Good night and thanks." He walked out of the door followed by Livy.

Eleanor could hear her husband's voice as he descended the stairs saying, "I'll see you first thing in the morning about this. God, think of it! Haines of all people! It's the dirtiest mess I've ever run into."

CHAPTER TWENTY-FIVE

ALL the way home, driving along the quay, Walter felt lightheaded, as if a great weight which had been sitting on the top of his head for two days had been removed. He had taken the first step, the proper step, in the long and intricate process of making Germaine acceptable as the wife of a Foreign Service officer. Frank McEwen, to whom he had told the whole story carefully, straightforwardly, exactly, without coloring the facts to suit his ends, had listened attentively, taking his notes, showing no signs of alarm, suspicion, or favor. When it was over he had thanked Walter for his frank exposition and had asked for an opportunity to interview Mlle. Brisson before writing his report.

It was a relief to Walter to have come clean, as was expected of him, and to know that Germaine would confirm every word of it. Oh, there would be suspicions and uneasiness in the beginning. The fear of Communist infiltration was such a pervading one in Washington that there were bound to be hysterical voices of caution. But in the final analysis he would be given good marks for his part in the story, he felt certain. After all, had he not made a prompt and full report? And—what was much more to his credit—had he not brought a Commy agent over to the other side, where she could be useful as a means of determining their organization and methods?

Then there was that other bit of news. That had come just before he had had his talk with McEwen and had served to strengthen his resolve and steady his voice during the recital. Livy had told him in confidence that he was to be appointed as chief of mission to The Hague. He felt certain that Livy, to have received the nomination of Ambassador to the Netherlands, must have considerable influence both with the Secretary and the White House. This meant that he had also been cleared for the post by Ambassador Sherrill. Livy was a realist who saw things as they were. He wanted Walter because he was confident that Walter could produce sound and searching dispatches which he could sign without fear of embarrassing questions from State or Treasury. Once he had heard the story, the true story, fully and frankly, from Walter's own lips, and had met Germaine—that was important because she was her own best advocate—he would pull every wire to have the marriage sanctioned.

And, of course, Mrs. Locke would help. He felt certain of her support, for it had been so obvious at the picnic that she liked Germaine and approved of her. A woman could do a lot in a situation like this, more than a man, because she didn't rationalize the truth but felt it, sensed it, and that was the only way to get at the truth about people; for ratiocination could only weigh actions and words, and they were only a portion of the factors involved. That had been his own weakness before he met Germaine. It was the reason why he had never fallen in love before, because he had had to dissect each girl like a butterfly on a board. It was his nature. This time he had allowed himself to be swept along on a strong current of emotion, with the result that he had found her, found himself, found something that was more profound, more precious than anything that could be reduced to words or symbols.

Christian was that way, too, he thought. He was the ultimate in rational man. That was why he was still skeptical about Germaine, still suspected that she was playing him for a sucker. He would have to talk to Christian—both he and Germaine should do it together—quietly, calmly over a drink, and with the Abbé along, too, if he wanted to join them. As a matter of fact the Dominican ought to be there, for he was the one who knew the whole history and was a friend of Germaine's father. Those priests had a way of sensing the truth, of knowing when it was spoken.

He parked the car on the quay side and walked up the three flights to his apartment, humming a tune—the adagio from Beethoven's Seventh. He opened the door, threw his hat on the console, and called her name as he went into the living room. As a rule, at this hour, she was in the tiny kitchen, cooking their dinner, and her response to the habitual call was always, *"Je viens dans un instant, mon amour,"* in a throaty, cadenced voice. He waited to hear it, holding his breath in anticipation, but there was no sound, no answer. He called again, louder, and again nothing but silence within the apartment, made more acute by the faint, familiar street sounds of Paris. He went through the dining room into the kitchen. She was not there, nor was there any evidence that she had begun her culinary preparations. The pots and pans were hanging in shining rows, like an illustration of geometric progression. No vegetables were on the counter, no stick of bread on the table. He looked at his watch, thinking that he might have misjudged the hour. Six-fifteen. By this time, as a rule, the food was there, ready to be cooked for a seven-thirty dinner. Could it be that she had delayed her shopping until late? If so, it would be the first time. She had always been waiting for him, that is, except for the one day when he had come home early after his lunch with Christian and the Abbé.

He went quickly into the bedroom, a slight, sudden fear tightening the muscles around his heart, but he laughed when he saw that all her clothes were there, and her toilet articles and face creams. He called himself a louse, a skunk, for having had the fear, for even allowing it to enter his consciousness. Going back to the living room, he noticed for the first time that the cocktail tray had not yet been put on the coffee table. That was strange. That was unlike Germaine, who was always so thoughtful, so precise, so regulated in the timing and order of her care of him. Every evening he had returned from the Hôtel Talleyrand to find the tray there, with the bourbon, the bitters, the sugar, the lemon peel, the little pitcher of water, the thermos ice bucket, and the two old-fashioned glasses. In the beginning she had taken a Bourin, not liking whiskey, but eventually he had weaned her to the taste, making them weak on whiskey and strong on sugar and water until she had become as addicted to her evening toddy as any young matron of Covington, Kentucky.

Still rationalizing her absence, fighting off any recurrence of the fear, he went back into the kitchen and prepared the tray himself, carrying it to the living room and placing it in its accustomed spot. He did not mix himself a drink, preferring to wait for her return and thus repay her loving care with a touch of gallantry. He lit his pipe, walked over to the center window, and looked again at his watch.

Half past six. Odd, but not alarming. He lifted his gaze to the Square de l'Ile de France, the prow of the ship, remembering that night when she had first come to his flat after the dinner at La Méditerranée, how they had stood together at this very window before they had played Ravel's "La Valse." Or was it the Fauré sonata? It was the Ravel, he recalled, because they had agreed on that during dinner. He would play it now, as a reminder to greet her return. He put the record on and sat down in his favorite chair, at the end of the coffee table, in front of the tray, facing the door to the foyer. He listened, not so much to the music, which filled the room and was inescapable, as for the sound of her footsteps on the stairs.

The coda ended and the room was suddenly, painfully silent, except for the click of the phonograph turntable halting its gyration. He knew that the record took about seventeen minutes to play. His watch confirmed the estimate by showing ten minutes to seven. The period of gallantry had ended. He mixed himself an old-fashioned and drank it down quickly to drown the fear, to help him fight against its persistent, ever increasing demand for recognition. He sat there numbly, no longer smoking, unable finally to dam the flood of queries that flowed into his mind. Where could she have gone? What could have detained her? Or, more to the point, who could have detained her? Had she met one of her former comrades? That man Fantin, the one who called himself The Twilight? Had they found her and caught her? Was she being held a prisoner, awaiting a Party trial? Maybe Christian or the Abbé had gone back on their promise and told the Deuxième Bureau. Maybe it was the police who had picked her up.

At half past seven he went back to the bedroom and made a careful inventory of her clothes. He wanted to know, felt he ought to know, what she was wearing, in case—well, in case. He knew every article, better than he knew his own clothes: each dress, each blouse, each skirt, each pair of shoes, all of which had been discussed, argued about, admired, criticized until they had become fixtures, recognizable landmarks of the growth of their love. They were not many, only a few, but well chosen; classic, but enough in the mode to lend the dignity of gentility to her radiant beauty. Each garment was present and accounted for, even the new gray suit of sharkskin worsted which Nino, in the rue du Faubourg St. Honoré, had made her for the special price of fifty thousand francs and which she always wore if she had to go out in the afternoon. The only thing missing was the worsted suit, the "Party suit" he had called it after her confession, when she had admitted that she had only worn it while marketing or on Party business.

He pulled her battered suitcase down from the top of the wardrobe. That's where she had put it away after that all-night bout of anger, argument, whiskey, renunciation, and love-making, saying as she did so, "From now on only to be worn for *marché* mornings." Monday. Was Monday a *marché* morning? Yes, it was. Always, after the week-end, the cupboard was bare, and Mondays had been the replenishing mornings, sometimes on the Ile de la Cité and sometimes at Les Halles, and always with the string bag. Often she had left the flat when he had, refusing a lift in his car, preferring to walk like the other housewives.

He went back to the kitchen to see if the string bag was hanging in its place on the hook beside the door to the dining room. It was not there. He searched carefully. It was not anywhere. Then she had gone to the market with her bag as usual, and in the morning, for she was wearing the worsted suit and the old worn shoes, both of which, she had proudly argued, helped to keep the prices down. The impact of this deduction was like an electric shock. It froze him for an instant; then he felt his body swaying and grabbed for the door frame to steady himself. Something had happened to her, and the thought made him feel sick at his stomach. He walked, stumbling, holding on to the backs of chairs and the door frames to the living room and sat down heavily in his chair.

He poured some whiskey into his glass and drank it down. What could have happened? He must try to think, try to get his mind in order, stop it from darting around aimlessly like a bird in a room, so that he could plan what to do, what action to take.

He let the whiskey calm the nerves of his stomach while he lit a cigarette. Getting himself in hand, though not enough to stop the gnawing fear that penetrated all thinking, he began to list the possibilities: an accident—hit by a car or a bicycle and lying now in a hospital, unable or unwilling to give her address and telephone number; the contingencies he had already thought of, that she had been picked up by the comrades of her apparatus or by the police, or—no, that he could not believe or even contemplate, it was too preposterous, too unfair. But there were other, parallel propositions which could not be excluded. For example, believing her attachment to him either as mistress or wife would be bound to wreck his career, even though she had repudiated the Communist Party, she had either vanished from him and them to find herself a new life, or maybe to return to her father in Toulouse; or, in the depth of her anguish and love, she had sought, in the traditional manner, the comfort and oblivion of the Seine. The last had to be considered, of course, but he felt it remote. She was not the suicidal type. She had too much sense, too much courage, was too much of the typical French woman, the *débrouillarde*.

He crushed out his cigarette and walked to the bedroom with sudden decision. Sitting on the bed, he dialed the number of Christian de St. Avit.

"Thank God I found you at home," he said when Christian's voice answered. "I've got to see you, to talk to you. It's urgent."

"You mean this evening?" Christian asked.

"Yes, at once, as soon as possible."

"What has happened?"

"I'd rather not discuss it on the telephone. Could you possibly come to see me?"

"Certainly. Whenever you say. I am just about to sit down to dinner. Why don't you come here? We can have coffee and a liqueur together."

"No, I can't do that," Walter said impatiently. "I'm sorry, but I don't dare leave my apartment. Please come here after you've eaten."

"But my dear fellow, of course I shall come," Christian said solicitously.

"Could you bring your friend, the Abbé d'Albret?"

"Well, I don't know. I shall telephone to him, and if he is at home and free to come I shall be happy to bring him."

"Thanks, Christian," Walter said, unable to hide the sense of relief from his voice. "I'm sorry to have to ask you to do this, but it's desperately important."

"I can imagine," Christian said. "I shall be there in about an hour."

The hour went by on heavy, leaden minutes. Walter did not want to drink any more, he wanted his mind to be clear, as clear as it could be with its harassments, doubts, and fears. He smoked continuously, one cigarette after another, not caring for his pipe, not having the patience now to fill it, tend it, keep it drawing smoothly. He put away the cocktail things, replacing them with highball glasses and a bottle of Scotch. Then he lit the lamps, but he did not draw the curtains at the windows, hoping that the light in the room might serve as a beacon to her. Ideas of action came to him and were dismissed, such as calling the police, the morgue, Mme. Nicole. As long as Christian was coming he had better wait for his counsel. He was a Frenchman and would know what, if anything, could be done. He kept hoping—hoping that she would come in the door, safe and unscathed, before Christian arrived. Then they could laugh and get slightly tight together, and the pressure on his heart would cease as he held her in his arms.

When he heard the click-click of the street door and the sound of footsteps on the stairs, he rushed into the foyer and opened the door to the corridor. He listened, and his heart sank as he heard two male voices. He recognized Christian's high-pitched tenor.

"*Bon soir, Christian et Monsieur l'Abbé,*" he greeted them as they reached the third-floor landing. "*Vous êtes bien gentils de—*"

"In the service of a friend anything is a pleasure," Christian interrupted in English.

Walter took their hats, placing them on the console, then ushered his guests into the living room.

"What is the matter, my dear Walter?" Christian asked as he sat down on the couch. "Has Mlle. Brisson been pinched by the police?"

Walter's face clouded with anger. "So you told them, did you?" he said.

"I will excuse that remark on the grounds that you are upset," Christian said coldly. "I gave you my promise that we would not speak to the police until you had had an opportunity of convincing us that she had forsworn her allegiance to the Bolshevics. Please do not question my honor, nor that of my friend the Abbé."

"Why did you ask if she had been pinched by the police? What made you think they were looking for her?" Walter asked, ignoring Christian's touchiness.

"My dear Walter," Christian replied, "it was obvious from

your voice on the telephone, and from your refusal to talk except here in your flat, that something had happened to Mlle. Brisson. I am right, am I not?"

"Yes," Walter said dejectedly. "You are right. She appears to have left here this morning to go to the *marché* and has not returned. But what made you think it was the police?"

"I merely mentioned it because I thought it might calm your fears," Christian said. "For, after all, that is the best thing, not the worst, that could have happened to her."

The Abbé, who was sitting in the chair facing Walter, reached out and put a hand on Christian's knee. "May I interrupt to say that I have a very great interest in this affair," he said. "I think I explained that to Monsieur Haines the last time we met. Now, according to my friend Christian, many things have taken place in the life of Mlle. Ninon Santerre since we had our little talk. She has, I understand, resigned from the Communist Party, denounced their beliefs, and agreed to become your wife. Is that true?"

"Entirely true," Walter answered.

"Would you care to tell me precisely how this came about?" the Abbé asked. "The details might help me to solve the problem of her unexplained absence this evening."

Walter, hesitatingly at first, his confidence returning as the recital developed, told the story of that afternoon, evening, and night when he had come home after the lunch at Christian's apartment. His memory, clarified by his fear, brought back all the arguments, the long discussions, the dialectics, the ultimate choices, and the final decision. Stirred by the emotion of that terrible night in which every word had been to him so true, so honest, so beyond dissembling or ulterior motive, he forgot his audience; his voice became dramatic, surcharged with earnestness. He believed, and the strength and purity of his belief was as clear and solemn as a tolling bell.

When he finished there was a silence; then the Dominican gathered his white robes and stood up. "I thank you, Monsieur Haines," he said calmly, looking at Walter with an intense, piercing gaze. "The Church thanks you. You have done what we have striven to do. Your love has accomplished it. She was not ready yet to return to the love of Jesus and the Blessed Virgin. It needed the first step, the love of a good man, an honest man. The rest will be easy. She is saved."

"Yes, Father," Walter said. "She's saved from the Communists, to that I'll swear. She'll never go back to them, never, not willingly."

"You believe, then, Abbé, that her conversion is sincere?" Christian asked.

"As completely as Monsieur Haines believes it," the Abbé replied. "Her words, as we have heard them recited, are not those of a deceiver."

"Well, then, I think we ought to have a drink," Christian said. "I owe it to you, Walter, to drink to your happiness without the reservations I made to Derek's toast at the picnic."

"Yes, but dear man, she's gone, she's not here," Walter pleaded.

"Never mind," Christian consoled him. "Put your faith in the good Abbé d'Albret. Now that he knows her soul is clean, he will find her, you mark my words."

"To do that, I must be going," the Abbé said. "No time is to be lost."

"But you must have a whiskey before you go," Walter said. "I apologize for not offering it sooner."

"Thank you, not now," the priest said. "Stay here and have your drink, Christian. I shall call you in the morning."

"No, I'll take you in my car," Christian said, jumping up. "I'm in this, too, and you may need my help. Good night, Walter."

Walter saw them to the door, then walked back into the living room. He had not eaten, but his hunger was not for food, only for the crumb of hope that they had thrown to him.

CHAPTER TWENTY-SIX

ELEANOR was surprised to hear her husband's voice on the floor below, talking to Julien. It was only six-thirty and he had told her that he would be home late, as he had to drop in at a cocktail party the Italian Delegation were giving for their Minister of the Treasury. She was sitting in the little library that looked out into the branches of the horse chestnuts which lined the Boulevard Jean Mermoz and were now in full flower. She had just left the children and had settled down for a quiet hour with Roger Martin du Gard when her reading had been interrupted by the sound of Sam's voice and his step mounting the stairs.

"Have you already been to the Italians?" she asked as he entered the library.

"I'm not going. I came home instead to have a talk with you." He picked up a chair and carried it over to the window, putting it down where it faced his wife's. He looked tired and angry, his skin taut on his jawbone, and his brow furrowed.

"What's the matter, Sam, has something gone wrong?" she asked, disturbed by his expression and the unusual and ominous statement that he wanted to have a "talk" with her.

Before sitting down, he went back and closed the door.

"Hadn't we better have Julien bring the cocktail things up before you start?" Eleanor said.

"No," he said abruptly. "I've already told Julien to bring them up in half an hour. I want to talk first."

"Yes, dear," she said soothingly, still wondering what the news could be, hoping that something had gone wrong with the ambassadorship. She put a bookmark between the open pages on her lap and closed the book, then looked up at him expectantly.

"I have just come from a long and disturbing session with Walter Haines," he said gravely.

"Oh dear," Eleanor said involuntarily, catching her breath and putting her hand on her bosom.

"He confirmed what McEwen told me, every word of it," Sam went on. "I felt it was only fair to give him the chance of telling the story to me before I ordered McEwen to check with the French police. We started at four o'clock in my office and we didn't finish until a quarter past six. I tell you, Eleanor, I never want to go through anything like that again."

"McEwen had the story straight?" she asked, trying to appear calm.

"In every respect," Sam said. "Walter made a clean breast of it, told us everything: how St. Avit had recognized the girl when Walter had taken him home for a drink after your party; how he had lunched with St. Avit and heard her history from a Dominican monk; how he had returned to his apartment and faced her with the facts and learned from her own lips that it was true. Then came the astounding part. God, Eleanor, it's beyond my comprehension how a sober-minded young fellow like that could make such a complete jackass of himself."

"What do you mean?"

"Asking the girl to marry him!" Sam almost shouted. "Why, it's unbelievable, idiotic, doesn't make sense. Can you imagine anyone so stupid that he would propose to a girl who acknowledged that she was a Communist spy, sleeping in his bed for the sole purpose of obtaining classified information for the enemy?"

"But she renounced the Party . . ."

Sam uttered a bark of scorn. "That's what *she* said. It was just a shrewd gambit to extricate herself from a jam. Secret agents in her category don't—"

"Why did she confess?" Eleanor asked. "She didn't have to. She could easily have denied everything and accused Christian de St. Avit of being what you said he was, an *agent provocateur*."

"Don't be silly," Sam said scornfully. "When Walter told her that St. Avit was going to report her to the Sûreté, she knew the jig was up and she was smart enough to counter that move with a confession."

"Sam, you haven't met the girl or you couldn't say that," Eleanor protested.

"Thank God I haven't! It's bad enough that Frank knows she was on that picnic of yours. That was a very grave error, Eleanor, and it may come back to bite us yet. I thought you had more sense—"

"Than to invite your assistant and his fiancée?" Eleanor said indignantly.

"Yes, when you knew she was his mistress."

"That was none of my affair. Besides, it's usual among the younger generation."

"Do you know where he met her?" Sam asked belligerently.

"No. How should I?"

"He picked her up in some joint that night he showed Senator Donegan the town."

"Walter Haines showed the Senator Paris night life?" she asked in amazement. "I can't believe it."

"That's what he told us, and it will give you a faint idea of what an unstable character we've been dealing with," Sam said judicially. "Furthermore, remember that the Senator met this girl. The implications of that should be obvious."

"You mean the Senator might be accused . . ."

"No, I might, because you invited the girl to that picnic. You know how they are, some of those senators, they'll damn anyone by association. They'll say that because he was my assistant and because you had her around, we are both involved in Commy activities. Oh, God, if we can only keep this story out of Washington until my name has been confirmed by the Senate!"

"I should think that Donegan could stop any such story as that," Eleanor said.

"Eleanor, you'll drive me mad. Donegan is a Democrat. That is why those Republicans would like to get their dirty hands on this."

"You've always defended those Republicans," Eleanor said with a feigned look of innocence.

"Let's not go into that," Sam said, with a gesture of impatience. "They've been useful, but I don't want them to be useful at my expense, just because my wife was silly enough to—"

"See here, Sam," Eleanor said sharply, "I'm not going to have you trying to link me up in this. I have done nothing to compromise you, so let's keep to the subject and leave me out of it."

"It's only that damned picnic," Sam said irritably. "If you hadn't asked her—"

"Oh, stop harping on the picnic. If it hadn't been for the picnic I wouldn't have heard the story. What about Walter? Has he agreed to break off his engagement? Did you talk him out of it?"

"We didn't have to talk him out of it. He sees the light now, I think."

"He no longer believes her?" she asked, incredulous.

"How could he? She has skipped."

"What do you mean?"

"Just what I said. She has left him, flown the coop, disappeared."

"Oh, no!" Eleanor gasped. "Oh, how awful! Poor man!"

"Damn lucky man, if you ask me," Sam said bitterly.

"He loves her," Eleanor said softly, to herself.

"He's a weakling, a spineless fool."

There was no use in trying to defend Walter. She knew that Sam was incapable of understanding. It was clear to her now, clearer than it had ever been, that Sam had never loved anyone but himself. "I could have sworn . . ." she started to say, then changed her mind. "Does Walter think she has gone back to her Party comrades?" she asked.

Sam gave a dry, hard laugh. "He thinks she had been kidnapped by them because she turned traitor, but, of course, that is just wishful thinking."

"It could be possible."

"You had better stop being so damned romantic about a dangerous spy. Just wait until the police catch up with her, then you'll learn a few cold facts about these Commies."

"The police have been notified?" she asked.

"Frank is there now, telling them the whole story."

Eleanor sighed and shrugged her shoulders. "Poor Walter," she said. "He'll take this very hard."

"He has no one but himself to blame," Sam said sanctimoniously. "He has demonstrated conclusively that he is not temperamentally fitted for the Foreign Service."

"Sam, that's a cruel and unfair thing to say," Eleanor said sharply. "How was he to know that she was a Communist agent? He's a young man, a bachelor, with a right to fall in love—"

"No responsible officer of our government has any right to be sucked in as he was," Sam said pompously. "And to believe her repudiation after she had confessed—why that was so stupid as to be treasonable."

"Will McEwen make a report to the State Department?"

"I suppose so, through security channels; but I shall make my own report, directly through the Embassy."

"Just the facts, of course."

"With my recommendations."

"And what will they be?"

"Just what I said, that Walter Haines is not fit material for a Foreign Service officer."

Eleanor stood up, the book on her lap falling to the floor. "Sam, you wouldn't do that!" she exclaimed, horror-struck.

"Indeed I will. It's my duty," he said self-righteously.

"It will ruin his life," she cried.

"And whose fault is that?"

"Not his, for God's sake! Just think what you're doing, condemning him without trial, without evidence, even."

"It was his own evidence, given freely. He has convicted himself."

"How do you know that she was not sincere when she said she would give up Communism because of her love for him? How do you know that they haven't kidnapped her because she had turned against them? Can't you wait until the police have found her? Can't you wait for the facts?"

"Even if she had been kidnapped because she had turned against them, which is highly unlikely, it would not alter my view of Haines. He is still emotionally too unstable to be a good security risk."

"So you are going to recommend that he be fired from the

Service?" she asked, looking at him with incomprehension and loathing.

"Tomorrow morning."

Eleanor picked up the book from the floor and placed it on the table in the center of the room. Her hands were trembling and she felt faint. Drawing herself up, she took a deep breath before starting to speak. "Sam," she said speaking slowly and carefully, "you have accused me of many things— of lacking ambition, of being a romantic, of having no social sense, of preferring the company of artists and wits to that of bankers and businessmen. You have worried that I was not up to the role of Livingston Locke's wife, and you have tried your best to coach me in the words and gestures—"

"Oh, for God's sake, Eleanor, stop sounding off like a tragic heroine," Sam interrupted impatiently.

"Not this time, Sam," she went on. "This time I'm not stopping at your command. I'm going to sound off, and you're going to listen. Yes, Your Excellency, the tragic heroine is going to speak her own lines this time, this one, last time. Walter is not the one who has convicted himself. It's you, Sam. You, in your inimitably selfish way, have confessed your own despicable, mean weakness. You want to be an ambassador. Like a spoiled child you want this new bright toy more than anything else in the world, and you'll get it, surely you'll get it, because you'll grind your heel on anyone who might possibly jeopardize your chances, even if the person is innocent, is loyal, is worthy, is brighter, more intelligent than you are. Because you are afraid that this affair with Walter's girl might be found out and used against you in the Senate, you are going to beat them to the punch by condemning Walter Haines, consigning him to oblivion so that you can prove by the date on the dispatch that you were the first to cry wolf—"

"Listen, Eleanor—" Sam said, rising to his feet, his face livid with anger.

"Don't interrupt me. There's not much more," she said coldly. "I'm no longer interested in your denials, your protestations of innocence. You are so self-deceived that you even believe in your own virtue. But *I* don't, Sam. I know you. I know to an exact degree how far the poison of ambition has rotted your soul, your integrity, your honesty. But let me tell you this, if you write that report condemning Walter Haines, you'll have to live with it on your conscience until you die." She turned and started for the door.

"What the hell are you talking about?" he roared like an angry bull. He lunged forward and grabbed her arm as she reached for the door handle. "What do you mean . . . ?"

She wheeled on him like a tigress. "I mean that I'm leaving you."

His face went white. "By God, Eleanor, you can't do that."

"I'm doing it. I couldn't live a day longer in this house and keep my self-respect."

He realized that she meant it, that she was bitter and angry, and he sensed, with that cunning of the trader, that his only hope was to calm her with the honey of reason. The incredible defection of Walter Haines had been bad enough, but to have his wife leave him at this moment would be the *coup de grâce*. He saw the whole dream of his ambassadorship irreparably shattered, falling to bits about his head. "Come, come, Eleanor," he said, with affected gentleness, as if trying to placate a stubborn child. "Steady now. I can understand how upsetting this has been for you. It is a horrible thing to have happen to a man you liked and admired. I appreciate that. But you must remember, dear, that your first duty is to your husband. If you should do something now that was impulsive and foolish, public opinion would jump to the conclusion that I was implicated with Haines. You can easily see what effect that would have on the Senate . . ."

She pulled her arm from his grasp and opened the door. "Maître Peyraud, my lawyer, will get in touch with you." She had not thought of a lawyer before. The name had just come to her, an inspiration.

When she reached her room she called Christian on the telephone. "I must speak with you," she said, her voice trembling. "It's very important."

"Of course," Christian said anxiously. "I shall come at once to your house."

"No, not here. Anywhere, but not here. Could you meet me somewhere for a cocktail?"

"Certainly, wherever you say. How about my apartment? It is quiet here. We can talk without fear of being overheard."

"Where is it?"

"Number 146 rue Spontini, on the third floor."

"I shall be there in about a half-hour. Thank you, Christian," she said, and hung up.

She dialed the number of the Hotel San Regis and ordered a suite for an indefinite period, then rang for her maid, telling her, when she came, to pack a suitcase with her night clothes, a *tailleur*, shoes for the morning, and a change of underwear. While the maid was packing, she changed quickly into a black taffeta cocktail dress and patent-leather pumps.

Julien was out in the street, trying to hail a taxi, as she looked at herself in the hall mirror. Her face was paler than usual and her eyes were fever-bright. Oh, Lord, she thought, what am I doing? What about Colin and Charlotte? I must have them. I'll agree to anything, anything at all, but not to lose them. They are mine, and I love them.

CHAPTER TWENTY-SEVEN

"WHAT is the matter, my dear Eleanor? You look very upset," Christian said as old Etiennette ushered Eleanor into his yellow living room.

"I had to see you," Eleanor said breathlessly. "Please, Christian, mix me a martini while I gather my wits."

He led her to a large fauteuil, one of three that surrounded a small circular table in a corner of the room. When she was seated, he offered her a cigarette from his gold case and lit it for her. "This is an honor—may I say, an undreamed-of honor—to have you here as my guest," he said as he went over to a sideboard at the far end of the room, where the cocktail shaker, already filled, was waiting for him to put in the ice. He was wearing pumps and a green velours smoking jacket.

"Tell me," she asked anxiously as he came back to her with the shaker and two glasses, "is it true that Germaine Brisson has left Walter Haines?"

"I regret to say that it is true," he answered, beginning to realize the cause of her anxiety.

"What was the reason? Do you think she lied to the poor man? Did she never really . . . ?"

"No, she did not lie," Christian said gently and rather sadly. "I am convinced of that. She truly denied her party."

"Then, where is she? What has happened to her?"

Christian shrugged his shoulders. "I should like very much to know. There are many of us who are searching for the answer."

"The police?"

"The police—and others."

"She must be found, Christian. It's desperately important," Eleanor said fervently.

"I realize that. We can't let them get away with this. She is too useful to be lost to our cause."

"Oh, and for Walter's sake. If she isn't found, if she can't prove her conversion, it will be the end of him."

Christian put his glass down on the table and looked at her. "You think he will take his own life?" he asked.

"No!" she almost cried. "He won't do that. He's far too solid and brave to do that. But our government, our State Department, will throw him out and he'll be ruined; he'll never be able to get another job."

"Do they know?" Christian asked in surprise.

"Of course they know. He told them everything. He's that kind. He felt it was his duty."

"Did he tell them that she had denied the Communist Party?"

"Certainly," she said. "But you don't think for a minute that they believed him. They laughed at him, said he was a romantic adolescent, that she was pulling the wool over his lovesick eyes. One can understand how they felt. It does sound like a fishy story when you tell it in cold blood."

"Who are 'they'?" Christian asked. "Who are these people to whom Walter spoke?"

"The security officer of the Embassy and . . ." She stopped.

"Your husband," he added.

Eleanor said nothing. She turned her head, hoping that he would not see the tears welling in her eyes.

"I see. I understand," Christian said slowly, thoughtfully. "Your husband does not believe Walter, nor does he approve of your defense of him, so you have come to me to urge the necessity of her return in order to prove his innocence. Well, let me tell you, my dear Eleanor, that everything possible is being done to find her. This case is receiving the personal attention of the very highest authorities."

Eleanor wiped her eyes and held out her glass for Christian to refill. "Have they any clues?" she asked.

"Not as yet," he answered, filling her glass.

"This is a real tragedy, Christian."

"It is indeed, as strange and as complex as one by Sophocles. There are so many people involved."

"Only Walter Haines, really," she said sadly.

Christian smiled. "You are not being honest when you say that."

"Perhaps not, not quite."

"May I ask a question? You don't have to answer if you don't wish to. Why are you so anxious for Mlle. Brisson's return when you are in love with Walter?"

"Why, Christian!" Eleanor said in shocked surprise. "How can you think such a thing! Really! It's a preposterous notion!"

"I'm sorry if I have offended you," Christian said apologetically. "It was jealousy, I suppose, that made me suspicious. That you should come here at this hour of the day to seek help for him seemed to indicate that you cared more for him than for your reputation."

"I care more for decency and justice than I do for my reputation," she snapped angrily.

"Forgive me, Eleanor," Christian pleaded. "I should have

known. I should have sensed your motive." He lifted his glass to her. "I admire you, my dear, extravagantly."

"I'm not looking for admiration," she said, the flame of her anger diminishing swiftly. "I'm looking for help for two fine people whose devotion to each other has brought them to the brink of disaster."

"And that help you will get, to the limit of my poor ability," he said humbly.

"Thank you, Christian," she said, smiling to reassure him that her rancor had vanished. She got up from her chair. "Now I must be running along and let you eat your dinner."

"Would you care to share it with me?" he asked, pointing to the table at the far end of the room, which was set for two.

"Mercy, you didn't tell me that you had a guest coming," she said, somewhat startled.

"That second place was set in hope," Christian said. "In hope that you might grace it."

She took a deep breath and held it while she weighed the question, then she turned to him quickly, with a grateful smile. "I accept with pleasure."

Etiennette served them like a fluttering, solicitous mother hen, urging them to larger helpings, filling their glasses with wine, commenting on the chic of Eleanor's dress and on the becomingness of her skullcap of black straw.

Both Christian and Eleanor tried their best to keep the conversation light and urbane, but it was a strain. The turmoil of Eleanor's thoughts continued, the terror of her decision striking her periodically like an arrow through the heart, stopping her speech in the middle of a sentence, making her suddenly unable to swallow. The children were the cause, the sole cause, of this recurring stab of fear. Should she, for their sake, have put up with anything, with cruelty, deceit, ambition, an embassy in The Hague? Was the cause of decency worth their displacement, their mental anguish, their loss of roots? Could she alone, with her love and kindness, cushion their shock, bring them up as adjusted individuals who would understand and condone? It was a terrifying prospect, but there was no alternative now. She could not return, unless, of course, Sam would agree not to report adversely on Walter. But even then, could she face going on with him, knowing what he was, despising him, knowing that he had only acceded to her wishes because he was afraid of what the world might say if she left him? She looked at Christian, who was telling her in quiet, measured words how rare and honorable a character Walter Haines was, and how much the world, the free world, needed men of his intelligence and integrity, and she knew that she could not go back to Sam Locke.

They took their coffee at the little table where they had sat for cocktails. When he had poured the brandy and lit her cigarette, he sat down opposite her and said, "You know, Eleanor, this Sophoclean tragedy in which you and I suddenly find ourselves as dramatis personae is inspired by a force as evil as it is insidious. Its purpose is to sow discord, destroy love, wreck the lives of individuals, in short, create a chaos which will enable it to enslave the mind and soul of man. If we don't watch out, if we don't keep ourselves firmly in hand, it will do just that to us. You judge me, I presume, at least your husband does, as an idle, inconsequential remnant of a defunct class that lives on dreams of past grandeur and has no more place in the modern world than that clock by Clodion on the mantel there which has even forgotten how to keep correct time. To all outward appearances I am that and nothing more. But I ignore outward appearances, my dear Eleanor, as you are ignoring them now. I have my own ideas of what use I can be to France, to the battle of the individual to think and behave as he chooses. I have an income, modest, but sufficient for my needs, enough so that I do not have to earn more, to pile more francs on those I have. Therefore I am free to pursue my own quests, and the first, the primary one on which all others depend, is the unmasking, the tracking down, the defeat of the evil forces of Soviet bolshevism within our society. There is no difference between this Christian you see and the Christian who called himself Captain Capet in the days of the Maquis and the F.F.I. It is the same man, fighting the same sort of tyranny."

He drained his coffee cup and picked up his *ballon* of brandy. Eleanor said nothing. She sat there, smoking constantly with short, nervous inhales, watching him.

He smiled at her shyly and went on. "You are wondering why I am boasting to you, endeavoring to justify myself. You are thinking, Here is his weakness, he is unsure of himself. Well, I agree with you, it is odd and contradictory. If I am as emancipated as I claim to be, why should I trouble to dissect myself for your benefit? The answer is complex. I want you to know that I can help to prevent that wrecking of lives and destruction of love which the Bolshevics desire by showing you that I am more than passively engaged in the search for Mlle. Brisson, that you have come to one who is loyal to the things you believe in, one who is fighting for them. Then, of course, there is the more direct and human reason—I want you to think well of me."

"I would have understood that reason without your telling me," Eleanor said, looking into her *ballon* as she swirled the brandy around.

"When I told you that I admired you extravagantly," Christian said, "I was purposely understating my feelings."

She looked at him with an attempt at a sympathetic smile. "Do you mind, Christian, if we don't go into that now? You have been so kind, so understanding, so helpful that I don't want to hurt your feelings. Perhaps you can guess what I've been through, what I'm going through, and realize that—well, that anything that touches on sentiment is like vinegar on the wound."

"I'm sorry, Eleanor," he said humbly. "I didn't realize that it was as serious as that."

"It couldn't be more serious. It's final."

"You mean that . . ."

"I've left him, Christian," she said defiantly, with a toss of her head. "I've left Sam Locke for good and all."

"You are very brave, Eleanor," he said.

"No, it wasn't courage, it was just a sudden realization that we had nothing in common, spiritually or morally." She drew a deep breath and her hands started to tremble again. "Oh, if you only knew, if you could have heard him go on about Walter and the effect of all this on his ambitions. . . . Well, there's no use going into that. It's over and done. He has ruined a man, and in doing so he has lost a wife and an ambassadorship." She smiled at him sadly. "There it is, Christian. Now you know."

"Where are you going? Where will you live?" Christian asked calmly.

"For the moment I shall be at the San Regis in the rue Jean Goujon. I'm going there now. My suitcase is in the hall. I brought it with me in a taxi."

"And the children?"

"Oh, that's what frightens me." She struggled to hold the tears back, but they came in spite of her. "I must have them. I've got to have them. In the morning I shall call René Peyraud. Do you think he will help me?"

"He will do anything, everything. You see, Eleanor, a good thing about our little band is that we stick by each other, for better or for worse. In a case like this where you, one of us, have acted in behalf of probity, there will be a solid welding of our forces in your defense."

"God bless you for saying that, my dear Christian," she said, sniffling. "I can't leave Colin and Charlotte. I just can't. You can see that, can't you?"

"Nor will you, even if we have to kidnap them," he said resolutely.

Eleanor got to her feet, dabbing her eyes with her handkerchief. "Now get me a taxi like a good fellow."

"Nothing of the kind," he said, standing up. "I shall drive you myself. My car is in the street below. Just give me a second to change my jacket." He ran out of the room.

Eleanor walked out into the foyer and mended her face with a touch of powder before the mirror. Her breath was still coming in gasps, the sobs she had tried to control.

When Christian emerged from his bedroom in a jacket that matched his trousers, he put both hands on her shoulders and looked at her earnestly. "You are a wonderful, wonderful woman," he said, then pulled her gently toward him and kissed her forehead. Her head fell forward on his shoulder and she sobbed without restraint. He put his arm around her, gently stroking her neck, her back, as one would soothe a child. "My love," he whispered.

"Oh, Christian, Christian!" she moaned, then lifted her head and looked at him. "I'll never be able to thank you."

He kissed her forehead again. "Yes, you will," he said, smiling; then, releasing her, he picked up her bag and opened the door.

CHAPTER TWENTY-EIGHT

FROM where he lay with his arms crossed behind his head on the pillow, he could see the first glow of dawn silhouetting the chimney-pots of the houses that faced on the rue Budé and the rue St. Louis en l'Ile. Through the open window of his bedroom came the distant sounds of the city's earliest activity: the arrival of the trucks at Les Halles, stuffed to the limit of their capacity with vegetables, cheeses, strawberries, the end of their all-night journey from the truck farms of the Ile de France. Like the opening passage of Zola's *Fécondité*, Walter thought. And then his gut twisted again, remembering the sound of her voice, her rich contralto voice, soothing, encompassing, covering him like a warm blanket as she read those sentences, making him see it, the creaking wagons, the tired horses, the sleepy drivers, through French eyes, through her eyes.

This was the second white morning after the second white night since Christian and the Abbé had come to tell him. They had not stayed long, tactfully, discerningly leaving him to hug his agony alone. When they had telephoned, he had opened a new bottle of Scotch, but with the shock, the solar-plexus punch, he had forgotten to offer them a drink. The next morning, one morning ago, the bottle was empty, but he might have been drinking sarsaparilla for all the effect. It had not even deadened the pain. All that night, all the next day, all last night, he had wandered from the living room to the bedroom, from the bedroom to the kitchen, and back to the living room through the dining room, sitting down once in a while when his knees gave out, or flopping on the bed—their bed—smelling the faint odor of her which still clung to the sheets, the pillow cases. He had not eaten. He had not even looked to see if there was anything to eat. There must have been enough nourishment in the whiskey—two bottles of it, for he had opened the second bottle yesterday and the last of that had gone during the night—to sustain him. He didn't feel tired, or even sleepy. It was only that sudden twisting of his gut and the hot saliva in his mouth and the giving away at the knee joints.

Now it was another day, the third day, the day when he would have to get up and put on his dark-blue suit and go to St. Sulpice, where they would wrap up his sorrow forever in an ancient ritual, chanted in singsong Latin. He wondered if he could face it, but he knew he had to, not for her sake, she would understand, but for Christian and the Abbé, who would expect it. He owed it to them.

Funny, he thought, that it isn't my carcass they will be saying mass for. By all that's right and holy it should be. He was the one who was fated, marked, branded for the stockyard. Like a skyrocket he had rushed up high, too high, too fast, and then he had exploded and was dropping now, empty, hollow, a charred cylinder, destined for the scrap heap. He had always believed that reminiscence was the signal of death. The drowning reviewed their lives in the brief moment before the water pushed the last oxygen from their lungs. The old, the sick, the doomed wrote their autobiographies in a final, desperate attempt to attain immortality, knowing there was no future, relying on the past. And that was just what he had been doing since the night before last, reliving every step of his life from Portsmouth to Paris, from the first memory of the haven of his mother's starched-cotton bosom with the watch pinned to it, like Mme. Nicole's, only plainer, just silver with no diamond on its case, to the sound of the Abbé's voice saying that he had identified her body at the morgue and that she had been slugged on the head, and then, with a cracked skull, tossed into the Seine, wearing the old suit and the old shoes and with the string bag still clutched in her left hand.

They had got her, and they had got him, because this was the sign, the sure sign, this remembering, this going back over his whole life. Not that it mattered. As long as she was gone there was no future, nothing to plan, no hopes, no figuring on means of supporting the economies of Europe, no promotions to Class 2, Class 1. He might as well sum up the skyrocket ascent, the shining meteor streak of it, and the beautiful burst of golden stars which was Germaine. Yes, that burst, that final beauty which had made them all say "Ah!" had to be pinned down in detail and in essence. He had been on the verge of writing it to his mother when Germaine had disappeared. Thank God he hadn't. That had been one time when procrastination had paid, for he would have had to write the sequel, and that would have been too great a shock for his mother, whose heart was not what it should be. Now he could write it as a completed episode, a story with a beginning, a middle, and an end, and he could so construct it that the tragedy would appear early, like the voice of doom foretelling the terrible dénouement, thus cushioning the impact, preparing her gently for the agony which she would understand.

He looked at his watch. It was twenty-five past six. He had to shave and take a bath and brush his teeth. The thought revolted him. Why must he make himself clean for a solemn rite over the cracked shell she once lived in and which was no longer hers? He realized that it was a stupid argument and got up stiffly from the bed. His arms ached from holding them crossed under his head. On his feet, he felt dizzy and his knees started to give way under him again. I've got to get something in my stomach, he thought, something besides whiskey. He stumbled into the kitchen, shook the kettle to hear if there was water in it, put it back on the stove, and turned on the gas. Taking a can of Nescafé down from the shelf, he looked into the icebox to see if there was any cream. He found the brown *pot de grès* in the back and smelled it. It was sour. All cream in Paris is slightly sour, because it gets that way coming down on slow trains from Normandy, but this was really sour. *Tant pis,* he said to himself, it's thick and it's sour, but that's all there is, there isn't any more. When they knocked her on the head, all the sweetness went out of the cream, out of me, out of life. The bloody world is sour and I'll drink it and like it. He put a heaping teaspoonful of Nescafé in a big kitchen cup and drowned it in boiling water, then he dug a spoon into the cream and ladled it into the coffee. He stirred it, but it didn't mix, it just floated on top in big oily blobs. "To hell with it," he said out loud, drinking it down so hot that it scalded his throat and biting into the sour clots of cream.

It was just before eight o'clock and he was putting on a clean white shirt when the telephone rang.

"Is this Walter Haines?" an American voice asked.

"What do you want?" Walter said cautiously, afraid it might be a fellow from one of the news agencies.

"This is Frank McEwen. They just called me from the Sûreté to tell me that—"

"They took their own sweet time, didn't they," Walter interrupted impatiently. "They knew it the day before yesterday."

"How did you know?"

"A friend of her father."

"How did he know?"

"He identified the body."

"Gee, I'm glad about this, Mr. Haines," McEwen said.

"I'm not interested in your feelings, you tactful bastard," Walter said and hung up.

Christ almighty, Walter thought, and they call him a security officer! He couldn't find a pimple on his own nose. So he's happy, is he! Happy that her poor, cracked, waterlogged body has vindicated my story that she had renounced the Party. They didn't believe me. They thought I was a mushy adolescent who had fallen for a subversive tart, and they have to have death, murder, to prove to them that she was better than they are. Well, to hell with them, to hell with all the cloak-and-dagger kiddies, with all the ambassadors, with all the dedicated dumbbells, with all the politics and all the phony balances of payments.

His gut began twisting again and his knees started to wobble. He sat on the bed and waited for the spasm to stop. Oh, Germaine, he thought, you are all I had, all I will ever have. You kept my knees braced and my gut in line and my heart beating strong and steady with the love you poured into me. Give me just a little now, just enough to get me into the car and across the river, so that Christian and the Abbé will know that you are in me, part of me.

When he had himself in hand again, he finished dressing and made himself another cup of Nescafé, with the clots of sour cream. He didn't like the cream, it ruined the coffee, but he had an idea that there must be some strength in it which would help him to get through the morning.

It was nine o'clock when he finished the coffee. Still too early, he thought. The mass was not until ten-thirty, but there was no use hanging around the flat. He might as well wait at St. Sulpice. It would be quiet there and maybe he would be able to think—think about her, think about the letter to his mother, which would be a record of the skyrocket's burst, of the bright, graceful stars, of the beauty and the awe of it.

The parking lights of the car were still on, and the starter turned over slowly, showing that the battery was on its way out, but the motor caught and he warmed it up for a minute or two before putting it in gear. He turned into the rue Le Regrattier and went around the block and over the Pont de la Tournelle. He drove slowly, feeling lightheaded, seeing the street and the traffic as something remote and apart from him. Turning right on the Boulevard St. Germain, he drove carefully until he had passed the Café Flore, where he made a U-turn and stopped at a florist he knew. He realized now that he should have ordered something suitable, one of those big rings, or a horseshoe, all wired up so the flowers didn't droop; but he had not thought of it, he had not thought of anything except her alive, and his skyrocket trajectory. He bought all the white roses and white lilac they had, three dozen of the roses and a big bunch of lilac. The slavey of the shop, an untidy little girl in a soiled white apron, helped him carry them to the car and lay them on the back seat. Both the proprietress and the girl were obviously impressed by the size of the purchase. They didn't often come that big in the medical quarter.

He gave the slavey one hundred francs and drove off, turning up the rue de l'Odéon and passing the Bar Condé where they had met for a drink that night in April. He remembered how suspicious he had been, not that she was a Commy agent, but that she was a tramp, out to get his money. His gut began to turn as he entered the rue St. Sulpice, so he stopped the car at about the same spot where he had parked it that night, and waited until his muscles relaxed before he started on to the church.

Carrying the flowers in was more than he could do in one trip. He brought the roses in first, walking up the right side of the transept, looking into the chapels to see which one was prepared for a mass. He found the one at last, the Chapel of St. Vincent de Paul, on the left side. A coffin was at the foot of the altar steps, the pedestals which supported it entirely hidden by rings and sprays of flowers. He laid the roses gently on the top of the casket and then went back to the car to fetch the lilac. The only other people in the church were a few women kneeling before the main altar, praying.

After he had arranged the lilac, also on the lid of the casket, at the foot, he parked the car and came back to the chapel. He noticed now that two rows of chairs had been ranged on the floor of the transept facing the chapel. Taking one from the end of the row, he placed it apart, nearer to the chancel rail, and sat down. Candles were burning at the altar and on the four tall candlesticks at the four corners of the coffin. The church was cool, almost cold, and the smell of flowers was strong and infinitely depressing. Why was it, he thought, that flowers were used to honor the dead? Death could be good, it could be bad. His father's death had been bad because it had been the end of a slow disintegration, a sordid finality to the running down of a body that had strained itself with overwork and worry. Death in action was different. Man against man, man against the elements, man against any danger facing him, died as a man should die, in glory. But hers was not that. Hers was the worst of all, the knock on the head from behind when there was no chance for courage, no hope for glory. It was a dirty death, a stinking death. Maybe that was why the flowers were used, as a deodorant, to cover the stench. The heavy sweet-sick smell of them was paralyzing, creeping inside one like an insidious gas, weakening the will to move, to think. He tried to conjure up a picture of her, her face, her eyes, her hair, but it was no use, she was not there, her image would not appear. All that he could see was an endless rising of skyrockets, shooting up, bursting, stars glittering, descending, vanishing. . . .

A voice was chanting unintelligible words. The rockets had gone and he was aware once more of the heavy scent of flowers. Quickly he straightened up, realizing, ashamed, that he had fallen asleep, with his head dropped forward almost to his knees. A priest in an embroidered chasuble of white and gold was standing, facing the altar, one hand upraised, the other on the open pages of a book propped up on a small gold lectern. Even though he could not see the face, he knew at once that it was the Abbé d'Albret. He turned his head slightly to see if Christian might be there in the row of seats. What he saw startled him, for not only was Christian there, but all the "little band," as he called them, were kneeling, their heads bowed.

Lowering his head, he clasped his hands together tightly between his knees. His diaphragm fluttered with a desire to cry, not for Germaine—he had done that during those nights and he knew that no tears would bring her back—but because these people had come for his sake, to demonstrate their loyalty, their friendship. Christian, dear good Christian, he thought, has done this. He has herded them together, brought them in a body, the brave Captain Capet at the head of his band. The tears choked him, and he tried to make a sob sound like a cough, but he knew that he had not fooled them. He must get himself together.

He took an inventory of the faces he had seen during his quick glance. There had been Mrs. Locke, Christian, Mme. de Tonville, Brigadier Dunglass, Lady Lettice, Peyraud, and, in the front row, two men, older men, whom he did not recognize. He wondered if one of them could be Professor Santerre. The Abbé was facing them now—without looking up. Walter could tell from the sound of the chanted Latin phrases. There was also the creaking of the leather of the acolyte's shoes on the stone floor, and then, as the Abbé carried the steady tone-thread of his chant, there came the brittle sound of something sprinkled on the flowers, his flowers.

Will it never end? he thought. Why do they have to go on and on? I must escape. I must leave before they do. I cannot talk to them, listen to their words of sympathy, take their earnest handshakes. It would be too much. Then he wondered at Livy's wife's coming. Could it be that Livy had changed his attitude, now that he knew the truth? Had there been time enough for McEwen to tell Livy, and for Livy to call his wife? He wanted to believe that she had agreed to come before Livy had told her, before she had learned the truth from Christian.

The voice of the Abbé ceased its chanting. There was a silence, except for the soft tread of feet passing in front of him. This is the moment, he thought, the moment to make a break. He started to rise, but a hand on his shoulder restrained him. The touch of the hand was light, but his knees were so weak that it was enough to sit him down.

"I shall go with you, in your car," Christian whispered in a tone of command.

"It's no use, Christian, I can't do it," Walter said, still not looking up.

Six men in black suits were now lifting the casket to their shoulders, and two more were gathering up the flowers.

"You do not have to go to the grave," Christian said. "You can sit in the car. Don't argue with me, Walter. Those are orders."

"I can't talk to them, Christian."

"We understand that. It is only Professor Santerre who wishes to shake your hand. You must do that for Germaine's father."

The others followed the casket out of the church, headed by the Abbé. Walter sat in his chair until he heard the last echo of their footsteps; then Christian took his arm and said, "Now you will come with me."

When they emerged into the sunlight of the Place St. Sulpice, the men in black suits were easing the coffin into an automobile hearse. The members of the coterie were walking slowly across the plaza to their cars. One of the two older men who had sat in the front row was standing on the curb, watching Walter and Christian as they came out of the church. He was a sturdy, thickset man with masses of unruly sandy hair. Except for the thick lenses on his spectacles, which proclaimed the scholar, he might have been a merchant or a stock broker. He came forward and put out his hand to Walter.

"I have no words," he said in English.

"There are no words," Walter said, shaking the extended hand.

Then Christian walked with Walter to his car, saying as they walked, "You need some food. You look like the devil."

CHAPTER TWENTY-NINE

IT was on the dot of nine when Walter walked into his office. He nodded to Janice Callery and Miss Kleinholz, who were drinking coffee from paper cups, and went into his own room, closing the door.

"He must have been sick. He looks awful," Kleinholz said.

"Poor guy, I feel sorry for him," Janice said. She had written Livy Locke's confidential report to the Department and attributed Walter's two-day absence and his pallor to the fact that the Communist agent he had been living with had run out on him, thus proving her guilt. But she had not told any of this to Kleinholz, nor had she any intention of telling her.

"So do I," Kleinholz said. "It's no fun being sick in a place like Paris."

The buzzer gave out two short blasts and Janice picked up her notebook and the folder with the night's classified cables and went into Walter's room.

"Sit down, Janice," Walter said. His voice sounded hollow and hoarse. "I want you to take a letter to the Chief of Foreign Service Personnel."

Janice put the cable folder in front of him before sitting down. "Maybe you'd better read the top cable first," she said.

Walter opened the folder and read: "Walter P. Haines, Class 3 F.S.O., currently assigned on special duty to O.S.R.,

E.C.A., will report to the Embassy to France for temporary duty pending further assignment." He read it through a second time, but there was no shock, just a dull impact as he realized that they had beaten him to the punch. McEwen had cabled the story, he thought; not the end, just the story as he had told it, and it had frightened them into immediate action. This transfer to the Embassy was a sort of detention while they made a fuller, more complete investigation. He didn't blame them. On the strength of what they knew it was a serious case.

"I'm sorry about this, Mr. Haines," Janice said, as if she meant it.

"Not that it matters," Walter said.

"Of course it matters," Janice protested. "It was just a piece of hard luck."

Walter looked up at her with surprise. "What are you talking about?" he asked, not suspecting that she knew anything about Germaine. "Where is the hard luck?"

"I know the whole story. No one else around here does, not even Kleinholz."

Walter smiled bitterly. "Mr. Locke told you, eh?"

"You won't tell him I told you, will you?" Janice asked, worried.

"I won't tell him anything, not any more."

"Well, listen, he didn't tell me—that is, not like you mean. He dictated a report to me, that's how I know."

Walter sat there smiling, the same bitter smile. So Livy had sent in his own report, afraid that McEwen might muff it, he thought. He wanted to be sure that the Department knew that he, Livy Locke, the shining white knight, was there defending his troops against the onslaught of the enemy. "So he gave them the works," he said, as if to himself, "the whole sordid story."

"It's not a sordid story, Mr. Haines," Janice said feelingly. "You shouldn't say that. It's a beautiful story. It almost made me cry. That was really wonderful of you to ask her to marry you. And to think that she left you. . . ."

"She never left me," Walter whispered hoarsely.

"That's what Mr. Locke wrote."

"Yes, of course he wrote it. He didn't know, none of us knew. But it isn't true, Janice."

"Oh, good. Then she came back?"

Walter drew in his breath deeply. "Yes, she came back. Mr. Locke knows it now."

Janice leaned across the desk and turned the page of the cable book. "Read that one," she said.

Out of habit Walter obeyed. The cable was marked "Personal and Confidential" and was addressed to Livy. It read: "The President has sent the nomination of S. Livingston Locke as Ambassador to the Queen of the Netherlands to the Senate. Unless unforeseen questions arise confirmation can be expected within ten days."

Walter wondered if the last sentence was mere official caution, or if it referred to himself, to Livy's report. It wasn't likely that the Department would tell the Appointments Committee about that. But the Treasury might, or the FBI. However, McEwen's final message would put it right.

"Did you know it?" he heard Janice ask.

"Yes, he told me about it," Walter mumbled.

"There's nothing like knowing the right people."

"What do you mean?" Walter asked, without interest.

"I mean like Senator Donegan."

"Oh, yes, I see what you mean."

"No, Mr. Haines," Janice said precisely, "I don't think you do see what I mean. Senator Donegan likes you, doesn't he?"

Walter shrugged his shoulders. To politicians "like" and

"dislike" were words of expediency. Donegan had "liked" him because he had shown the Senator the town. Yes—a shiver shook his whole body—that was the night he had met . . . He snapped the lid on his thoughts. Janice was speaking.

"Do you get me, Mr. Haines? You might need a friend in Washington."

The telephone rang and Janice picked up the receiver. "Mr. Haines's office," she said. "Yes. May I say who wishes to speak to him?" She handed the receiver to Walter. "It's Mrs. Locke."

"Walter," Eleanor said. Her voice sounded anxious. "I had to talk to you. I called your apartment, but there was no answer. You should not have gone to the office. Christian says you're in no fit condition to work."

"I have no intention of working," Walter said. "I just came in this morning to settle up a few things."

"Then you are taking a leave of absence?"

"You might call it that."

She hesitated. "Listen, will you lunch with Christian and me today?"

"I'd rather not, not today. I don't feel up to it yet, Mrs. Locke."

"I understand perfectly, but I wish you would. Christian is quite firm about it. He says I must command you to come to his flat at one o'clock."

"Christian has been a true friend."

"He still is, and he will expect you."

"I'll see how I feel."

"And one more thing, Walter . . ."

"Yes."

"Will you promise me something?"

"What is it?"

"Will you promise me not to take any steps, any irrevocable steps, until you have talked to us?"

"You are asking a good deal, Mrs. Locke."

"Is four hours out of a lifetime much? And please don't call me Mrs. Locke ever again. I'll see you at Christian's at one. Now, if Miss Callery is there, I'd like to speak to her."

"Just a moment," Walter said into the telephone, then handed the receiver to Janice. "Mrs. Locke wishes to speak with you."

Walter sat numbly wondering what possible advice Eleanor and Christian could give him that he had not already considered and rejected. The sound of Janice's voice repeating "Yes, Mrs. Locke. I understand, Mrs. Locke," came to him only distantly, like the street sounds in the rue St. Florentin. He was too removed within the core of his own sorrow to take notice of outer reality. Not even the click of the receiver on its base, or the breathless "Well, what do you know!" exhaled by Janice entered his consciousness.

"Never mind about that letter . . ." he started to say.

"My God, she's left him!" Janice blurted out.

Walter looked at her uncomprehending. Who had left who? Had the girl gone mad?

"She's at the San Regis," Janice went on excitedly. "She wants her mail sent there."

"Do you mean Mrs. Locke?" Walter asked, incredulous.

"She came right out with it. She said, 'Mr. Locke and I are no longer living together. Until further notice, please have any letters or messages sent to me here at the San Regis. I have already advised Ambassador Sherrill.' Those were her very words." Janice stood up. Her hands were trembling. "What's happened to this office? It's jinxed. First you, and now Mr. Locke. Oh, golly, and I did so want to go to Holland with him!" She walked hurriedly out of the room, dabbing her eyes.

What a strange thing for Eleanor to have done, Walter thought. Could it be my fault? Could it have been the report? Ah, well, he would learn the answers at lunch. There was no need to speculate. But what had made Janice say that about wanting to go to Holland with him? Did she think that he might not be confirmed? Janice probably knew more about these things than he did. Maybe the Senate wouldn't fancy a man whose wife had left him. Maybe Donegan . . . Yes, the ubiquitous Mike. He had "liked" Eleanor too.